REPTILIAN

JOHN J. RUST

SEVERED PRESS
HOBART TASMANIA

REPTILIAN

ONE

"Dammit, Ozzie! Shut up, already!"

The barking outside fell silent.

For about five seconds.

"Shit." Phil Welsh heaved his paunchy body off the worn sofa. He stomped out of the living room and through the kitchen to the back door. Ozzie continued to bark.

He flung the door open. "Shut up!"

The black and white border collie looked at Welsh, then turned back to the high grass running along the property. The dog growled.

"What the hell is it now?"

Ozzie's gaze remained fixed on the grass. He growled again.

Welsh scanned the high grass and shook his head. It was too dark to see anything. Maybe there was a fox or coyote out there.

"Get in the house."

Ozzie turned to him again, then back to the grass.

"Get in here."

With a short, almost frustrated *"woof,"* Ozzie trotted up the back steps and inside.

"Stupid dog." Welsh shook his head. This was the third night in a row Ozzie had barked up a storm. It made him wonder if anything really was outside.

Well I sure as hell ain't gonna look for it in the dark.

He settled back into his sofa, the TV tuned to the Braves/Brewers game. Welsh gulped his beer, frowning as he saw the Atlanta batter swing and miss.

"Gomez goes down swinging, strike three," said the announcer. "His slump continues. Oh-for-two tonight and one for his last sixteen at-bats."

Welsh watched an unsmiling Gomez shake his head and return to the dugout.

"Aw, poor baby." Big deal, the guy wasn't hitting worth a damn. He'd still collect his million-dollar paycheck and sleep in his big mansion later tonight.

All for playing a fucking game.

Meanwhile, Welsh busted his ass working any odd job he could to pay the bills and keep his house. That seemed less likely each passing day. He was way behind on his mortgage payments. The fucking bank bombarded him with calls and letters threatening foreclosure.

Welsh looked up at the ceiling, shaking his head. Amy had always been good with the finances. Everything just went to shit after she passed two years ago. The towing company he worked for closed. Jobs were scarce in this part of South Carolina. He couldn't even scrape together enough money to put his two daughters through college. Chloe and Vanessa both left home and went down to Charleston to find steady work, which they did.

Though Vanessa worked as a stripper. The thought made Welsh want to roar and throw his bottle. What kind of father lets his daughter become a stripper?

One who's pathetic.

Welsh sank deeper into the sofa. He barely paid attention to the game.

Ozzie sprang to his feet and growled.

"Don't even start --"

The dog barked and dashed for the back door.

"Oh for God's sake, what is your problem?" Welsh pushed himself to his feet.

Ozzie kept barking, pawing the door.

"Shut the hell up already."

The dog didn't obey.

Welsh looked up at the ceiling, shaking his head. He stomped to the closet and grabbed his Weatherby PA-08 shotgun. Maybe it was a coyote. He had seen one trot across his front lawn about a month ago. The damn things were all over the place. He remembered hearing something about the state government offering bounties to kill coyotes to keep the population manageable. A thousand bucks. Maybe he should get in on that. He could certainly use the money.

"Move," Welsh grumbled at Ozzie and threw open the door. He scanned the backyard and the tall grass bordering it. He saw nothing, heard nothing.

Ozzie raced down the steps and into the tall grass.

"Ozzie!" Welsh ran down the steps. "Ozzie! Get ba-"

Something roared from the grass.

Welsh froze, his chest tightening. He'd never heard a sound like that, almost like a long belch inside a garbage can. He couldn't

2

imagine what sort of animal could make a noise like that, but whatever made it sounded big.

Really big.

Ozzie barked. A section of grass jerked back and forth.

Welsh swallowed against his rising fear. "O-O-Ozzie?" He could barely get the words out.

The barking continued, more urgent, more threatening.

Another sound overwhelmed it. A sharp, high-pitched hiss that turned into a bubbling growl.

Ozzie yelped and cried.

Welsh's muscles locked up in terror. More grass jerked back and forth. More yelps and hisses followed.

Then he heard nothing.

"Ozzie?" He said it in barely a whisper. His heart pounded. Sweat drenched his body.

The thing growled again. Grass bent forward. Welsh's brain screamed at him to run. Fear kept him rooted to the spot.

Something burst out of the tall grass. Welsh's eyes bulged.

It had to be over seven feet tall, bulked up, with a stubby snout. The eyes blazed blood red and locked on him.

The thing growled and charged.

Welsh screamed and pulled the trigger.

TWO

Pinehurst, North Carolina. Jack Rastun had never even heard of the place until a couple of months ago. He certainly never expected to be in the small town on vacation.

Not so much a vacation as a weekend excursion. Pinehurst hosted an annual marathon at the exclusive Forest Creek Golf Course, and somewhere among the rolling greens and multitude of trees was his girlfriend Karen Thatcher, and a few hundred other runners. It would be her last full marathon of the year as she looked ahead to next April, and her first appearance at the Boston Marathon.

He took another slug of water from his bottle and wiped the sweat from his brow. Up and down this part of the course, spectators stood or sat in lawn chairs, several fanning themselves. It wasn't even noon and the temperature had to be over 80. And of course, you couldn't forget the suffocating humidity common to the south. How many runs and field maneuvers had he been on at Fort Bragg and Fort Benning in this weather? Drenched in sweat, downing water and salt pills. Calling for a medevac when someone collapsed from dehydration.

It was fucking miserable, but you dealt with it.

"Hey, Jack. Is that a cool-looking house or what?"

Rastun turned to the 11-year-old girl with a round face and dark brown hair sitting in the lawn chair next to him. He followed Emily Thatcher's gaze to one of the upscale mansions bordering the golf course. It sported a brick facade, large windows, and slanted roofs and dormers.

"Yeah, it does look pretty nice."

"You think we could live in a house like that someday?"

He tilted his head, thinking. With the money he and Karen made on their book deals for the sea raptor expedition, they could certainly afford it.

"Who knows?" he replied. "Maybe. But not one by a golf course."

Emily scrunched her face. "How come?"

"Because some places like this want you to be a member of the golf club when you buy a house, and playing golf is about as fun as watching grass grow."

Rastun felt the same about soccer, but didn't say it, since Emily was one of the top players on her youth team.

A smile formed on his face as he stared at Karen's daughter, noting how she said "we" when talking about living in a house. It was further proof how much he'd become part of Emily's life. Up until a year ago, he never gave much thought to being a father. Even when he'd been engaged to Marie, they rarely talked about having children.

Luckily, Emily had taken to him quickly. The girl never knew her father, and the more time Rastun spent around her, the easier it became to fill that role. Plus, Emily was easy to adore. She was smart, fun loving, and well behaved – usually.

Applause and cheers went through the crowd when two female runners rounded the trees and loped toward the finish line.

"Mom coming?" asked Emily.

Rastun leaned forward, squinting. "Nope. Not yet."

Ten minutes and seventeen runners later, he spotted her. The slender figure, the smooth round face, the firm legs. He smiled wide as Karen approached the finish line.

"Here she comes." He stood and snapped several pictures with his phone as Karen ran past them.

"Yay, Mom!" Emily threw a small fist into the air.

"C'mon." Rastun took her by the hand and maneuvered through the crowd. More than once he looked around with discerning, suspicious eyes. He couldn't help but think of the Boston Marathon Bombing from a few years ago. Granted, this marathon was nowhere near as large or as famous. The odds were against anything like that happening, but his experiences in Iraq and Afghanistan, and on the sea raptor expedition, taught him it always paid to be a little paranoid.

No bombs went off as Rastun and Emily neared the finish line near the clubhouse. A couple of marathon volunteers helped Karen over to the wooden porch. She plopped down, soaked with sweat, mouth hanging open, gulping down oxygen. She looked like she'd keel over at any moment.

But who wouldn't look that way after running 26 miles?

One volunteer handed Karen a bottled water when Emily hugged her. "Hey, Mom."

"Hi, sweetie," she replied in a breathless voice.

"Good job, babe." Rastun rubbed her arm, slick with sweat.

Karen just nodded and took a gulp of water. She slowly rose to her feet and began walking. Actually, the way she walked reminded

Rastun more of a zombie shuffle. While most people thought the thing to do after a marathon was collapse, as a cross country runner back in high school, he knew better. You had to move for about ten to fifteen minutes after a race to get your heartbeat and blood flow back to normal.

He left Karen alone to do her cool down as other runners crossed the finish line. When she returned, well, she still looked like hell, but less so than before.

"You doin' okay?" he asked.

"Better." Karen didn't sound out of breath when she spoke.

"You did great, Mom."

"Thanks, sweetie."

"Yeah, hell of a run," said Rastun.

"I could've done better. I was about forty seconds off my average time. Second marathon in a row that's happened. What's goin' on?"

"It's called old age." Rastun gave her a wry grin. "Hell of a thing, isn't it?"

Karen shot him an evil glare. While she was only three years older than him, he still couldn't help needling her about her age.

At least, on those occasions when he felt brave.

"Forget the couch, you're sleeping on the floor."

Rastun shrugged. "For one night, it was worth it."

"I meant for the week."

"Well now you're just being cruel." Rastun smiled again and hugged her. "Average time or not, you did good. How many other people can do this?"

"Thanks, but enough of the hugging, please. I feel like someone dumped a garbage can full of sweat on me."

"You were expecting something different after running twenty-six miles? C'mon, let's get you to the car. I've got bananas and Gatorade waiting."

"Thanks."

They crossed the parking lot, Karen leaning against Rastun's shoulder as they walked.

"First you don't want me to hug you 'cause you're sweaty, now you're pressed up against me. Make up your mind, woman."

"The hugging was something intimate. This is to make sure I stay on my feet."

"Wow, what will the diehard feminists say? Having to lean on a man to make it through the day."

Karen snorted. "Screw 'em. None of them just ran a marathon."

When they reached their rental SUV, Rastun opened the rear hatch. Karen sat on the bumper while he grabbed a portable cooler.

The ringtone on his phone blared Nightwish's "Dark Chest of Wonders." He checked the display.

RANDY E.

"Hey, Doc."

"Jack," replied Randy Ehrenberg, the cryptozoologist who led the sea raptor expedition. "How's everything in North Carolina?"

"Fine. Karen just finished the marathon. Came in nineteenth."

"Good for her. Hey, I wish I was calling to just shoot the breeze, but this is actually work related."

"What is it?"

"The Lizard Man."

Rastun recalled the name from Ehrenberg's weekly familiarization classes at the Foundation for Undocumented Biological Investigation on the world's numerous cryptids. "That's the one down in South Carolina."

"Yeah," replied Ehrenberg. "First popped up in 1988 around Scape Ore Swamp in Lee County."

"Don't tell me someone actually found it." Rastun tacked on a brief, soft chuckle.

"Actually, someone did."

THREE

"Is that some kind of dinosaur?" Emily gaped at Rastun's iPad. "Cool."

"The jury's still out if this is real." Rastun sat next to Karen on the bumper of their SUV as they watched the video Ehrenberg emailed them. It showed a large, bipedal creature with dark green skin and a lizard-like head.

"I'm gonna start by saying this thing is not fake," said a male voice off-camera. "It attacked me in my backyard. Took three blasts from my shotgun to put it down. I know you guys at the FUBI look for monsters like this. That's why I sent this video to you, not the cops. They'd just take it away from me. You can't do that, 'cause you're not cops. You have to make a deal with me. So here it is. I want a hundred thousand dollars. Give me my money, this thing's all yours. Ball's in your court."

The man kept the camera on the Lizard Man for another thirty seconds. Rastun noticed dark red patches on its scaly torso. Dried blood, he assumed. *Or red food dye, if it's fake.*

The video went to black.

"Okay," Rastun said to Ehrenberg, whom he had on his phone's speaker. "We saw it."

"So what's your verdict?"

"I didn't see anything that looks like CGI," said Karen. "Of course, if all you want to do is show a dead monster, you could fake it with a mannequin."

"If it is a mannequin, they did a pretty good job with it," Rastun pointed out. "That makes it almost impossible to tell if this is fake or legit."

"I hope it's real. That would be so cool." Emily practically beamed. An image formed in Rastun's mind of Karen's daughter, fifteen years down the line, following in their footsteps and working for the FUBI.

"If it is real, we need to find a better name for it," said Ehrenberg. "Lizard Man is just too unimaginative."

"So I take it whoever made this video is close by, otherwise you wouldn't have called us," said Rastun.

8

"He is. The man's name is Phil Welsh. He lives outside of Bishopville, about ninety miles or so from where you're at."

"You got his address?"

"I do. Of course, Welsh said he'd only give us the body if we paid him the hundred thousand."

Rastun's brow furrowed. "You didn't really agree, did you?"

"Roland Parker agreed to pay for it out of his own pocket," answered Ehrenberg.

Rastun let out an aggravated breath. He thought the billionaire philanthropist who helped set up the FUBI had more sense than that. "When word gets out that Parker paid this guy, every crazy with a camera is going to send us videos demanding money to see whatever bogus cryptid they created. If we pay them like we're paying this Welsh guy, we're going to file for Chapter Eleven by the end of the year."

"Don't worry. He's only doling out twenty-five percent of the money. If you confirm this creature is real, we'll give him the rest."

Rastun still didn't like it. He didn't see that discouraging future hoaxers. Better to get some money than none at all.

Still, Roland Parker was the boss. It was his call, whether he agreed with it or not.

"Sorry if this ruins your trip," Ehrenberg added.

"No, we're good," said Rastun. "The marathon's over, and we were just going to relax for the rest of the day."

"Good. Parker wired the money via Western Union." Ehrenberg gave him the address to their office in Pinehurst, then Welsh's address.

"I'll pick up the money and head to Bishopville ASAP."

"You mean *we'll* head to Bishopville?"

Rastun looked at Karen. "Forget it. You're in no shape for this."

"Jack, c'mon."

"No. You've run enough marathons to know how much it takes out of you, and how important recovery is. Tell me I'm wrong."

Karen frowned. "You're not wrong."

"I can come." Emily bounced on the balls of her feet.

"Sorry, kiddo. I need someone to stay behind and look after your mom."

"Aww." Emily pouted.

Truth be told, he didn't want an 11-year-old girl with him to see someone who, for all he knew, could be crazy.

"Thanks for doing this, Jack," said Ehrenberg. "Call me as soon as you confirm if this is a hoax or not."

"You got it, Doc."

Rastun pocketed his phone. "C'mon. I'll get you two back to the hotel, make a supply run, and head to Bishopville."

Karen pushed herself off the bumper, slowly. "Good luck. Hope this doesn't turn out to be a hoax."

"It better not be, otherwise I'm gonna be pis --" He bit his tongue, glancing at Emily. "Um . . . really mad."

FOUR

Rastun glanced at the empty passenger seat as he drove south on U.S. 1. He would definitely miss Karen on this assignment. Not just because she was his girlfriend. They had become a great team in the field. Karen had proven herself smart, resourceful, and brave.

On the flip side, he had control of the satellite radio. That meant he could tune it to the heavy metal station.

Ninety minutes, one hundred miles, blasting Iron Maiden, Metallica, Lacuna Coil, Pantera, and Trivium as loud as he wanted. He was in heaven.

Rastun stopped at a Wal-Mart for some necessary supplies, including a Whetstone hunting knife. He hadn't brought his Glock or any other weapons on the trip. He had no idea if Phil Welsh was an all right guy or a nutcase. If the latter, he wanted to have something to use to defend himself.

He also called Arthur Sherlock Dunmore, a former Ranger and current deputy U.S. marshal whose help proved invaluable during the sea raptor hunt.

"Sorry to bug you on a weekend, but I need some background on a guy named Phil Welsh. Lives in Bishopville, South Carolina."

"What makes him so special?"

"He sent the FUBI a video. Claims he shot and killed the Lizard Man down here."

"Lizard Man? Seriously?"

"That's why Randy's sending me to Bishopville, to see if this is serious."

"Sea monsters, bigfoot, now lizard men." Sherlock made a sound between a grunt and a chuckle. "You definitely do not have a normal job."

"Normal jobs are overrated," Rastun replied.

"So anything in particular you're looking for on Welsh?"

"Whatever you can find. I just want to see what type of guy I might be dealing with."

"I'll see what I can find and get it to you ASAP."

Rastun had reached the city limits of Bishopville, bobbing his head to Motorhead's "Hellraiser" when Sherlock called back.

"No real red flags on our man. Out of work tow truck driver. Two daughters, both college age. His wife passed away a couple of years ago."

"Any criminal record?"

"A couple of speeding tickets. He was also cited for drunk and disorderly a couple of years ago. Coincides with the death of his wife, so I can understand that."

Rastun nodded. Welsh didn't sound like a serial killer. Just a guy down on his luck with two girls he'd probably like to put through college. A hundred thousand dollars would help big time.

Still, he wouldn't completely let his guard down.

He drove through Bishopville proper, eyeing a sign at the edge of downtown with the face of a snarling reptile.

WELCOME TO BISHOPVILLE. HOME OF THE FAMOUS LIZARD MAN.

Well, they wouldn't be the first town to take advantage of a resident cryptid to promote tourism.

Rastun headed west. The small cityscape quickly vanished, replaced by trees, occasional houses, and farmland, some of which looked like they hadn't seen crops in years.

"You have arrived at your destination," chimed the GPS.

He stared through the windshield. To call it a modest house would be kind. Much of the wood siding was peeling or rotted. Part of the gutter dangled from the roof. An old, faded red pickup sat in the dirt driveway. The overgrown grass looked more brown than green. The Southern states had had a relatively dry spring, and now suffered through a heatwave.

He checked the display screen. The temperature read 92 degrees.

Rastun stepped out of the cool, air conditioned SUV and into the all-enveloping heat and humidity. He took a long pull from his water bottle and walked up to the rundown house. A pang of sympathy went through him for Phil Welsh.

Unless this turned out to be a hoax, then that sympathy would go bye-bye. All the time he spent driving down here, and all the time he'd spend driving back, was time he could have spent with Karen and Emily.

He knocked on the door.

"I'm comin'," said a voice from inside.

The door opened. A paunchy man with black hair and a beard stood before him.

"Phil Welsh?"

"That's me."

"Jack Rastun, FUBI." He showed him his credentials.

Welsh's eyes widened. "Jack Rastun? You're the guy who killed that sea monster in New Jersey."

"That's correct."

"Damn, I didn't know they were sending you." Welsh shook his hand. "Come in, come in. You want anything? I've got some beer in the fridge."

"No thank you. I'd like to see the creature you told us about."

"You got my money?"

Rastun took off the small backpack he'd purchased on his trip here. He pulled out a money pouch and handed it to Welsh. The man opened it and looked inside.

"This doesn't look like a hundred thousand dollars."

"It's not," said Rastun. "It's twenty-five thousand dollars."

Lines etched into Welsh's face. "I told you people, if you want that Lizard Man, I want a hundred thousand."

"Do you know how many videos the FUBI gets every day? Do you know how many are fake? My bosses sent me here to confirm you have an actual cryptid and not some mannequin you painted green."

"Trust me, it's real."

"Then show me. If it's real, you get the rest of your money. Otherwise, I'm outta here."

Welsh sighed, his shoulders sagging. "All right. Deal. C'mon. I got it out in the shed."

Rastun followed him to the backyard, taking out his phone and hitting the video feature. He stated the time, date and his name.

"I'm at the residence of Phil Welsh outside Bishopville, South Carolina, to verify his claim that he shot and killed the cryptid known as the Lizard Man of Scape Ore Swamp and is in possession of its body. This is Mr. Welsh." Rastun aimed the phone at him.

"Um, hi."

"You said you're keeping the creature's body in your shed?"

"Yeah. But before you see it, you may wanna check that out."

He pointed to an indentation in the dry grass. A footprint. A damn big footprint.

Rastun videotaped it, then snapped several stills. In one shot he planted his foot next to the print. Next, he got a ruler from his pack, laid it next to the footprint, and snapped another picture. Like all field personnel in the FUBI, Rastun took an intensive two-week class at the *FBI* Academy at Quantico on evidence collection and preservation. One of the things the instructors told him was to always use something to show the scale of whatever object you photographed.

"Length of the footprint is roughly sixteen inches," he said when he resumed videotaping. "Three toes, more claw-like than rounded."

He noticed something out the corner of his eye, a mound in the middle of the lawn with a small white cross.

"Who's buried there?"

"My dog, Ozzie," answered Welsh. "That thing killed him." He swallowed. "Tore him to shreds."

"Sorry." Rastun gave him a sympathetic nod. He also made a mental note to possibly exhume the dog for forensic examination.

"So, the creature. It's in there?" He pointed to a shed with peeling paint and rotting wood.

"Yeah. C'mon."

A stench surrounded the shed, like rotting meat. When Welsh threw open the door, the stench was much worse.

Rastun hacked. So did Welsh. He waved a hand in front of his face.

"Sorry. This thing fucking reeks."

"And keeping it in a shed when it's ninety degrees out doesn't help." Rastun wrinkled his face.

"I know, but I didn't have anywhere else to put it. I sure as hell wasn't going to keep it in the house."

Rastun couldn't blame him for that.

He began to doubt this was a hoax. Most hoaxers never took into account recreating the smell of a cryptid.

He stared at the shed, grimacing. *Suck it up, Jack. If you can get through the tear gas chamber in the Army, you can get through this.*

Rastun approached the door. The rotting meat odor plastered itself over his face. His nostrils burned. Nausea slithered through his stomach.

I think I'd rather be in the tear gas chamber.

He fought through the discomfort and entered the shed.

The creature lay before him, bloated, the torso covered with dried blood. The skin was dark green, similar to an alligator's. The head reminded him of an iguana's, if said iguana had its eyes in the front instead of the sides . . . and if it had razor-sharp teeth.

Rastun slowly moved his phone's video camera up and down the body, then took several still shots. Its legs resembled those of a velociraptor's, only thicker, and ended in clawed, three-toed feet. Just like the footprint outside.

The hands also ended in claws. Sharp ones. He remembered from one of Ehrenberg's cryptid classes that the Lizard Man had allegedly damaged several vehicles around Lee County. Claws like that looked like they could rip through the thin metal bodies of cars and trucks.

And do a nasty number on human flesh.

He resumed video recording and set his phone on the ground. "I'm going to do a hands-on examination to determine if this creature is real or a mannequin."

Rastun removed some latex gloves from his pack and slipped them on. Outside, Welsh coughed while looking on.

Rastun knelt down, face twisting from the foul stench. He waved away a cloud of flies and placed a hand on the creature's chest. His instructors at Quantico would probably scold him for compromising evidence, but this wasn't a murder investigation, and putting his hands on this thing was the only way to prove whether or not it was real.

Rastun pressed down, then ran his hands over the chest, neck, shoulders, and sides. A bolt of shock and excitement went through him. He didn't feel rubber or plastic or the metal of a zipper. He felt rough, scaly flesh.

Next he looked over the patches of blood. He'd seen enough gunshot wounds to know these weren't done with a can of spray paint or food dye.

Rastun took the ruler, held it next to the creature's feet, hands, and snout and snapped pictures. Then he laid next to it and had Welsh take a photo.

"How does this look?" He showed Rastun the image.

"Looks good." The creature was over seven feet tall, making Rastun look like a midget by comparison. Not that he'd ever been a big guy. The media liked to call him a real-life action hero. Unlike Hollywood action heroes, Rastun did not stand over six feet tall with a square jaw and bulging muscles. He came in at 5'10 and about 170 pounds. A very lean, very firm 170 pounds.

He'd proven many times in the past that his size did not make him any less deadly.

"Well?" Welsh looked anxious.

"Mister Welsh, it looks like you're going to get the rest of your money."

A huge grin spread over Welsh's face.

They went back inside, where Rastun interviewed Welsh at the kitchen table. He ran through everything that happened the night he shot the Lizard Man, including the vocalizations it made.

"It was like, I don't know, a combination of burping, growling, and hissing. Really weird stuff."

Interesting description. Rastun put his phone away. "I think that should do it. I'll give FUBI Headquarters a call. They should have a team out here in another day or two."

"Along with my money?"

"You'll get your money, Mister Welsh. This is a pretty significant discovery. It would have been nice if we had a living specimen."

Welsh cut him off. "Hey, the thing was coming at me. What, I was supposed to sit there and let it rip me apart like it did Ozzie?"

Rastun held up his hands in a calming gesture. "I'm not questioning your actions. Trust me, I've run into my fair share of people who sit in offices and think they know how to act in a firefight better than me. From what you told me, this was a justifiable shooting."

"Damn right it was."

Rastun stood and shook Welsh's hand. "Thank you for your time, Mister Welsh. Like I said, we'll have a team here in a day or two to collect the creature's body."

"You may also want to check around this area."

"Why's that?"

"After I shot that thing, I heard some more of those weird growls coming from the field. That monster I killed, I think it's got friends."

FIVE

Maybe I'm too paranoid.

Welsh stared out the back window, shotgun in hand. By the glow of the porch light, he could tell the shed was still the same as when he last checked it twenty minutes ago.

He went back to the living room. The TV was on, but he paid little attention to it. All he could think of was his big day tomorrow. Jack Rastun and the FUBI team would give him the rest of his money for the Lizard Man. He could finally let the world know about it. Reporters would interview him. He'd probably appear on talk shows. Did they pay their guests?

You better believe I'm gonna ask for money.

He wondered if he could get a book deal like Jack Rastun. Welsh had seen a few interviews with him talking about *Warriors and Monsters: The Jack Rastun Story,* which made *The New York Times* Best Seller list. Welsh wasn't a big reader and certainly no writer. But those publishers would probably hire a real writer to do his book. So long as he got his cut, he was fine with that.

He stared at the phone, wondering if he should call Chloe and Vanessa and tell them the big news. No. Rastun had told him to keep this under wraps.

"You start telling people a secret, there's no guarantee they'll keep it," he had said.

Good advice, especially with kids today. They didn't know shit about keeping their mouths shut. As soon as they saw or heard something, they immediately blabbed it to the world on Instagram or Twitter. Instead, he'd surprise his daughters with big fat checks and show them their old man was not a pathetic loser.

Welsh went to the kitchen for a beer. He stopped at the fridge, then went to the rear window. Again, everything looked fine with the shed.

He grabbed a beer and took a long pull from it. He imagined all the things he could do with the money he was going to get. Putting his daughters through college came first. After that, a new house for him. He also wanted a new dog. Ozzie had been a pain in the ass at times, but still, he'd been an okay dog. Maybe this time he could –

A loud bang rattled the walls.

Welsh swung around. Another blow shook the house.

He put his beer on the sink counter and brought up his shotgun. "Who's there?"

No response.

His heart pounded as he checked out the window. There was no one outside. The shed looked fine.

BANG!

Welsh jumped. His hands shook. Again, he looked at the shed.

Can't let anything happen to that monster.

Sucking down quick breaths, he moved to the door. He reached for the knob, trying to force his hand to stop shaking.

It didn't.

Welsh grabbed the knob, tensed, and swung the door open. He rushed outside.

"Get out! Get out n-"

The enormous, dark figure turned. Welsh focused on its blazing, blood red eyes.

He racked the shotgun.

Something slammed into his back. Pain exploded throughout his body. He flew off the steps and slammed into the ground. Welsh cried out. He couldn't feel the shotgun in his hands. He rolled onto his back. Pain slashed his insides. He closed his eyes and clenched his teeth. What the hell had hit him?

Welsh forced his eyes open. Another large figure leaned over him. He opened his mouth to scream.

Teeth tore into Phil Welsh's throat before he could make a sound.

SIX

"You weren't kidding when you said this guy lived in the ass end of nowhere."

Rastun looked over to Ehrenberg, who stared out the window of their Suburban as they drove down the country road. Only fields and trees flanked them. The last house they passed was two miles back.

"I guess some people really like their peace and quiet," said Karen.

"He better enjoy it while it lasts." Rastun knew as soon as the FUBI announced they had the body of the Lizard Man, the media would invade Bishopville. Welsh was sure to have cameras and microphones shoved in his face.

He glanced at the rearview mirror, looking at Karen. She seemed a bit worn out, not just because of having run a marathon two days ago. She had flown back to Virginia with Emily to drop her off with the parents of her best friend from her youth soccer team, then hopped a plane with the rest of the FUBI expedition to fly to nearby Columbia.

Still, he knew Karen would gut it out and do her job.

Rastun checked the GPS. They were a mile from Welsh's house. He activated the hands-free phone. His first call to Welsh before they left Columbia went to the answering machine.

So did this call.

"Mister Welsh, this is Jack Rastun again. Are you there?"

He waited a few seconds. No one picked up.

"We're a couple of miles from your house. We should be there shortly."

Rastun hung up.

"You'd think the guy would be home for something like this," said the short, lean Hispanic man sitting next to Karen. Alfonso Herrera, a former sergeant in the Army Rangers. Rastun had done a tour with him in Afghanistan and tapped him as a field security specialist. Another FSS sat in the back, even shorter than Herrera. Norgay, a Nepalese who'd served 22 years in the Gurkhas. Rastun knew the reputation of that group of soldiers who'd served Great Britain for nearly 200 years. Hiring him had been a no-brainer.

Rastun pulled into the dirt driveway of Welsh's home. A rental truck stopped behind him, with Pete McClure, another field security specialist who'd been a company commander in the 82nd Airborne, and Dan Plank, a graduate from American University and field investigator-in-training. The truck carried a freezer to preserve the Lizard Man's body.

"McClure. Norgay. Secure the area," Rastun ordered.

"Yes, sir," replied McClure.

Rastun didn't expect trouble in the hinterlands of South Carolina. Still, after what happened on the sea raptor expedition, he knew there were people out there who'd go to extremes to get their hands on a cryptid. He wasn't going to be caught off-guard again.

"Everyone be sure you have your masks." Ehrenberg held up a white surgical facemask. "From what Jack says, this cryptid is pretty rank, probably more so being in that shed and this heat for a few days."

Herrera scrunched his face in disgust. "Now I'm really looking forward to this."

Rastun looked over the house. Hopefully, the money Welsh got would help him...

"Hold up." His left hand snapped up.

Everyone stopped.

"What is it?" asked Ehrenberg.

"The window's broken there." Rastun pointed. "Look what's under it."

A DVD player lay on the grass a few feet from the shattered window.

"What the heck happened?" asked Karen.

"I doubt it's anything good. Herrera, with me. Everyone else, stay here. Keep your comms open."

Rastun drew his Glock and advanced toward the house. Herrera was a few steps behind and to the right, his handgun also out. Welsh hadn't answered his phone. A DVD player had been thrown out the window. Could it be a robbery? Could the robber or robbers still be here?

He directed Herrera to the front door while he approached the window. Rastun peeked inside.

The living room was a mess. Lamps, furniture, and picture frames lay strewn about the floor. He looked to Herrera, who tried the doorknob.

"It's locked."

Rastun knocked away the remaining glass in the window with the butt of his pistol. He climbed inside and quickly got to his feet, Glock up. If anyone was still in the house, they'd have heard the breaking glass.

Herrera climbed in next. Using hand signals, Rastun directed him to search the left side of the house.

Couch and chair cushions had been torn apart. Stuffing covered the floor like thick piles of snow. A wrecked TV lay against the wall.

Next, Rastun went to the kitchen. The refrigerator door was open. A few cabinets had their doors torn off. Boxes, broken glass, and food littered the tiled floor.

"Living room and kitchen are clear," Rastun radioed. "Completely trashed, but clear."

"Same story with the bedroom and bathroom," replied Herrera.

"Copy. I'm going to check the backyard."

The rear door lay on the floor, a huge dent in the top half. Rastun peered out the open doorway.

"Backyard clear." He was about to step outside, then stopped. His gaze came to rest on a large patch of red in the grass.

Blood.

"Herrera."

"Go, sir."

"We've got blood in the backyard. A lot of it. Get over here."

"On the way."

Rastun noticed a trail of blood across the grass. It ended by the shed.

"Doc?" he radioed Ehrenberg.

"Here, Jack."

"Call Nine-One-One. Looks like we've got a serious situation here."

"I'm on it."

When Herrera arrived, they followed the blood trail to the shed. One of the doors hung from its hinges. It swung slightly in the breeze, creaking with every movement. Rastun expected it to fall off at any second.

He crept along the door, listening for any sounds coming from inside. All was quiet.

He drew a breath and swung his body halfway around the door, Glock raised.

The Lizard Man was gone.

Another body had taken its place, the shredded, bloody body of Phil Welsh.

SEVEN

"Who could have found out about Lizard Man's body being here?" Ehrenberg leaned against the grill of the Suburban, arms folded. "We took all kinds of precautions to keep this discovery quiet."

Rastun let out a sharp breath as he stared at the house. "I hate to admit this, but maybe we've got another leak inside the FUBI." He hoped that wasn't true. It had been a pain in the ass rooting out all of Gunderson's moles following the sea raptor expedition. He didn't feel like doing that again.

"I'll tell you," Herrera grimaced. "I don't think I've ever seen anyone as messed up as that poor guy, and I saw some pretty nasty stuff in Afghanistan. I mean, if someone wanted that Lizard Man, why not just do a double-tap to Welsh's chest and cart the damn thing off?"

Rastun didn't respond. He just stared at the grass, thinking of Welsh. Like Herrera, he'd seen all manner of mutilation during his Army days. People with their stomachs and chests blown open, or faces torn apart by bullets or shrapnel. He'd seen guts splayed out on the ground, men trying to scream with their jaws ripped away.

Welsh's death was as horrific as any of the ones he'd seen in Iraq and Afghanistan. But while those had been done by guns, grenades, and bombs, what happened here seemed more . . . animalistic.

Karen snapped pictures of the expedition members and Welsh's house. Rastun figured it was more to keep her occupied until the police got there than anything else.

A few minutes later, a white car with black and gold detailing approached, followed by a second one. They pulled behind the FUBI vehicles. Two Lee County Sheriff's deputies got out, one tall and black, the other of average height and white.

"You the monster hunters?" asked the tall deputy.

"We are. Doctor Randy Ehrenberg." He shook the deputy's hand.

"Deputy Clay. That's Deputy Wills. The detective and the crime scene techs should be here soon. I have to ask, has anyone been in the house?"

"That would be the two of us." Rastun pointed to himself and Herrera. "We saw the inside trashed and crawled through a window to see if anyone was hurt. We also checked the backyard and the shed. That's where we found Mister Welsh."

Clay nodded. "Okay. We have to secure the crime scene. Be sure to tell the detective you went through there."

"I will."

The deputies walked past him toward the house. Rastun caught Wills muttering, "Civilians tramping through a crime scene. Blefary's gonna have a meltdown when he hears that."

He groaned. *That's reassuring.*

The deputies were still putting yellow crime tape around the property when two more sheriff's vehicles pulled up. A man and woman emerged from one, carrying bulky silver cases. Crime scene techs, Rastun assumed. A large dark-skinned man got out of the second vehicle. He appeared to be in his mid-to-late forties, about 6'3 with a large paunch. His face was compact and he didn't smile. He looked like a guy who'd never smiled in his entire life.

"You're from the FUBI?" he asked in a gruff voice.

"We are." Ehrenberg shot him his trademark wide smile. "Doctor Randy Ehrenberg. Pleasure to meet you." He stuck out his hand.

The large man stared at it for a moment, then gave it a brief shake. "Detective Bruce Blefary." He pulled out a notebook and took down everyone's names. "So who discovered Welsh's body?"

"Myself and Herrera," Rastun answered.

"What time was that?"

"About eleven-thirty."

"So why are a bunch of monster hunters so interested in a guy living out in the sticks?" Blefary paused. "Don't tell me. Phil Welsh found the Lizard Man."

Ehrenberg rubbed the back of his neck. "Well, actually . . . "

The expression on Blefary's face grew harsher. "Are you shittin' me?"

"Absolutely not." Ehrenberg shook his head. "Mister Welsh emailed us a video of what he claimed was the body of the Lizard Man. Jack happened to be nearby, so I sent him here to check it out."

Blefary turned to Rastun. "When was that?"

"A couple of days ago."

"And was it a real monster or some guy in a suit?"

"It was real."

"Mm-hmm." Blefary sounded like he didn't believe it. "So where was Welsh keeping this thing?"

"In a shed in his backyard."

"Is it there now?"

"No," Rastun answered. "Someone took it."

"Of course." Blefary scribbled in his notebook. "Anyone have any idea who took it?"

Everyone answered, "No."

Blefary turned back to Rastun. "You sure that thing was real?"

"I felt it, looked at the bullet holes -"

"Bullet holes?"

"Mister Welsh claimed the beast charged him, so he shot it."

Blefary slapped his notebook against his thigh. "So some guy allegedly blows away a monster, stuffs it in his shed, and you don't think to call the police?"

"We did consult with our legal department," Ehrenberg jumped in. "Everything indicated Mister Welsh acted in self-defense. The animal he shot was not on the endangered species list, since up till now it hasn't been proven to exist. Plus, given what happened during our expedition to find the sea raptor, we thought it would be best to keep this under wraps."

"You thought?" Blefary barked out. "Just who the hell do you think you are? You're not law enforcement. You're not even an official federal agency. You're civilians. Civilians who may have kept knowledge of criminal activity to themselves!"

"Now, Detective." Ehrenberg held up a calming hand. "Like I said, we checked and double-checked with the FUBI lawyers, and they could not find any evidence Mister Welsh committed any crime."

"Of course some damn lawyer would say that. At least tell me you didn't tamper with any evidence."

"We tried not to," said Rastun.

Blefary's head snapped toward him. "What do you mean, 'You tried not to?'"

"When I looked through the window and saw the living room trashed, I climbed inside with Herrera and searched the house."

Rage flared in Blefary's eyes. Rastun sensed an eruption coming.

Ehrenberg tried to head it off. "Detective, please. Jack explained to me he only went inside to see if anyone might be hurt. A rather logical assumption given the condition of the living room. I'm sure even the police would have done the same thing. The first priority is to ensure the safety and welfare of people, isn't it?"

Rastun's eyes shifted between Ehrenberg and Detective Blefary. The cryptozoologist had a talent for diffusing tense situations with his easygoing manner and well-chosen words.

"You're right, Doctor. The police would have. Not untrained civilians!"

Rastun frowned. Ehrenberg managed to diffuse tense situations *most* times.

"I wouldn't call us untrained," said Rastun. "Herrera and I are former Army Rangers. We both served in Afghanistan."

"This isn't Afghanistan and you're not Rangers anymore. You're civilians. Civilians who don't know shit about what to do when you come across a crime scene!"

Karen stared daggers at the detective. Plank shrank away, doing his best to turn invisible.

Rastun stood there, unfazed. Six years in the Army, he'd dealt with his fair share of screamers. Some worse than Blefary.

Blefary pointed at Karen's camera. "Did you take any pictures of this place?"

"A few."

"Then I need that camera for evidence." He grabbed it out of her hands.

"What the hell?" Karen snapped.

"Hey!" Rastun stomped toward him. "Watch yourself, pal."

"Back off!" Blefary's free hand hovered near his holster. "Back off, right now!"

Karen snatched her camera back.

Blefary whipped his head around, his expression a mix of shock and anger. "Lady, you are interfering with a police investigation."

Karen pulled out a small wafer-like object from the camera, then held it up. "Memory card. This has all the pictures I took, so you don't need my whole camera."

She tossed him the card. Blefary fumbled it once, then caught it against his chest.

"Next time, how about do something my daughter knew how to do when she was five."

"What's that?" asked Blefary.

"Say please."

Blefary glared at Karen. She didn't look intimidated at all.

The big detective eyed the rest of the FUBI team. "I want you all to stick around the area. I may have more questions for you later."

"That won't be a problem, Detective," said Ehrenberg. "The FUBI wants us to investigate whether there are more creatures like the one Phil Welsh killed."

Blefary scowled. "Just make sure your investigation *does not* interfere with my investigation."

"I wouldn't dream of it."

With one final scowl, Blefary stalked off toward the house.

Rastun watched him go, shaking his head. A few months ago, his team had gone down to Florida to search for the Skunk Apes. It took a week to find them, the easternmost colony of Sasquatch discovered to date. Unlike in New Jersey, there'd been no attacks by cryptids on humans. All in all, a relatively easy operation.

The same wouldn't be true here.

EIGHT

Alex Cassian jerked upright in bed. Sweat soaked his compact body. He rubbed his face, the whiskers of his thick brown beard scratching his palms.

It was the nightmare again, the one that had stayed with him since childhood.

He slid out of bed and shuffled through his Coachmen RV, trying to push the horrific images out of his mind. Never an easy thing to do. How could anyone forget something like that?

Cassian put on shorts and a t-shirt for his morning jog. He made sure to carry his Smith & Wesson SD40. He was in a remote area of Georgia. Was conceal and carry legal in this state?

Who the fuck cares? There were dangerous people, and things, in this world. Cassian knew that first hand. He'd be damned if he'd entrust his safety to some pantywaste gun-hating politician.

He took off down the forest path, the trees blocking the rising sun. The air, while not cool, wasn't blistering hot. That would change in a few hours.

When is this damn heatwave gonna end?

He put in six miles before returning to his RV. Next came the rest of his morning regimen of push-ups, sit-ups, pull-ups from the sturdy branch of a nearby tree, and free weights.

Cassian showered, but not for long. The water tank was getting low. He needed to refill it. Today.

After he dried off and changed, he grabbed a microwavable breakfast from the small freezer and tossed it in the oven. Images of the nightmare assaulted his mind as he waited for his food to heat up. Would there ever be an end to it? Maybe if he accomplished his mission. But what if that didn't do it?

It doesn't matter. They have to pay.

He sat at the U-shaped table, shoveling processed scrambled eggs and sausage into his mouth, and checking his laptop. The sighting maps had nothing new. Next, he combed various news sites for any mysterious deaths or disappearances involving politicians, scientists, or truth seekers like himself. Nothing there. Same with any UFO sightings or animal mutilations in the south. He did find a story about a SpaceX launch scrubbed due to technical problems.

Technical problems my ass. Cassian knew *they* had sabotaged man space exploration. *They* ended the lunar landings and decommissioned the space shuttle fleet because of the potential threat both programs posed.

Maybe he should go to SpaceX's headquarters in California, see what he could uncover. But he hated leaving the South. This was the center of *their* activity. He was so close to uncovering the truth, destroying their operation, he could feel it.

Cassian typed news for South Carolina into the search engine, specifically looking for any out of the ordinary stories involving Lee County.

His eyes widened at the headline, FUBI SENDS "TOP TEAM" TO FIND SC LIZARD MAN.

He leaned closer to the screen and read the article.

(Bishopville, SC) They gained notoriety for ending the deadly rampage of the sea raptor in New Jersey last year. Now cryptozoologist Dr. Randy Ehrenberg, field security specialist Jack Rastun, and photographer Karen Thatcher have another potentially dangerous monster to find.

Officials with the Foundation for Undocumented Biological Investigation confirmed that the three, along with other FUBI personnel, have been sent to South Carolina to search for the Lizard Man of Scape Ore Swamp. This comes as the Lee County Sheriff's Office is investigating the murder of a 47-year-old man west of Bishopville who claimed to have the body of the legendary creature in his possession.

"Jack Rastun happened to be in neighboring North Carolina when Mr. [Phil] Welsh contacted us about his discovery," said FUBI Director Edward Lynch. "We sent him to Welsh's home, and he confirmed the body was authentic."

When FUBI personnel arrived at Welsh's residence two days later, they discovered his mutilated body and no sign of the purported Lizard Man corpse. Sheriff's investigators said they have no suspects in Welsh's murder.

"There is the possibility that other creatures like the one Mr. Welsh supposedly had are out there," said Lynch. "We want our top team there to find them."

Neither Lynch nor the Lee County Sheriff's Office would say if they believed Welsh's death might have been caused by one of these creatures.

The Lizard Man has been described as a half-human, half-reptile creature first reported in 1988 by a local teenager. Since then, numerous people have reported seeing it throughout Lee County, with some claiming it was responsible for damage to their vehicles.

"Well, good news, bad news."

The good news, he had a very good lead on another one of those monsters. The bad news, the FUBI was involved. They thought the Lizard Man some dumb animal and would try to keep it alive. They had no idea the truth behind those things, how they had to be exterminated.

Except Jack Rastun. He had killed the sea raptor, which had to be one of *their* experiments.

Cassian clasped his hands together, staring over the laptop's screen, thinking. Could Rastun have known that? Could he be waging his own covert war against *them?*

He looked to his bed, thinking about the hidden compartment that contained his trophies. He smiled at the thought of adding one more.

And this time, he would have none other than Jack Rastun helping him.

NINE

"Looks like reinforcements have finally arrived." Rastun started across the lobby of the Bishopville Econo Lodge as two men and two women entered.

"Yeah," replied the large, muscular man with close-cropped dark hair and horn-rimmed glasses. "Second time in a year I gotta make sure some monster doesn't eat your ass. This is gettin' ridiculous."

"I'm touched by your concern." Rastun slapped Wendell "Geek" Hewitt on the shoulder. "Still, glad to have you here."

"Of course you are. You'd be lost without a damn good NCO to keep you out of trouble."

"He doesn't need an NCO to keep him out of trouble any more. He's got me." Karen shot Geek a wry grin.

"Then I guess I'll go back home."

Karen chuckled and gave Geek a hug.

Rastun turned to the tall black man with a solid build. "Nice of the Marshal's Service to cut you loose for this." He shook hands with Sherlock.

"Not a problem. Your boss figured you could use a law enforcement liaison."

"The way this expedition's started off, we could use all the help we can get." Rastun was grateful that help came in the form of the two former non-commissioned officers. Geek and Sherlock had spent two decades each in the Army, and Rastun had served with both men. Without them, he doubted he would have survived the sea raptor expedition.

"Hi, Jack," said one of the women. She was thin with a narrow yet attractive face and a long brown ponytail.

"Hi, Petal." There was the slightest hesitation before he said the name. It felt unnatural to call an adult woman that, but it wasn't a nickname. Mr. and Mrs. Garland had actually named their daughter Petal thirty-plus years ago. Both were big-time earthy, granola-chewing types, and she followed in their footsteps.

She also happened to be a damned good biologist with degrees from UCLA and the University of Washington.

"Have a good trip?" he asked.

"We made it here safe and sound, so I'd call it good."

Rastun grinned and looked past Petal to the stocky woman with short black hair and a round, intense face. "Who's the newbie?"

"She's my sidekick from Aster." Geek referred to the company he worked for, which made equipment for the military and law enforcement. "Alana Kurowski, this is the one and only Jack Rastun."

"It's nice to meet you, sir." She shook his hand.

"Likewise. What do you do at Aster?"

"I'm a field tester, just like Geek."

Rastun could tell right away from the woman's bearing she was ex-military. "What branch were you?"

"Marine Corps. Four years."

"MOS?" He used the acronym for Military Occupation Specialty.

"Sixty-One sixteen, tilt-rotor mechanic."

"Can you handle yourself if things get hairy?"

"I'm a Marine, sir. I've been under fire in Afghanistan, and I've fired back at the Taliban SOBs who were trying to kill me."

Rastun stared at her for a few seconds, nodded, and turned back to Geek. "I like her."

"You think I'd come out here with somebody who never sets foot outside their lab? They'd be an easy snack for this Lizard Man."

Ehrenberg curled his lips and shook his head. "Yeah, we're definitely going to have to give this cryptid a new name."

"You can have a contest. The person who comes up with the best name gets to come with you on your next expedition." Geek stared at the ceiling for a moment. "On second thought, considering what you all deal with, maybe an FUBI t-shirt and a gift card are better."

Ehrenberg responded with a quick laugh. "Well now that you're all here, we can do some actual work."

Rastun was ready for that. The group had spent much of yesterday studying sighting maps of the Lizard Man and tracking down witnesses for interviews. Most of their descriptions matched the creature Phil Welsh had shot. One man showed him and Karen a photo of a blurry, dark shape amongst the trees he swore was the Lizard Man. Even with all Karen's photo enhancement programs, they couldn't identify the shape with any certainty.

"It could be a bear, a hunter in camouflage, or a tree stump," she had said.

They entered one of the hotel's conference rooms, where Plank had set up the computer for the Power Point presentation and laid out bottles of water. Once everyone sat down, Ehrenberg began.

"This is our quarry. The Lizard Man." He put up one of the stills Rastun had taken of the dead creature.

"Holy shit," said Alana. "It looks like something out of *Star Wars*."

"Extraterrestrial is one of the theories surrounding it," Ehrenberg explained. "I happen to think it's more terrestrial-based, maybe some evolutionary offshoot of dinosaurs."

"Or the evolutionary dead end for dinosaurs." Petal gazed at the others. "Many scientists believe because of the ratio of size between a dinosaur's brain and its body size, they never could have evolved into an intelligent species. Or at least, intelligence approaching our level."

"Given the shape of its head," Ehrenberg ran a finger over the screen, "it would seem to indicate a larger brain. It could have a Sasquatch or chimpanzee level of intelligence, or close to it."

"You know." Alana leaned back, still gazing at the image of the creature. "I've heard of the Jersey Devil and the Abominable Snowman. I've never heard of this Lizard Man. When did this thing pop up?"

"The first documented sighting was summer of 1988," Ehrenberg answered. "A local teen was changing a tire when he claimed the creature attacked him. We were hoping to interview him, but it turns out he was murdered a few years ago, apparently something to do with a drug deal. A few witnesses we did interview probably misidentified a known animal, and two, I think, were outright liars."

"What about the other witnesses you interviewed?" Sherlock reached for his water.

"Their descriptions were close to the creature at Phil Welsh's house, and after Jack's inspection of the body, I don't think there's any doubt the Lizard Man exists. Now we just have to find a live specimen."

Sherlock looked across the table at Rastun. "You're sure Welsh didn't fake this?"

"If that body was fake, Welsh wouldn't have lived in a rundown house in the middle of nowhere. He'd be making a ton of money as a special effects artist in Hollywood. He also told me the night he shot the Lizard Man, he heard more hissing growling around his home. He thought there were more of them out there."

"So you think more of these lizard men killed Welsh?" asked Geek.

"We don't know." Rastun shook his head. "But whoever, or whatever, did it looked like they wanted to kill Welsh fifty times over."

"Yeah, the captain's not exaggerating," added Herrera. "That guy was ripped to shreds."

"Sasquatch travel in social groups," said Petal. "That usually isn't the case with reptiles, though there is evidence to suggest some species of dinosaurs, particularly the smaller carnivores, operated in packs. It's possible more lizard men were in the area when Phil Welsh shot and killed its pack member."

A doubtful look settled on Sherlock's face. "It sounds like you're talking vengeance, something that requires thought and planning. I don't see animals capable of doing that."

"On the contrary." Petal folded her hands on the table and looked at the marshal. "There was a study done at the Max Planck Institute for Evolutionary Anthropology in Germany that showed if one chimpanzee stole another's food off its table, that other chimpanzee would deliberately try and collapse the offending chimp's table."

"There have also been reports of chimpanzee attacks on humans in Africa, possibly in response to a loss of territory," Ehrenberg chimed in. "There's also the story of a poacher in Russia who shot and wounded a tiger in the nineties. The tiger allegedly tracked him over two days, staked out his cabin, and killed him."

"So it's possible the same thing could have happened to Welsh," said Karen.

"Yeah." Ehrenberg nodded. "It's possible."

Rastun leaned back in his chair, staring at the table in thought. He'd heard other animal revenge stories over the years. Had they really been acting out of vengeance, or could it be simple self-preservation? He didn't know. He doubted anyone truly did, and they wouldn't unless they could read an animal's mind.

But Rastun would not completely dismiss the notion. No soldier worth a damn underestimated their opponent. Especially when that opponent was a seven-foot-tall reptile with razor-sharp claws.

"The first thing we need to do," said Sherlock, "is get with the Sheriff's Office and examine the evidence they collected from the crime scene. Who's the lead detective on the case?"

"A lieutenant named Blefary," answered Rastun.

"What's he like?"

"He's a prick," said Karen.

Sherlock looked at her, then to Rastun.

"I'm not gonna disagree with her."

"It has been . . ." Ehrenberg bobbed his head back and forth, as though considering his next word, "difficult to get any information from him."

"How so?" asked Sherlock.

"I've called his office three times. I'm still waiting for him to return those calls."

Sherlock's stoic expression didn't change. "Don't worry. I'll convince Blefary to share his evidence with us."

"I wish you the best of luck," said Rastun.

"Just be sure to wear earplugs," Karen added. "This guy likes to yell, a lot."

"I've dealt with yellers before. I'll survive."

"So, Geek." Ehrenberg looked at the big ex-sergeant. "What fancy toys did you bring us from Aster Technologies?"

"Probably the biggest thing is the Flapjack."

"Did you bring some syrup, too?" Ehrenberg grinned.

"Funny, Doc. The Flapjack is our new quadracopter drone. Comes with both FLIR and thermal imaging cameras. This part of South Carolina has a lot of forests and farmland. That should come in handy finding monsters that don't want to be found."

"And if we do find 'em?" asked Rastun.

"We brought the same loadout we had in Point Pleasant. Flash/bang grenades, tranq and toxin darts. I also threw in a few extras like rubber bullets and a net gun. We're ready to take this thing down, one way or another."

"Just be ready to lug everything," added Alana. "We were going to bring Aster's new robo-mule."

"What the heck is that?" asked Karen.

"It's a tracked, load-bearing platform meant to transport heavy gear for Marines and soldiers. Your Ag Department guy nixed us using it."

Rastun stifled a groan. Alana referred to Nathan Hipper, their liaison with the Department of Agriculture. Rastun had developed an instant dislike for the man during the sea raptor expedition. Hipper was the typical government bureaucrat. Risk-adverse, rule-obsessed, and incapable of adapting when things went wrong.

"What was his problem? The robo-mule's paint wasn't environmentally friendly?"

"Actually, it was the fire danger here," Alana answered Rastun. "He said it's really hot and dry. If the robo-mule hit a rock and threw a spark, we could be looking at hundreds, maybe thousands, of acres going up in smoke."

"I know you won't like hearing this, Jack," said Ehrenberg, "but I have to agree with Hipper on this. I spent a couple of summers during my college days on Forest Service fire crews. He's right when he says one spark can cause a major wildfire."

Rastun nodded. He'd seen how dry the vegetation was around Welsh's home. He begrudgingly had to admit Hipper made a good call.

For once.

"We also have to be careful with firearms," Ehrenberg added. "A muzzle flash or a hot cartridge can also start a wildfire."

"Okay, you heard the man." Rastun looked to his field security specialists. "Glocks and rifles only in absolute life or death situations. If we come across any lizard men, we use tranqs first. If that doesn't work, hit it with a toxin dart. Trust me, it'll put down any cryptid faster than a bullet will."

"It sounds like we're set." Ehrenberg clapped his hands together. "We do have to see the mayor this afternoon before we head into the field. We'll start near Phil Welsh's home and work our way north. If we don't find any sign of a lizard man . . . which we'll call it until someone can think of a better name, we'll go to one of the sighting hot spots. These creatures are likely nocturnal, so we'll concentrate our searches from late afternoon into the night." His lips tightened for a moment. "And after what happened to Phil Welsh, I probably don't need to tell you to exercise extreme caution out there."

An image of Welsh's mutilated body hovered in Rastun's mind. *You definitely don't have to tell me that, Doc.*

TEN

Karen was right.

That's what Sherlock thought when he met Detective Blefary. The permanent scowl, the eyes that seemed to view the world with mistrust and anger, the aura of a pending eruption.

He did look like a prick.

"You the marshal?" Blefary muttered as he looked up from his cluttered desk, one of four in this common office for the Lee County Sheriff's Detective Bureau.

"Arthur Sherlock Dunmore. It's a pleasure to meet you, Detective Blefary." He extended his hand.

Blefary stared at it, then grunted and gave it a brief, perfunctory shake. He didn't offer Sherlock a seat.

Sherlock, on his own, lowered himself onto the worn, padded chair in front of the desk.

"So why's the Marshal's Service interested in this case?" asked Blefary.

"Actually, they're not. I'm on loan to the FUBI to act as their liaison with local law enforcement."

Blefary grunted again. "Did that nutjob Ehrenberg send you over here?"

"He did."

"Tell him I've got better things to do than help him look for make-believe monsters."

"I think this might be more than make-believe. I assume you saw the video Phil Welsh sent to the FUBI?"

"I did. Have you been on YouTube lately? You seen how many bullshit videos are on there? Especially the ones with monsters and aliens."

"Captain Rastun performed an examination of the creature's body," said Sherlock. "He confirmed it was authentic."

Blefary let out a harsh sigh. "And I'm supposed to believe him because he's famous?"

"Being famous has nothing to do with it. Jack Rastun is an experienced Army Ranger and a decorated soldier."

"That doesn't mean he can tell the difference between an 'actual lizard man,'" Blefary used his fingers to make quotation marks, "and a mannequin."

"Have you found anything in Welsh's background that suggests he knew how to make a first-rate mannequin?"

Blefary's jaw stiffened. "He could have a friend who does."

"Uh-huh."

The detective's scowl deepened. "Look, Marshal, I'm busy. So what do you want?"

"To review the Welsh case."

Blefary let out a short, sardonic laugh. "What? That crazy so-called doctor thinks the Lizard Man actually killed Phil Welsh?"

Sherlock maintained a neutral expression, but his aggravation at Blefary's insults grew. Rastun was one of the most competent, capable, and honorable officers he'd ever served with. While Dr. Ehrenberg had his eccentricities, he considered the cryptozoologist smart and passionate, definitely not crazy.

"Well, if you're that interested," Blefary continued, "go to the reception office and ask for the police report."

"I already did. But we both know there are lots of things left out of police reports so as not to jeopardize an investigation."

"And that's the stuff you want to see, I assume?" Blefary narrowed his eyes.

"Yes. Autopsy reports, crime scene photos, list of witnesses or POIs." Sherlock used the term for Persons of Interest.

"Then you mention it to your monster hunter buddies and they blab it to the press."

Sherlock put up a calming hand. "You have my word, one cop to another, any sensitive evidence I come across, we will keep it compartmentalized."

"You'll forgive me if I'm not the most trusting of souls," replied Blefary.

"Detective, I assure you, the FUBI is not here to interfere with your investigation. But there is evidence that an as yet unknown animal may be responsible for Phil Welsh's death."

"Do you really believe that?"

"I'm approaching this as I do any case, without any preconceived notions. If it looks like a human being murdered Welsh, I will not bother you any more. But if it was a lizard man, then the FUBI has experience dealing with such creatures. It makes sense for us to work together."

"Work together?" Blefary crossed his arms. "Do you want to know what the Welsh case has become? A damn circus. Ever since his death got linked to the friggin' Lizard Man, every damn reporter in the world's shown up here. Satellite trucks parked up and down the street, morons with microphones yelling questions at me and anyone else who comes in or out of this building, dumbass people calling us or sending emails telling us we need to kill these monsters. One of our deputies pulled over a pickup full of drunk dumbfucks who were going Lizard Man hunting. If I agree to help the FUBI, this becomes an even bigger circus. Thanks, but no thanks."

He turned to his computer, ignoring Sherlock.

Sherlock stifled a sigh. He'd hoped to do this the nice way. He'd always tried to avoid coming off as the heavy-handed fed when working with local cops.

Right now, however, he didn't seem to have a choice.

Plus, Blefary was such a prick he would not feel bad about it.

"I'll be sure to mention this to Roland Parker."

"Who?"

"He runs one of the country's largest investment management firms, big-time philanthropist, and he's one of the men who founded the FUBI."

"That's nice."

"When I give him my report, I'll be sure to tell him about the lack of cooperation from the Lee County Sheriff's Office. If there is another lizard man out there, and it did kill Phil Welsh, that lack of cooperation might prevent us from finding it."

"If this stupid monster really exists," said Blefary.

"A lot of people around here think it does," Sherlock slid forward in his seat. "They want it found. What are they going to think when they hear the Sheriff's Office is not helping the group that discovered the sea raptor and several Sasquatch colonies across the country? It could be embarrassing to this department, embarrassing for your sheriff."

Blefary's eyes shifted from his screen to Sherlock.

"When is Sheriff Haddix up for re-election?"

"Next year."

"It might be hard for him to hold on to his office if people thought he wasn't doing all he could to catch the Lizard Man. I wouldn't want to be the detective who may have cost him the election because he wouldn't honor a request from a fellow peace officer."

Blefary glared at Sherlock as he continued. "What do you think the sheriff would do? Demote you? Reassign you to some crap detail? You might think you can put up with it until he leaves office, but who's to say the new sheriff won't look at you as someone who might create another controversy for this department?"

The detective's fleshy face tensed. He drew a couple of deep breaths, then picked up his phone.

"Captain, it's Blefary . . . I've got a U.S. Marshal named Dunmore here. He's working with the FUBI team looking for the Lizard Man . . . Yeah, he wants access to everything pertaining to the Welsh case . . . No, this isn't an official investigation by the Marshal's Service . . . Yeah, but, Captain, he's got connections with higher ups at the FUBI. They could raise a stink with the Sheriff about this, or go to the press . . . I know, but you know how folks around here are worked up about this Lizard Man bullshit. It won't look good for the Sheriff if it gets out we weren't helping the FUBI . . . I know it's bullshit, but that's not what most civilians think. Civilians who might vote for the Sheriff . . . No, I don't want to be on the bad end of that shitstorm either . . . Okay. I'll send him over."

Blefary hung up. "Captain Grammas's office is down that hall and to the right. He's in charge of the Detective Bureau. He'll set you up with the proper authorization."

"Thank you, Detective," said Sherlock. "I appreciate it."

Blefary grunted.

After seeing Captain Grammas and picking up the authorization forms, Sherlock left the Sheriff's Office. Trucks and vans from various TV stations lined the street in front of the red and green, one-story building. Smartly dressed reporters, along with their camera operators, milled about. Sherlock avoided eye contact and headed for the sidewalk. He hoped the press would ignore him.

"Sir! Sir!" one of them shouted. "Are you investigating the Lizard Man Murder?"

Seriously? 'Lizard Man Murder?' Anything for ratings, he figured.

"Are you with the Sheriff's Office?" a second reporter shouted.

"Has the cause of Phil Welsh's death been confirmed?" asked another reporter.

Sherlock gave them the answer he'd been told to give the press while at FLETC, the Federal Law Enforcement Training Center. "No comment."

The reporters kept shouting questions. He ignored them and kept walking to the next block over, where the Lee County Coroner's

Office was located. The first thing he wanted to do was see Phil Welsh's body and look at the autopsy report.

He showed his badge and paperwork to the receptionist, who led him to the coroner's office. A thin man with slicked back graying hair and glasses sat at the desk, typing on a computer. He wore a white dress shirt and a plain red tie. Several degrees and certificates hung on the wall behind him.

"Doctor Porter?"

"Yes?"

"Deputy U.S. Marshal Arthur Dunmore." Sherlock showed his badge.

"Marshal?" Porter's eyes widened behind his glasses. "We normally don't get visits from federal agents." He paused. "I can't even remember the last time that happened here."

"Actually, I'm working in conjunction with the FUBI. I need to see everything you have on the death of Phil Welsh." Sherlock handed the coroner his paperwork.

"So you believe he was killed by the Lizard Man?"

"I'm reserving my opinion until I've seen all the evidence."

"Ah, a man after my own heart." Porter smiled.

Sherlock nodded. He took an instant liking to the coroner. He felt he'd have an easier time working with him than Detective Blefary.

Porter led him to the morgue. They walked between a couple of steel examination tables to a row of slide-in refrigeration units.

"I hope you have a strong stomach, Marshal?"

"I was in the Army before I became a marshal. I saw some pretty bad stuff in Iraq and Afghanistan."

"Uh-huh. Still, I hope you have a strong stomach."

Porter grabbed the handle of the steel door labeled 5 and pulled it out.

Sherlock grimaced. Nausea burned in his stomach.

Welsh's throat had been completely torn out. Half his face was gone, both ears and one eyeball missing. Chunks of flesh had been ripped out of his chest, stomach, and thighs.

"I'll admit, this ranks right up there with some of the worst things I saw on any of my combat tours."

Porter nodded. "I've been doing this for twenty-eight years. I've handled really bad traffic accidents, small plane crashes, even one young man tortured to death with a blowtorch. But this is one of the worst conditions I've ever seen a body."

Sherlock clenched his teeth, staring at the savaged pile of flesh that had been Phil Welsh. He tried to imagine him as he'd been before his death. Some might have called him greedy, demanding a hundred grand from the FUBI for the Lizard Man body. Sherlock saw him as a man down on his luck. Wife dead, no job. Had he been thinking about how that money would turn his life around? Would he have gotten his life back on track if he'd lived?

He put those thoughts out of his head. Time to concentrate on the job.

"What was the exact cause of death?"

"Severing of the external and internal jugular veins and the carotid artery," said Porter. "Though it would probably be more accurate to say they were torn apart. He likely died within twenty to thirty seconds."

"So all the other injuries were post-mortem," said Sherlock.

"That's correct."

"Do you know the exact time of death?"

"Sometime between nine p.m. and midnight on the eighth."

"Any idea what the killer or killers used?" asked Sherlock.

"It wasn't a straight-edged weapon like a knife or an ax. I also ruled out saws and chainsaws. I did find a few jagged lacerations that appear to be claw marks, along with some teeth marks."

"So it's likely this was an animal attack?"

Porter tilted his head to the side. "The claw marks were too big for a coyote or a dog. The same is true for the victim's dog we exhumed. The only animal in these parts that could do this sort of damage is a black bear, but most of them live in the northwest corner of the state or along the coast. We only have a couple of reported sightings in the county every year, if that."

"What about a dog pack?"

"I've done autopsies on people mauled to death by dogs. They were in pretty bad shape, but even the worst one doesn't compare to what happened to this poor fellow. Besides, the claw marks don't match those of any dog or bear. Dogs, in general, have four toes and bears five. Whatever did this had three claws, indented farther apart than a bear's or a dog's."

Sherlock lowered his head, thinking. "What about a person trying to make it look like it was the Lizard Man?"

Porter bobbed his head from side-to-side. "Perhaps. It would seem an elaborate way to kill someone, especially considering some of the trace evidence the crime scene technicians found on Welsh's body."

"What was it?" asked Sherlock.

"Skin samples." Porter faced him. "At least, I believe they're skin samples. I sent them to the state crime lab in Columbia for DNA analysis, but I swear they look like scales."

ELEVEN

Are we all gonna fit in here? Rastun thought as he stood in the doorway of the mayor's office. Four people were already seated in the small space, a civilian and two black, middle-aged police officers in front of the dark brown wooden desk. Behind it sat a heavyset, gray-haired man. Bishopville Mayor Bud McAllister. He introduced Rastun and Ehrenberg to the others. Herman Sawyer, chairman of the Lee County Council, Police Chief Byron Gibson, and County Sheriff Tom Haddix.

McAllister pointed a hand to two chairs at the back of the room. Rastun took the one up against a bookshelf, barely a couple of feet behind Sheriff Haddix. He'd been in armored personnel carriers roomier than this.

You'd think the mayor would have a bigger office. Then again, this was Bishopville, not Philadelphia or Los Angeles.

Sawyer twisted in his seat to face Ehrenberg. "So how long will it be before you find these things?" The anxiousness in the lean, mustachioed man was evident.

"I'm sorry, Mister Sawyer. I can't answer that."

"What do you mean you can't answer that?" Sawyer's right hand snapped up in the air. "Is it going to take a couple of days? A week? Longer?"

"I'm sorry," Ehrenberg replied in a calm voice, "but looking for a cryptid is not something you can put a timetable on. They do have a knack for staying hidden."

"Well this one isn't staying hidden. It's killed one man, it's got folks 'round here scared. You need to find it and find it quick."

"We will do everything possible to track down these lizard men," Ehrenberg assured him.

Sawyer's eyes bulged. "Lizard *men?* How many of these damn things are out there?"

"I can't say for sure." Ehrenberg shrugged. "But whenever people refer to any cryptid in the singular, it's always a misnomer. Many have been sighted for hundreds of years, so there has to be at least a small population so the species can propagate."

"So how many does that take?"

"At minimum, several dozen. Maybe as many as one to two hundred. Given the number of sightings over the years, and the small area where they've occurred, I can't see it being more than that."

Sawyer gaped, not blinking. "Are you serious? There could be hundreds of these monsters running around?" He turned to Rastun. "And how many security people did you bring?"

"Including myself, four."

"Four?" Sawyer's tone was one of disbelief. "Four against a couple of hundred monsters?"

"It's unlikely we're going to run into every single lizard man in South Carolina at once. The Sasquatch social groups we've encountered have never numbered more than a dozen. We're well trained and well armed. We can handle them."

Sawyer's face tightened. The man didn't seem convinced. He looked at the Sheriff. "You have to help them. Send your men out into the woods and find those things."

"Herman." Haddix, a tall, broad-shouldered man, held up a hand. "You know we don't have the manpower to cover all the forests and swamps around here, neither does Byron. I do have extra patrols around the area where Phil Welsh was murdered."

"I think you two can spare more of your officers for this search. This isn't Charleston or Columbia. Bishopville won't go to hell because we have a few less police on the streets." Sawyer stabbed a hand toward the floor. "This is our number one public safety emergency. We need to find all these lizard men and kill them."

"Mister Sawyer, we are not going to massacre this entire population," said Rastun. "If we do identify the creature that killed Phil Welsh, we will put it down. As for the others, we'll tranq them, attach GPS collars to them, and study them."

"And we're all supposed to go about our business with a bunch of monsters living right on our doorstep?"

"It's similar to a lot of people out west who live with mountain lions or bears near them," Rastun replied.

"Well I'd say a seven-foot-tall lizard man is a hell of a lot more dangerous than a bear or a mountain lion."

"The sightings for this cryptid go back nearly thirty years," Ehrenberg told him. "Until now, there has never been a report of a physical attack, let alone a death."

"And now there's likely to be more." Sawyer's voice climbed with each word.

Rastun ground his teeth, his frustration with the politician mounting. The man seemed determined to work himself up into a panic attack. His gaze shifted to the Mayor McAllister, who had yet to utter a word. Perhaps he wanted to let everyone have their say before weighing in. He'd seen officers do that in the Army. Heck, he'd done it on more than one occasion.

"The number of wild animal attacks on humans a year is small, especially fatal ones," said Rastun. "You're more likely to be killed by a dog than a bear or a mountain lion, or a lizard man."

"And you know this how?" demanded Sawyer.

"My parents have been running the Philadelphia Zoo since I was in high school. I worked there every summer when I was in school. I picked up a thing or two about animals."

Sawyer folded his arms, gaze locked on Rastun. "Well . . . what about the sea raptor? How many people did it kill in Jersey?"

Rastun wanted to roll his eyes. Sawyer had probably seen too many movies and TV shows that made it look like predators couldn't wait to take down the first human they came across.

"There are always exceptions," said Ehrenberg. "The Jersey Shore shark attacks in 1916. The Tsavo lions in Uganda in 1898, and of course, the sea raptor last year."

"And now we have an exception here with the Lizard Man," Sawyer countered.

"All right, look." McAllister finally spoke, holding up both hands. "Before we go any further with this, do we know for sure that Welsh was killed by the Lizard Man?"

"Doctor Porter says there were slash marks on his body consistent with an animal attack," Sheriff Haddix answered, "but not from any known species. He also found what could be scales on Welsh's body. They've been sent to the state crime lab for further analysis."

"What about someone coming up with a way to kill Welsh to make it look like the Lizard Man did it?" suggested Chief Gibson.

"Seems a pretty elaborate way to kill an unemployed tow truck driver," said Rastun.

Gibson tilted his head to the side. "True. Still, I'd like to consider every possible scenario before we say with one hundred percent certainty a monster killed Welsh. Besides, that body he had, why was it gone? I can't see an animal carrying off one of their dead."

"Actually," Ehrenberg held up a finger. "Elephants, chimpanzees, and dolphins have all been observed tending to their dead. There's also a theory that Sasquatch may bury their dead, which is why no one has ever come across one of their corpses. The same could be true for lizard men." He furrowed his brow, eyes darting from one official to another. "Have you considered another name for this creature?"

Rastun stifled a laugh. Trust the Doc to add some levity to a meeting like this.

McAllister stared at Ehrenberg for a couple of seconds, then let out a small chuckle. A bit forced, Rastun thought. Maybe the guy was being polite.

"Well, if you find it, you can name it." The mayor turned to Rastun. "The body Welsh had, you're sure it was the real thing?"

"Yes, sir. The feel of it, the smell, the blood. That was a real animal. The Lizard Man's no longer a myth, and it looks like you've got more of them around here."

"Okay." The mayor thumped his desk. "Herman, Sheriff. Welsh's murder happened outside our city limits, so it's your ballgame. My suggestion would be, for an official position, that from all the evidence we have, Phil Welsh was apparently killed by an unknown animal. We can say the FUBI's looking into a possible connection involving the Lizard Man, but we don't come right out and say that thing did it, unless Doctor Porter says it, or Doctor Ehrenberg's people can find another one of these damn things. Sound reasonable?"

Sawyer, Sheriff Haddix, and Chief Gibson all agreed. Ehrenberg also had no problem, as did Rastun. It was true, after all. The Lizard Man certainly qualified as an unknown animal.

"I still say you need more men," said Sawyer. "Maybe the Sheriff can deputize them."

"I think for right now we're good on manpower," replied Rastun.

Sawyer's shoulders rose, his face stiffening with tension. "I don't agree. I think you need as many people as possible hunting down these things and killing them."

"Mister Sawyer," Rastun spoke in a firm tone. "The FUBI only kills animals as a last resort."

Sawyer rubbed his forehead. "Look, Lee County isn't all that big, and we're not swimming in money. We're trying to lure in more development, more business, to stimulate our economy. After what happened to Welsh, that's gonna scare away anyone who wants to come here. And it'll probably make people already here want to leave. You don't find and kill these things, the whole county could go down the drain."

Rastun squared his shoulders. "Mister Chairman. Like I just said, we only kill cryptids that pose an imminent threat to life."

"Then maybe you can capture 'em and ship 'em off somewhere else?"

"And what if they're vital to the local ecosystem?"

"They're monsters." Sawyer's hands shot out in front of him. "We don't need 'em here."

"Jack's right," said Ehrenberg. "Something the size of a lizard man will have large mammals as part of its diet. Deer, wild hogs. Take them out of the equation and those mammal populations will increase, meaning less food for other mammals. Then starvation and disease sets in."

Sawyer looked away, jaw stiff, not convinced.

"Considering the way you fellas handled the sea raptor situation," McAllister looked from Ehrenberg to Rastun. "I'll defer to your expertise on this. I'm sure the chief and the sheriff will give you whatever help they can."

"Of course." Haddix nodded.

"You bet," said Gibson.

The meeting broke up. Rastun gave a final handshake to everyone in the mayor's office, all of whom wished him luck.

Except Sawyer, who said, "Just find these things fast, before they kill someone else."

Rastun grunted an acknowledgement and headed into the hallway, followed by Ehrenberg.

"Don't pay any attention to Sawyer." The cryptozoologist jerked his head to the office behind them. "He's just scared."

"I know, Doc. The problem is, sometimes scared people do stupid shit."

***

Rastun's eyes burned with fatigue as he walked into the lobby of the Econo Lodge Inn with the rest of the expedition. Dawn was breaking over Bishopville. Most people would soon head off to work, but for him and the rest of the team, their day was done. They'd spent all night exploring the fields and woods near Welsh's property. They discovered a lot of trampled and bent grass. Whether it was caused by a lizard man or the Sheriff's Office crime scene techs had been difficult to determine. The dry, dusty ground also meant finding footprints from two or three days ago was highly unlikely.

In all, a rather unproductive day.

Just gotta look ahead to the next day . . . after a good night's sleep.

Or I guess in this case, a good morning's sleep.

"All right, gang." Ehrenberg fought off a yawn as he spoke. "I'll see you in the conference room at noon. No watching TV. Everyone straight to bed."

"Yes, Dad," said Geek.

Everyone headed to their rooms. Rastun stared at the bed through half-closed eyes. He just wanted to fall on it and go to sleep.

"I assume you wanna hit the shower?" said Karen.

"Do I smell that bad?"

"Hey, I'm soaked with sweat. I doubt you're better off. Why don't you go first while I upload my pics to our website and Facebook pages. Not that I've got much to upload." She checked her camera's screen, cycling through the shots. "Bent grass . . . Bent grass . . . ooh, trampled grass."

As uninteresting as it sounded, it was SOP for field expeditions to photograph any potential evidence of cryptids.

"Here's a good one." Karen angled the camera so Rastun could see the screen. The image showed him in a tan-olive-brown boonie hat and sunglasses with a serious look on his face.

"You know," she said. "You really need to smile more when I take your picture."

"I was tramping around the woods on a muggy night with nothing to show for it. What was there to smile about?"

"You were with me."

"Yeah, but you weren't naked. Now that would make me smile."

"Pervert." Karen playfully slapped his arm. "Go take your shower."

"Yes, ma'am." Rastun threw her a mock salute.

He stripped off his damp clothes and stepped into the shower. The warm water and lather from the miniscule bar of soap felt refreshing. When he finished, he toweled off and threw on an undershirt and a pair of red and white Philadelphia Phillies boxers. While Karen took her shower, he turned on his laptop to check his messages. Nothing too exciting in his personal email. His FUBI one, as usual, was loaded. The vast majority came from people he didn't know. Most were fans wishing him well in his search for the lizard men. A few people offered him their theories – which they presented as scientific fact – about the lizard men.

Their extra-terrestrials. There's been alot of UFO sitings and lizardman sitings in South Caralina since the 1980s. The two have to be conected.

Rastun rolled his eyes, wondering if this guy had ever heard of spellcheck.

Have you heard of the Hollow Earth theory? These things must come from underground. They could be scouting for a full-scale invasion.

The last one was just as amusing.

Captain Rastun,

I have credible information about the true nature of the lizard people. I am not exaggerating when I say they are a threat to every man, woman, and child in South Carolina. Please meet me tomorrow at 1 pm at the coffee shop on Main Street and I will explain everything.

Rastun let out a slow breath. *The price of fame, I guess.* Along with accolades and well wishes from sincere, normal people, he also attracted a fair share of nutbars.

He fired off a short update to Colonel Lipeli, then crawled into bed. He started drifting off to sleep when he heard Karen clear her throat.

She leaned against the wall, clad in only a Led Zeppelin t-shirt. *His* Led Zeppelin t-shirt, which she'd claimed as her own sometime during the past year.

"You asleep yet?" she asked with a wry grin.

"Obviously not."

"Good." Karen removed the t-shirt, balled it up, and threw it at his chest. He ignored it and stared at Karen, who stood naked before him.

"So, are you smiling now?"

Rastun was indeed smiling.

TWELVE

Where the fuck is he?

Cassian fidgeted as he sat on the bench outside the coffee shop. He clutched an iced coffee – his third so far – head whipping left and right.

No sign of Jack Rastun.

"C'mon, man. C'mon."

A young woman walked past, holding a little girl by the hand. She gave him a wary look.

"What?" Cassian snapped.

The woman picked up her pace.

He glared at her for a few more seconds before turning back to his coffee. No surprise she gave him a sketch look. He hadn't shaved in a week and hadn't cut his hair since . . . shit, how long had it been? His polo shirt and jeans had been bought at a thrift store. Everyone probably thought him a homeless man.

Maybe he should have gotten some better clothes for meeting Jack Rastun. He had a decent cash flow, but a good chunk of it went to food, weapons, and other necessary supplies. As for clothes, the cheaper the better. The money he saved getting secondhand shirts and pants could go to buying food and bullets.

And this sweet phone, which played one of his favorite podcasts.

"There is a war coming to our planet, folks," the voice of Darren Staub came through his earbuds. "It's not human versus human. It's mammal versus reptile. The Sasquatch have been out in the open for two years. Their habitats are no longer a secret. And we are going to discover their true origins. They are not of this world. The Sasquatch come from either another planet or another dimension."

Cassian nodded. This hadn't been the first time the talk show host had linked Sasquatch with aliens.

"Reptiles and mammals . . . like water and electricity," Staub continued. "No way the damn lizards are going to share the Earth with them. No room for two star-faring or dimension-hopping races on this planet."

A dull *thump* sounded away from the microphone. "Wake up, everyone! We need to throw in with Sasquatch. Mammals teaming up against reptiles in the coming Great Species War."

Cassian nodded more emphatically. Staub had put out this particular podcast a month ago. He wanted to listen to it again, make sure he didn't forget any important details when he talked to Rastun.

He finished his iced coffee and went back into the coffee shop for another. Cassian checked his watch while in line. Rastun was over an hour late for their meeting.

Maybe he's busy.

He's Jack Rastun. He can make the time to be here, especially with what's at stake.

Cassian returned to the bench just as an SUV parked across the street. He sat up, taking an anxious breath. Could it be him?

Instead, three teenage girls got out of the vehicle.

Damn. A frustrated breath shot out his nose.

The girls crossed the street and headed for the coffee shop. All three were thin and wore shorts. Cassian gazed at their legs as they passed.

The girls ignored him.

"I need a smoothie," said one girl, fanning herself with her hand. "It's hot as fuck today."

"It's been hot as fuck the last three weeks," said another girl. "When's it gonna cool off already?"

Cassian shook his head. Those girls had no idea what hot was. He did. So did Jack Rastun.

When the hell was he gonna show up?

Another half-hour passed. No Jack Rastun. His kidneys were ready to burst.

What if he shows up and I miss him?

He gritted his teeth and clenched his legs together. The pressure built and built till he could no longer resist. He jumped up, chucked his empty cup in the trash, and powerwalked into the coffee shop, making a beeline for the men's room.

Refreshed, he walked out of the restroom. A couple of customers in line gave him cautious, sideways glances. So did one of the baristas.

He locked eyes with one of the customers, a woman, who looked away. What? Just because he wasn't clean-shaven or wore nice clothes, she thought he'd snap and waste everyone in the place?

He hated them. Hated them for assuming he was some psycho because of how he looked. Hated them for their ignorance. No, not ignorance. Their stupidity. Their stubborn refusal to believe in the *real* threat to their lives.

Why do I protect these fucktards?

No, he didn't do what he did for them. He did it for himself.

He did it for his parents.

Cassian waited another twenty minutes. Jack Rastun still didn't show up.

"Shit." He stormed off, ignoring the stares from passers-by.

He must be busy. He fought to convince himself of that. It did nothing to quell his anger. How could Rastun ignore his email? How much clearer could he have been on the threat those monsters posed?

Cassian continued on for a mile-and-a-half until he reached the parking lot of a drug store. His Coachmen RV was parked in the middle of the lot. Three men sat inside. One of them, a string bean with a goatee, asked, "So did he show?"

"No," Cassian answered Doug Smith.

"Did you really think he was gonna show up because you sent him an email?" A short man with a firm build folded his arms. "This is Jack Rastun we're talking about."

"I told him how important it was," Cassian replied to Todd Lansford. "I told him lives were at stake. Everything he's been through, you'd think he woulda met me."

"Yeah, right," Lansford scoffed.

Cassian furrowed his brow. "What's that supposed to mean?"

"He's a celebrity, man. He doesn't give a shit about people like us any more. It's all about being on TV and writing books and shit. He probably just sits back and lets the grunts do all the hard work, like all officers do."

"Bullshit." Cassian slammed the RV door closed. "Jack Rastun's a hero. He won a Silver Star in Afghanistan. He went one-on-one with that sea monster and killed it."

"Yeah," said Lansford. "Then he got rich and famous and it all went to his head."

Cassian glared at him. Lansford always rode his ass whenever he talked about Rastun. He chalked it up to jealousy. Jack Rastun was the epitome of what a warrior, a hero, ought to be. It inspired him to pick up *Warriors and Monsters: The Jack Rastun Story,* one of the few books he'd actually read from beginning to end. That and Darren Staub's three novels.

"Um, I think I have some good news."

Cassian looked to a thick young man with glasses sitting at the table, a laptop in front of him.

"What is it?"

"I hacked in to the Lee County Sheriff's Office network."

"Way to go, man." Cassian fist bumped Weber Proly, the team's computer geek. The only one of the four without prior military experience, Proly had been a tub of lard when Cassian first met him. But after putting the young man through an improvised boot camp, his fat turned to muscle. Proly could now handle himself on a computer and in a fight.

"It was no sweat. They're no different from most government agencies. Their security's beyond lame. The equivalent of a screen door with a rusty latch."

"Still, good job. Get anything useful?"

"Not much," Proly answered. "Just some things they didn't put in the news, like they found traces of scales on the dead dude and some specks of blood in the field near his house. They're still waiting for the DNA results. We also looked over the coroner's report. He says an unknown animal killed that Welsh guy."

"Animal my ass," Cassian snorted. "This Welsh guy was gonna expose those slimy bastards to the whole world, and they killed him and took away that body."

"Maybe they'll go into hiding until this all blows over," Smith suggested. "Especially with the FUBI here."

"Nope." Cassian shook his head. "They brought in Jack Rastun, Randy Ehrenberg, and Karen Thatcher. That's their fucking first string. They found the sea raptor, they found those Sasquatch in Florida. The lizards might worry they'll find them, too. They may try and take out Rastun and his team, or worse."

He leaned against the wall. "We have got to get in touch with him before it's too late."

THIRTEEN

Pizza never tasted so good.

Much as Len Mankowski loved his wife, he was happy when it was her rehearsal night. Once a week, Pam practiced with the Choir Babes, a group of middle-aged women who performed at all sorts of events throughout the state. She enjoyed singing, and he enjoyed being able to eat whatever he wanted for dinner when she was gone. Pam had been on a serious vegan kick the last few months.

"It's better for your health," she had told him, "and there are some really tasty dishes, too."

None of them, though, were as tasty as a pizza, especially one with sausage, peppers, and mushrooms. He moaned in delight as he polished off his second slice just as the local news came on. It started with a recap of the debate between the candidates for mayor of Columbia. That was followed by a three-injury accident on I-20.

They didn't get to the "Lizard Man Attack" until after the first commercial break. The anchor took thirty seconds to say that the cops and FUBI had nothing new to report.

Mankowski grunted out a laugh as he chewed on another slice. *Lizard Man Attack.* What a bunch of BS. That's all anyone talked about at the AC repair company he worked for.

"I knew this would happen," said one technician. "I knew the Lizard Man was gonna rip apart someone one day."

"I'm keeping my pistol on my nightstand," said the receptionist. "Glock 37. One shot and that thing's going down."

"No one better have their AC break down outside the city at night," said another tech. "I ain't goin' out to fix it. Not after what happened to that guy."

Mankowski could only roll his eyes. He'd heard stories about the Lizard Man since he was a teenager, and dismissed them.

"They found Bigfoot and that sea monster," a co-worker told him the other day. "How can you say the Lizard Man doesn't exist?"

He could accept Bigfoot a lot easier than the stupid fucking Lizard Man. Apparently, though, he was in the minority. People were flocking to gun stores. Security companies had been flooded with calls. A group of dumbasses got busted by the cops for forming their own Lizard Man hunting party.

It was a person that killed that Welsh guy, not a monster. He was more than prepared for that, with his hunting rifle and two pistols. Welsh's house was only three miles from his. This far from Bishopville, if something went down, you couldn't wait for the cops to show up. You had to take care of it yourself.

Hopefully, the cops would find this psycho and lock him up.

Mankowski finished off his pizza. He folded the box, stuffed it at the bottom of the garbage can, and covered it with other trash. The last thing he needed was Pam getting on his ass about eating something "unvegan."

He settled down in front of the TV and clicked on the Braves game. They were up in Philadelphia tonight.

They only played one inning before a downpour hammered Citizens Bank Park.

Wish we had some of that rain. He couldn't remember the last time it had been so hot and dry around here.

Mankowski flipped through the channels, finally settling on a rerun of *NCIS.*

Something pounded the back door.

Mankowski jerked in his chair.

Another *bang* shook the walls.

"Who's there?" His heart slammed against his chest. He stood, his legs shaking. He took a tentative step forward. Another.

Gun. Get your –

The door exploded. Heavy footsteps pounded across the kitchen.

Mankowski hyperventilated. His brain screamed for him to move.

He stood in place, shaking, terrified.

A large, scaly shape stalked into the living room.

Mankowski screamed as it charged him.

***

Pam Mankowski smiled as she neared her house. Practice had gone well tonight. The Choir Babes were ready for Bishopville's annual 4th of July celebration coming up in a few weeks. She just hoped there would be fireworks. Vicky's husband worked for the fire department, and they were as nervous as a long-tailed cat in a room full of rocking chairs. One spark could set off a major forest fire.

Maybe we'll get some rain by then.

She started to turn into the driveway, wondering what garbage Len stuffed into his mouth tonight. Much as he tried to hide it, she knew he ate very non-vegan dinners when she was at choir practice. Well, maybe cheat days were all right. But not many.

She hit a button just above the sunglasses holder. The garage door slid up.

Two large shapes stood in the garage. She slammed on the brakes as one of them pushed over the tool chest.

The shapes turned to her.

Pam stared at them, mouth agape, shivering.

One of the shapes ran at her. She screamed as it jumped on the hood.

A fist slammed against the windshield. Spiderweb cracks spread across the glass. Blazing red eyes stared down at her. Pam shrieked louder. She threw the car into reverse. Tires squealed. The shape slid off the hood. The car bounced out of the driveway and tore off down the street. Pam kept screaming. She had no idea how fast she was going.

Len. Oh my God, Len! Was he okay? Was he . . .

No, no, no.

She slammed on the brakes. With trembling hands, she fumbled through her purse for her phone. Pam yelped when her finger pricked something. It felt like the tip of a pen.

She finally gripped her phone, ignoring the droplets of blood from her index finger. Her breaths came rapidly as she hit the button for 911.

"Nine-One-One, what's your emergency?"

"My house. They broke in. My husband . . . I don't . . . I don't know."

"Calm down, ma'am. What's your address?"

Pam gave it. "Please send someone. My husband's home. Oh my God, send every cop you have. They almost got me, too."

"Who almost got you, ma'am?"

Pam took a shaky breath. "Lizard men. They were lizard men!"

FOURTEEN

"You're about fifty yards from it," Rastun heard Alana say in his earpiece. He took a careful step forward, Aster 7 dart gun up. The forest was heavy with trees and brush. Whatever Alana's drone detected on its thermal imager was well concealed.

And big.

He kept his focus straight ahead. He sensed rather than saw Karen moving to his left and Dan Plank to his right.

"Forty meters," reported Alana.

"I still can't see it."

"Trust me, it's there. Wait. It's turning toward you."

Rastun's left fist snapped up. Karen and Plank halted. Rastun kept the dart gun leveled.

"Now it's moving away from you," said Alana.

He charged forward. Something leapt out from behind a tree ahead of him. He halted and lowered the weapon. "False alarm . . . again."

"What was it?" asked Alana.

"A deer. Looks like a white tail."

He watched the animal bound deeper into the dark woods.

Plank moaned. "Man, how many times is this gonna happen? Every time that drone finds something, it's either a deer or a coyote or a fox. When are we gonna find some friggin' lizard men?"

Karen turned to the field investigator-in-training. "This is part of the investigation process, Dan. You have to look for days, sometimes weeks, before you find what you're looking for, and that's if you're lucky."

Plank slouched. "This is gonna take forever."

"Hey," said Rastun. "You're looking at a guy who once spent three weeks humping across the mountains of Afghanistan looking for a group of Taliban fighters."

"Three weeks?"

"Yup. We found them, eventually. You just need some patience."

Plank moaned again.

"I take it they didn't have a course called Patience One-oh-One at American University," said Rastun.

Plank tramped on ahead. "I wish we'd find this damn thing already."

Rastun shook his head as the young man continued through the darkened forest.

"You can't blame him too much." Karen patted his shoulder. "His generation wants everything right this second."

"Well, he's going to be sorely disappointed when he learns that's not how the world works." Rastun started forward, then turned back to Karen. "And what's with this, 'his generation' bit? He's not that much younger than me."

"Hey, don't you mean he's not much younger than *us?*"

"No. To him, you're ancient." Rastun grinned, bracing himself for the inevitable response.

Karen smacked him on the shoulder. "Remind me again why we're together?"

"Because I'm a bottomless pit of irresistible charm."

"Only in your dreams."

Rastun chuckled as they continued on, the rest of the expedition walking abreast at ten-yard intervals. He caught sight of Plank, head down, footsteps harsher than before.

"Eyes up, Plank. You won't see any lizard men staring at your feet."

"Uh-huh."

Rastun bristled. He'd been used to a reply of, "Yes, sir," whenever he gave an order. That rarely happened in the civilian world. He thought he'd finally learned to accept it, but times like this the discipline and procedures drilled into him since he was an 18-year-old ROTC cadet resurfaced.

At least Plank listened. The young man had his head up, looking left and right. Rastun only wished he could order him to have some patience. Without it, Plank had no future as a field investigator.

They pushed on past the trees and bushes. Crickets chirped. An owl hooted. A rabbit broke from the brush. There was an abundance of wildlife out tonight. He didn't take that as a good sign. If a large predator like the Lizard Man was around, all these animals would have gone to ground.

They took a break around eleven. Rastun, sitting against a tree with Karen next to him, finished a Cliff Bar when he heard the faint hum of Ehrenberg's satellite phone on vibrate.

"It's Sherlock," he said, looking at the screen.

The others gathered around him as he put the phone on speaker mode.

"Sherlock, what's on your mind?"

"There's been another attack."

Rastun felt his chest clench. Karen closed her eyes and lowered her head.

"Where?" asked Rastun.

"A house about three miles from where Phil Welsh was attacked."

"When did it happen?"

"The Sheriff's Office told me it couldn't have been more than three hours ago."

Ehrenberg drew a slow breath. "Anyone killed?"

"Affirmative. A man named Len Mankowski, fifty-three. Same M.O. as the Welsh murder. Body mutilated, house trashed. Thankfully his wife managed to get away."

"Is she okay?" asked Ehrenberg.

"Yes. Shaken up, of course, but not hurt. One of the attackers tried to bust through the windshield of her car. She drove away before they could get in."

"Did she positively identify her attacker?" Ehrenberg leaned closer to the phone.

"She claimed they were lizard men," said Sherlock. "Detective Blefary chalked it up to hysteria, and she was pretty hysterical when deputies found her."

"Where is she now?"

"Lee County Memorial Hospital."

"I thought you said she wasn't hurt," said Karen.

"She wasn't," Sherlock responded, "but when the police found her, she was having chest pains and trouble breathing. They thought she was having a heart attack. The paramedics said it was a panic attack. They took her to the hospital as a precaution."

"Do you think I could talk to her?" asked Ehrenberg.

"The Sheriff said he'd cooperate with our investigation, so that shouldn't be a problem."

"Good. I'll be at the hospital as soon as possible."

"I'll meet you there, Doc."

Ehrenberg pocketed the sat phone. "Petal. You're lead investigator until I get back."

"Cool."

"I'll go with you," Rastun said.

"Thanks, Jack, but I think I can find my way back to the car."

"C'mon, Doc, you know the rules. No one goes off on their own, especially with a hostile cryptid on the loose."

59

Ehrenberg gave a brief sigh. "Yeah, you're right." He looked at the others. "Stay extra alert. Those attacks happened not too far from here."

"Don't worry, Doc." Geek threw him a two-fingered salute. "We'll be ready if the shit hits the fan."

Ehrenberg didn't talk much during the hike back to their SUVs. Rastun figured the cryptozoologist was thinking of questions to ask Mrs. Mankowski. Or maybe he was thinking of her now late husband. Rastun certainly was. They were maybe ten miles away from Welsh's home, which put them 13 from the Mankowskis's house.

If only we'd searched toward the east instead of the west, maybe . . .

Maybe the lizard men would have killed that Mankowski guy anyway. He learned during his time in Iraq and Afghanistan you could play "what if" until it drove you crazy. It wouldn't change what happened. You just had to deal with it.

He drove to Bishopville, while Ehrenberg texted the FUBI higher ups about the latest attack. It was after 12:30 in the morning when Rastun spotted the series of one-story, rectangular buildings that made up Lee County Memorial Hospital. He used his Bluetooth to tell Sherlock they'd arrived. The deputy marshal met them at the main entrance.

"Can we talk to Mrs. Mankowski?" asked Ehrenberg.

"Blefary gave us the go-ahead, though he didn't look happy about it."

"A blowjob wouldn't make that guy happy," said Rastun.

Sherlock nodded. "He did have one stipulation. He wants me to record the interview and share it with him."

"No problem." Ehrenberg waved them to the door. "Let's go."

Apprehension twisted Rastun's insides as he walked through the corridors. He didn't like the thought of talking to Mrs. Mankowski so soon after her husband died. He wanted her to have time to grieve. But with a killer cryptid out there, they couldn't afford to wait.

Mrs. Mankowski sat on a table in one of the examination rooms. She was of medium build with curly brown hair, late forties or early fifties. Her head was down, shoulders sagging. A bandage covered the tip of her index finger. She wasn't hysterical, like she'd been when the police and paramedics found her. Rastun wondered if the woman had been given a mild sedative.

"Excuse me, Mrs. Mankowski?" Ehrenberg stepped toward her.

She sniffled and looked up. Rastun clenched his teeth when he saw the woman's red, tear-filled eyes. His heart went out to her.

Mrs. Mankowski blinked. "A-Are you Randy Ehrenberg, from the FUBI?"

"I am." Last year's sea raptor expedition had made Ehrenberg a household name. "And this is Jack Rastun and Sherlock, I mean, Arthur Dunmore from the U.S. Marshal's Service. Um . . . I just wanted to say we're sorry about what happened to your husband."

"Thank you." Mrs. Mankowski's voice cracked. She shuddered and pulled a tissue from the pack on her lap.

Rastun looked away. He wished he could be anywhere else but here.

Focus on the job.

"I hate to ask this," Ehrenberg tensed for a moment, "but I wanted to see if you were up to answering some questions about the attack?"

"The police already did that. But that detective . . ." She dabbed her eyes with the tissue. "He didn't believe me when I told him I saw lizard men. But I did. I did. You believe me, right? You hunt these things."

"I believe you." Ehrenberg gave her a sympathetic smile. "Do you mind if we record this?"

"No, that's fine."

Ehrenberg took out a camcorder from his pack, while Sherlock activated the audio recorder on his phone.

"I'm talking with Mrs. Pam Mankowski at Lee County Memorial Hospital about a reported attack by lizard men." Ehrenberg gave the time and date. "FUBI Field Security Specialist Jack Rastun and Deputy U.S. Marshal Arthur Sherlock Dunmore are present with me. Mrs. Mankowski, when did you first see your attackers?"

"I was coming home from choir practice. I guess it was around eight. I was pulling into the garage. That's when I saw them. They were in the garage, trashing it."

"How many?"

"Two."

"Can you describe them?"

"Big. They were so big. The head looked like a lizard's. And the eyes." She trembled. "Red. So red."

"What happened after you saw them?" asked Ehrenberg.

Mrs. Mankowski took a couple of shaky breaths.

"It's okay, ma'am." Rastun laid a hand on her shoulder. "Just take your time."

It took a minute for the woman to regain herself. "The one, it . . . it jumped on my car. My God, it was huge. A-Almost broke my windshield. I put the car in reverse and got out."

"What about the creature?" asked Ehrenberg.

"It fell off the hood."

"Do you know if it was injured?" asked Sherlock.

Mrs. Mankowski shook her head. "I don't know. I just wanted to get out of there. Then I thought about Len, and . . . I didn't even . . . I didn't even see if he was okay."

She broke down.

Rastun's jaw stiffened. He tried to think of comforting words, recalling all the times he dealt with grieving wives and mothers at memorials for fallen soldiers. "He was a good man," he'd always say, or, "He was a good soldier . . . He was a credit to his country." Rastun sometimes wondered if they had even heard his words, if they even mattered. How could simple compliments ease their pain?

And what the hell could he say to Mrs. Mankowski? He knew nothing about her husband. How hollow would his words sound?

He just let her cry. After a few minutes, Ehrenberg put an arm around her. "Mrs. Man . . . Pam, there was nothing you could have done. I think he would have been glad you got away safely."

"Thank you."

Mrs. Mankowski went through a few more tissues before she was ready to continue. Ehrenberg turned the camcorder back on.

"Did these creatures try to follow you?" he asked.

"No. I don't think so."

"Anything else you remember about them? A sound they made?"

"No."

"Jack." Ehrenberg handed him the camcorder, then took out his iPad. "I'm going to show you some images. Tell me if any of them resemble the creature you saw."

Ehrenberg called up a photo of a Sasquatch. Mrs. Mankowski shook her head. Next was a picture of a man in a leaf-covered ghillie suit used by hunters and military snipers. Then a bear, then another Sasquatch, then a CGI image of the Lizard Man with green, scaly skin, and red eyes. It had its maw open, revealing rows of sharp teeth.

"That's it." She tapped a finger on the screen. "That's what I saw."

Ehrenberg nodded, then took the camcorder from Rastun. "Did you or your husband notice anything unusual around your house over the past few nights?"

"Like what?"

"Strange noises, strange footprints. Unexplained damage to vehicles or your home."

Mrs. Mankowski shook her head. "No."

"Do you have a dog?" asked Rastun.

"We used to. Maxie. But she died a couple years ago."

Ehrenberg lowered the camcorder. "Mrs. Mankowski, thank you very much for your time. Again, you have our condolences."

"Thank you."

They exited the examination room, Rastun looking back. Mrs. Mankowski lowered her head and wiped at her eyes.

"Why the question about the dog?" Sherlock asked him as they entered the hallway.

"Phil Welsh told me his dog was barking up a storm just before he shot that lizard man."

"Poor woman." Ehrenberg leaned against the wall. "This is starting to turn into another sea raptor expedition."

"I wouldn't go that far," Sherlock told him. "A lot more people were killed in that one."

Rastun turned to the marshal. "Then let's make damn sure the same doesn't happen here."

FIFTEEN

"Get up! C'mon, get up, guys. You gotta see this."

Cassian's eyes snapped open. He sat up in his bed and looked to the kitchen table. Proly leaned close to his laptop, his face lit up in excitement.

"What the fuck, man? I was sleeping," groused Lansford. Both he and Smith lay on the floor in their sleeping bags.

"Forget sleeping. There's been another Lizard Man attack."

"What?" Cassian jumped out of bed and plopped down next to Proly. "When?"

"Last night, just west of Bishopville. Here, I'll play it for you."

After Lansford and Smith got to their feet, Proly clicked on a video on the website for Channel 19 in Columbia.

"A Lee County man is brutally murdered, and some believe the legendary Lizard Man is responsible," said the smartly-dressed male anchor. "Good evening, Columbia, I'm Connor Green.

"'Horrific.' That's how one official with the Lee County Sheriff's Office described the scene at a home outside Bishopville, where a man in his fifties was found dead around eight-thirty tonight. Law enforcement officials say there are similarities between this death and that of Phil Welsh, the victim of what has been dubbed 'The Lizard Man Attack.'"

Green introduced a female reporter on the scene. She talked of how the body had been 'badly mauled' and that the house where the murder took place was only three miles from Welsh's home.

"Sheriff's officials say the victim's wife was pulling into the driveway when one of the assailants rushed her car and shattered the windshield. She managed to escape with a minor injury and call Nine-One-One."

"Andrea, has the Sheriff's Office actually said that the Lizard Man was responsible for this attack?" asked Connor Green.

"The Sheriff's Office has avoided any mention of the Lizard Man, but they have stated that some unknown animal appears to be responsible for the death of Phil Welsh, and this attack seems identical to the one on Welsh."

Cassian grunted. "They still think this was an animal. Fucking blind sheep." He looked at Proly. "Did they give the names of the people who got attacked?"

"No. But this thing's a few hours old. Let me call up something more recent."

It didn't take long before Proly found an article from the *Lee County Observer* online.

"Here we are. The guy who got killed was Len Mankowski. His wife's name is Pam. Says here she was taken to Lee County Memorial Hospital."

Cassian leaned back in his seat. "Yeah, the news said she had a minor injury."

"Uh-huh." Proly straightened up, realization on his face. "Shit. You know what that means?"

Lips pressed in a tight line, Cassian slowly nodded. "Yeah. I do."

SIXTEEN

"Damn. They went all out for us."

Rastun gazed around the basement of the Lee County Courthouse. Boxes and crates had been pushed to the side, making way for a large table with several laptops and phones. A large video monitor hung from the wall above a whiteboard, with maps of the area taped to either side. A small refrigerator stood in the corner, along with a table for a coffee maker and cups. Two middle-aged men, volunteers with the Sheriff's office, staffed the FUBI's new command center.

"All that's missing is a spread of cheese and crackers," Geek whispered to him. "Or better yet, one'a those big-ass subs."

"Put in a request. The worst they can say is no . . . and they probably will."

Geek sighed. "Just kill my hopes, why don't ya, Cap'n?"

"Well, you can have your sub. I'm getting some coffee."

Rastun poured himself a cup of the black liquid, forcing his heavy eyelids back. After interviewing Mrs. Mankowski, he and Ehrenberg rejoined the rest of the expedition. They found some disturbed vegetation and what appeared to be a partial, clawed footprint, but otherwise came up empty.

He dumped two sugar packets into his cup and took a sip, grimacing. The coffee was warm, and somewhat bitter from the excess sugar. Right now he didn't care about taste. He needed something to keep him awake.

"Oh, I so need that right now." Karen shuffled next to him and got her own cup, also dumping in two sugars, yawning while she did it.

"You may want to add one more so you don't fall asleep at the meeting." Rastun took another sip from his cup.

Karen looked at him through half-open eyelids. "What I want is to be back in bed. We were out nearly all night, barely got three hours sleep, and Sawyer wants us here at nine for this stupid meeting?"

"Just gotta suck it up. I can't tell you how many times --"

"I know. How many times you stayed up twenty-four straight hours or more when you were in the Army 'cause you Rangers are all superhuman."

Rastun cocked his head. "You know me too well."

"I should." She flashed him a grin. "We've been together almost a year."

He felt a hitch in his breath as he stared at Karen's beautiful face. It had been nearly a year, the best year of his life thanks to this woman who possessed more spirit and toughness than any he'd ever known. How he'd gotten so lucky was beyond him.

"Yeah, well, after a year with you, I know if you don't get at least seven hours of sleep, you go through the day like a zombie, and a cranky one at that."

Karen frowned, then softly chuckled. "Too true, but I bet you still don't know what my favorite color is?"

Rastun's face scrunched in thought. "Um . . . blue?"

Rolling her eyes, Karen turned away from him.

"Yellow?" he said.

"Keep trying."

He let out a short laugh and followed her to the conference table.

The local officials began filing in a few minutes later. Mayor McAllister, Sheriff Haddix, Chief Gibson, and County Councilman Sawyer.

"Thanks for the set up." Ehrenberg shook all their hands.

"You're welcome," Haddix replied. "I thought it would be a good idea to coordinate all our efforts."

"Especially now that this thing has killed two people." Sawyer folded his arms, aiming a hard stare at Ehrenberg.

Rastun noted the tone of the politician. He couldn't tell if the man was upset over a second alleged Lizard Man death, or if he blamed the FUBI for not preventing it. If the latter, then Sawyer was a fool.

Then again, he hadn't thought highly of the county councilman after their initial meeting.

After getting coffee or water, everyone took their seats at the conference table. Ehrenberg and Petal began with the details of the interview with Pam Mankowski and the FUBI's unsuccessful search around her home.

"How is the poor woman doing?" asked Petal.

"She's all right, all things considering." The corners of Haddix's mouth turned down, probably in sympathy for Pam

Mankowski. "She's getting out of the hospital later this morning and going to stay with a cousin in Camden. One of my deputies is taking her back to her house to get some things."

Haddix folded his arms on the table. "We should have tip lines set up by early this afternoon. People can phone, text, or email their information to us."

Ehrenberg frowned. "I hate to say it, but you'll probably get more hoaxers than legitimate tips."

"We usually do with these things, but if just one of those calls turns out to be legitimate, it's worth it."

"Has Doctor Porter done his examination on Len Mankowski?" asked Sherlock.

"Just wrapped it up a couple of hours ago." Haddix shifted in his chair to face the deputy marshal. "Same as Welsh. It appears the attack was done by some animal."

"Or again," Gibson began, "someone who wants us to think the Lizard Man is ripping people apart."

"I think it's pretty obvious we're dealing with the genuine article," Ehrenberg countered, "given all the evidence we have."

Gibson tilted his head. "It's just as possible a person could have done this. Someone might have made a costume, complete with claws, and decided to go on a killing spree."

Petal scrunched her face in disbelief. "Why would anyone do that?"

"Why have some murderers kept parts of their victims as trophies or engaged in cannibalism? There are some very sick and twisted people in this world."

"Making Welsh their first victim is too much of a coincidence," said Rastun. "He said he'd keep quiet about having the Lizard Man's body."

Gibson shrugged. "Maybe he didn't. Maybe he blabbed about it at a bar and someone overheard him. They killed him and took the alleged Lizard Man body as some big prize. We're trying to retrace Welsh's steps in the days before his death, and to see if he had any connection to Len Mankowski."

Rastun bristled at the term, "alleged Lizard Man body." But with the corpse gone, it would be hard to convince skeptics like Bishopville's police chief it was the real deal.

"So what else are you doing to find the lizard men?" Sawyer let out a harsh breath. "Or killers dressed like lizard men or who or whatever's responsible?"

"Chief Gibson has agreed to loan us a few of his officers to help us patrol the area where Welsh and Mankowski were killed," said Haddix. "We also have a volunteer who owns a Cessna. He's agreed to do aerial searches."

"I set up several webcams and camera traps in the woods around Phil Welsh's home," Karen added. "After this attack we'll have to expand our coverage area." She looked to Ehrenberg. "I'll have to get the Foundation to overnight us some more webcams and camera traps."

"Order as many as you need." Ehrenberg shifted his gaze to Sawyer. "And with Geek and Alana's drone from Aster Technologies, we'll have a lot of electronic eyes peeled for the lizard men."

"Real eyes would be better. Lots of them. There are a lot of people in this county who like to hunt and camp. Let's have them volunteer and form a big search party."

"A big search party with a lot of members likely untrained in dealing with the sort of situations we do." Rastun leaned forward in his chair. "I also don't like the idea of a lot of scared people with guns out there who might shoot a tree stump, or another person, because they think it's the Lizard Man."

"I have to agree with Mister Rastun on that," said Haddix.

"Me too." Petal's hand shot up. "The last thing we need is people with itchy trigger fingers shooting creatures that had nothing to do with these attacks, maybe even wiping out the entire species in the process."

"Two people are dead, Doctor Garland," Sawyer snapped. "Now's not the time for this animal rights PETA bullshit."

Petal glared at him. Rastun started to open his mouth, about to come to the defense of his teammate.

"C'mon, Herman." Mayor McAllister held up his hand. "Settle down. It sounds like the Chief, the Sheriff, and Doctor Ehrenberg's people have a good plan to find these monsters."

"And how many people died in New Jersey before the FUBI found the sea raptor?"

All of Rastun's muscles clenched. He eyed Sawyer, rage boiling. He gritted his teeth, fighting not to go off on the fuckhead, all the while thinking of Dr. Malakov having her head ripped off in front of him, unable to help the scientist.

"A lot more people would have died if it wasn't for us." Karen shot back, her eyes narrowed.

"That's enough, folks." McAllister spoke in a firmer tone. He scanned the people at the table. "Arguing and throwing around accusations won't help us stop these lizard men from killing more people."

Silence settled over the table. Several people took slow breaths or looked down to calm themselves. Rastun forced his muscles to unwind, glancing at the mayor, grateful for his cool head.

"Sorry," Sawyer muttered, not sounding like he meant it.

A few more seconds of silence passed before Ehrenberg spoke. "What I want to know is, why now? There have been sightings of the Lizard Man since the late 1980s. There've been reports it damaged cars, but it never physically attacked anyone until now. So, what changed?"

McAllister folded his arms and leaned back in his seat. "Mmm." He retained his thoughtful look for a few moments before saying, "Any theories?"

"Maybe there aren't enough animals in their normal habitat," suggested Petal. "They could be searching other places for new sources of food."

The sheriff's phone rang. He took the call while the mayor answered, "I don't think lack of food is the problem. I know a lot of hunters around here. Most of them come back with a pretty sizeable deer or pig."

"What about human encroachment into their territory?" asked Rastun. "Have any new developments popped up around Bishopville in the last year or two?"

"Yeah." McAllister nodded. "Cedar Creek Homes. About a hundred houses. My firm actually handled the project."

"Where is it?" asked Ehrenberg.

McAllister pointed to one of the maps on the wall. "West of town, near the Camden Highway."

Ehrenberg walked over to the map. "Where exactly?" He traced a finger along the highway.

"Right there."

His finger stopped just north of a pond on the other side of the road. "Right here. The edge of Scape Ore Swamp, where the majority of Lizard Man sightings have been reported."

Sawyer took a quick breath and held it. McAllister grunted and looked away.

Sheriff Haddix set his phone down on the table. "That was Doc Porter. He got the DNA results back on the skin samples."

"What did they show?" asked Ehrenberg.

"They're reptilian scales, but they're not from any known species."

SEVENTEEN

Cassian learned many skills during his time in Marine Force Recon. Gathering intelligence, CQB – Close Quarters Battle – advanced first aid, how to survive in any environment.

But the one skill he had come to value the most was patience. Many people his age had no concept of it. They were part of the generation of instant gratification. If they had to tell a friend something, they couldn't just wait to see them face-to-face. They had to text them now. When they wanted food or some disgusting pseudo-coffee concoction, it had to be ready right at that moment. If they had to wait more than a minute for anything, they'd lose their pathetic little minds.

You couldn't be that way in the Marines, especially in Force Recon. Sometimes you had to wait hours, maybe days, or even weeks, for the enemy to show up. Then you just sat there and watched them, for hours, or days, or weeks, gathering every bit of information you could, and passing it along to other Marines who would erase them from existence.

And if Force Recon had to take direct action, they were more than capable.

Cassian had to do both this day. He had to exercise patience, wait for his target to show up, then eliminate it himself.

He couldn't have asked for a better location. The house was the only one on this stretch of road. He had settled beneath some bushes, his ghillie suit making him invisible to any cars that drove past. His position gave him a perfect view of the front porch. From 110 yards out, he didn't have to be a trained sniper to take out his target.

Smith was hidden two miles down the road, ready to alert him when the target's vehicle appeared. A 2013 Nissan Altima, red in color. Proly had learned that from hacking into the South Carolina Department of Motor Vehicles. Lansford was a hundred yards back in the woods, covering his rear, while Proly sat behind the wheel of the motorhome, ready to extract them.

Everyone was in place. All Cassian had to do was wait.

Hours passed without a sign of their target. The house sat deserted, yellow police tape flapping in the wind in front of the door. Even with the best trained warriors, the more time that went by, the more the mind wandered. Times like these, Cassian's mind wandered to one night in particular. That horrifying night when he was six. The night that changed his life.

He closed his eyes, projecting himself back in time. The fear, the screams, seemed as real now as they had been all those years ago.

That terror had overwhelmed him for most of his childhood. As he got older, it morphed into rage, and a desire for revenge. But would he stand a chance if he ever ran into one of those monsters?

He recalled that day when he was seventeen and passed by the Marine Corps recruiting office at a local mall. The poster that caught his eye had a man in black camo face paint covered in a leafy ghillie suit and the words SWIFT. SILENT. DEADLY. MARINE FORCE RECON.

That's what he needed to be to take on the so-called lizard men. The day after he graduated from high school, he joined the Marines.

Cassian spent three years in uniform. It would have been more if not for all the "discipline issues." Whatever. The Corps taught him all he needed to search out and destroy his enemies, and he'd honed those skills in Afghanistan. After his time in the service, he'd come back to South Carolina and took the fight to the monsters.

They thought they were safe, that everyone was blind to the truth. Well he was no longer blind, and he would show, once again, that they were not safe.

His phone vibrated. Smith texted him. *Cop car coming your way.*

Cassian lay still. He heard the engine from a distance. Then a white car with a lightbar appeared. He held his breath, nervousness bubbling up. He convinced himself his concealment was good. The cop wouldn't see him.

The car turned into the driveway of the Mankowskis' home. Maybe the police had to get more evidence.

The deputy exited the car, a stocky man with a shaved head. Cassian didn't move. He did what Force Recon Marines do best. Observe.

The deputy walked around to the passenger side and opened the door.

What the hell?

It was Pam Mankowski. No doubt about it. He had stared intently at her driver's license photo that Proly got for him.

Why the hell is a cop bringing her home?

Maybe the deputy was part of the conspiracy. Maybe he was bringing Pam Mankowski up to speed on what was expected of her as a new convert.

Shit. This complicated things. Pam Mankowski was his target, but if he shot her, the deputy's training would kick in. He'd go for cover and call for the cavalry.

The deputy led Pam Mankowski toward the front door.

Cassian tucked the Remington 798 against his shoulder and stared down the scope. He settled the crosshairs just in front of the deputy's face.

Lead the target . . . shouldn't be much bullet drag . . . gentle breeze from the southeast.

The deputy put his right foot on the first step.

Cassian let out his breath halfway and pulled the trigger.

The round drilled through the deputy's cheek. A trained Marine sniper would have put it through the target's temple, but with a .30-06 round, it was good enough. A cloud of red blasted out the other side of the deputy's head. He toppled to the ground.

Pam Mankowski stared at the deputy, wide-eyed, mouth agape. Like most civilians who experienced something unexpected, she froze in shock.

Cassian's second round tore through the top of Pam Mankowski's skull. Blood and brains spattered the side of the house. She fell on her back, dead before she hit the ground.

Cassian picked up the shell casings and slid backwards, deeper into the woods. When he could barely see the roadway, he rose and started running, texting as he did.

X-Point. Now.

He, Smith, and Lansford reached the extraction point without incident. Proly was waiting for them in the RV. Cassian glanced back in the direction of the Mankowskis' house. He couldn't help but feel bad for the wife. But he'd read and watched articles and shows about how the "lizard men" created hybrids by combining their DNA with a human's.

Pam Mankowski had been injured in last night's attack. Whether bitten or scratched, the damn monster had put its DNA into her. The transformation had begun, sort of like a werewolf. If he could take out any of their foot soldiers, or potential foot soldiers, he'd damn well do it.

Two down, and a lot more to go.

EIGHTEEN

A wailing siren caught Rastun's attention. He glanced at the rearview mirror to see a police car barreling down the rural road, red and blue lights flashing.

He pulled to the side. The cop car shot past him. So did another, and an unmarked SUV with flashing lights in its grill.

"Damn," Geek said from the backseat. "There must be some serious shit going on."

Rastun nodded and pulled back onto the road, looking at Sherlock in the rearview mirror. "Does this look like the kind of place where three cop cars hauling ass is normal?"

"No it does not." He pulled out his phone and called the Sheriff's Office. "I just passed three of your vehicles going down the Camden Highway. Is it anything serious?"

Several seconds passed. Sherlock's usual, stoic expression faltered.

This isn't good, thought Rastun.

"I'm sorry to hear that. What's the location . . . Are you sure . . . All right. Thank you for your help." Sherlock slowly lowered his phone.

"What's going on?" Karen's brow furrowed.

"Those cops are responding to a double-homicide. One of the victims is a deputy sheriff."

"Shit," muttered Geek.

"Oh my God." Karen put a hand on her chest.

Rastun's shoulders slumped. No wonder Sherlock reacted the way he did. Law enforcement was just as much a brotherhood as the military. The loss of one was felt by all.

"There's more," said Sherlock. "The murders took place at Pam Mankowski's house."

"What?" Rastun blurted. "Is she the other victim?" Dread welled up within him. He felt he already knew the answer.

"Yes."

"Did they say how they died?"

"No."

Rastun flexed his hands on the steering wheel, unconsciously speeding up. He thought about Mrs. Mankowski at the hospital roughly twelve hours ago. Tears in her eyes, trying to come to grips with her husband's death. The poor woman could barely hold it together.

Now she was dead, along with a deputy sheriff. Had a lizard man attacked them?

"Karen. Call Randy and tell him what happened, and tell him we're making a detour to the Mankowskis' house."

After Karen contacted Ehrenberg, the four drove in relative silence. A mile from the house, Rastun slowed. A LCSO car blocked the road, a pair of deputies standing in front of it.

He pulled to the side of the road and got out with the others. He recognized the deputies, Clay and Wills, who'd secured Welsh's house.

Clay greeted them. "Sorry, folks. You'll have to turn around. We have an active investigation going on."

"We know." Sherlock pulled out his badge. "Pam Mankowski and one of your deputies. Sorry for your loss."

Both Clay and Wills nodded, their mouths pressed into thin, tight lines.

"We interviewed Mrs. Mankowski early this morning about her husband's death," Sherlock continued. "This could be related to the FUBI's investigation. I'd like to talk to one of your detectives." He still held up his badge.

Clay and Wills looked at one another, then at Sherlock's badge.

"Sure thing, Marshal." Clay stepped to the side. "Lieutenant Blefary is handling the investigation."

Great. Rastun could imagine what the detective's reaction would be when he saw Sherlock. Blefary's perpetual foul mood had to be fifty times worse working a double-homicide where one of the victims was a deputy sheriff.

He watched Sherlock head down the road, not envying his friend for the reception he was likely to get. Rastun didn't even bother asking if he could accompany him. The FUBI wasn't a law enforcement agency. The cops didn't want civilians walking around a murder scene. So he stayed behind with Karen and Geek, the afternoon sun blazing down on them. He took a long pull from his water bottle when Karen spoke.

"I'm sorry about your deputy."

Both Clay and Wills thanked her.

"We all are," Rastun added. "Did you know him well?"

Clay lowered his head, shoulders slumping. That was enough of an answer for Rastun.

"We both knew him really well," said Wills. "Clark Spillman. Good guy. Been on the job for three years."

"Did he have any family?" asked Karen.

"He's living . . ." Wills shifted his weight. "He lived with this woman for about two years."

Rastun closed his eyes, imagining someone else grieving over the sudden, violent death of a loved one.

"I got him into the SO." Clay lifted his head, the pain in his eyes evident. "We were in the same National Guard unit. Did a tour in Afghanistan." He shook his head. "I can't believe it. Clark got through the whole damn deployment with just a couple of scratches, and he winds up getting shot right here." He spread out his arms.

Rastun straightened. "You said he got shot?"

"Yeah. Him and the lady."

He turned to Karen and Geek. Both looked as surprised as he did. He'd expected to hear Mrs. Mankowski and Deputy Spillman had been mauled, not shot.

"It's crazy," said Wills. "Last night her husband gets torn to pieces, then today she gets shot."

"I think suspicious is a better word than crazy," Karen told him.

Wills nodded. "Yeah, I think you're right."

"Well I hope you get whoever did this."

"Don't worry, ma'am, we will." Clay's tone left no doubt.

The group stood quietly, the deputies turning around a few vehicles. Rastun drank from his water bottle when he spotted Sherlock walking toward him, with Blefary behind him. When they reached him, Sherlock looked fine. Sweaty, but fine. Blefary was stooped and breathing heavy. Perspiration soaked his face and left large, circular stains under his arms.

"Lieutenant," Rastun greeted him.

Blefary took a couple of breaths. "If you were expecting some Lizard Man attack, forget it. Spillman and Pam Mankowski were shot."

"Any idea how it happened?" asked Rastun.

"Shot in the head, one round each, from a distance."

"When did it happen?"

"Maybe two, three hours ago," said Blefary. "A passing motorist spotted the bodies and phoned it in."

"Sniper?" asked Geek.

"Whoever did it was good," Sherlock answered, "but sniping wasn't their specialty."

"How do you know that?" Karen ran her water bottle over her forehead.

"Deputy Spillman was shot through the cheek. An actual sniper would have put that round through his temple. The bullet that killed Mrs. Mankowski would have missed if it had been a few centimeters higher. An actual sniper would have hit her square in the forehead."

"Real sniper or not, they're both dead," said Blefary. "Whoever it was knows how to use a gun, and well. Maybe a hunter or an ex-soldier." He flipped open his notebook and looked at Rastun. "You interviewed Pam Mankowski this morning?"

Now Rastun knew why Blefary hadn't screamed at them to go the hell away. He and Sherlock were two of the last people to see Mrs. Mankowski alive.

"Did she say anything to you about someone wanting to hurt her?" Blefary asked.

"No," answered Rastun. "The only thing we talked about was the Lizard Man attack."

Blefary grunted. Even with the news about the unknown scales, it seemed he still wanted to believe a person was behind Phil Welsh's and Len Mankowski's deaths.

"Did you notice anyone suspicious at the hospital?"

Both Rastun and Sherlock answered no.

"Have you or anyone at the FUBI had any previous contact with the Mankowskis?"

They all shook their heads, with Rastun adding, "We didn't even know them until last night."

"Mm-hmm." Blefary scribbled in his notebook, then wiped his sleeve across his sweaty forehead. "Can you recount what you all did today?"

"We went to the briefing at the courthouse, got some lunch, then headed out," said Rastun.

"Where did you have lunch?"

"A place called The Good Ol' Cafe. It's down the street from our hotel." Rastun noticed Karen stiffen, her eyes locked on Blefary.

"Can anyone outside your team confirm your whereabouts between the time you left your briefing and now?"

Karen let out an exasperated breath. "You've got to be kidding. You really think one of us shot that woman and that deputy?"

"I have to cover all possibilities."

"Well that's bullshit. Why the hell would we want to kill them?"

"Hey. I've got a dead deputy and a dead civilian back there. So I don't need any shit from you!"

"You're out of line, Lieutenant." Rastun stepped up to Blefary, eyes narrowed, just inches from the man's fat face. A fat face he really wanted to punch.

Blefary tensed and started to open his mouth when Sherlock stepped in the middle of them and held up his hands. "Let's everyone calm down." His tone was even.

"What?" Karen jabbed a hand at Blefary. "You're gonna let him accuse us of murdering two people?"

"Karen, please." Rastun put a hand on her back. She swung her head toward him, face blazing with fury. He gave her a stern look, mouthing, "Enough."

He, more than anyone, knew the reason Blefary's comments made Karen so incensed.

She exhaled loudly and turned back to Blefary. She glared at the big detective, but said nothing.

To Rastun's surprise, Blefary also kept quiet.

"You can call the hotel and the restaurant," Sherlock told Blefary. "They'll confirm we were there."

"I'll do that." Blefary took out his phone, looked up the numbers and called them. After two quick conversations, he pocketed the phone. "Your story checks out. You can go."

"Thank you, Lieutenant," said Sherlock.

Blefary walked away. Rastun saw the man's shoulders sag. He knew that had nothing to do with physical exertion.

"Lieutenant."

"What?" snapped Blefary.

"Sorry about Deputy Spillman."

Blefary stared at him. Several long seconds of silence passed before he muttered, "Thanks," and continued walking.

A twinge of sympathy went through Rastun. Blefary was an asshole, but he had just lost a man. He was all too familiar with that feeling. The guy had to be hurting.

"This is insane." Karen shook her head. "Bad enough we have lizard men killing people, now some lunatic's running around shooting people."

"All this has to be connected somehow." Rastun led them back to the SUV. "Mrs. Mankowski gets her head blown off the day after her husband's mauled to death. No way is this a coincidence, no friggin' way. But who did it and why?"

NINETEEN

Rastun stood under the tree, aiming a flashlight at one of the branches above him. Karen sat on it, mounting the last of their webcams. Even as he provided illumination for her, his eyes flickered around the darkening forest. He caught sight of Geek nearby, also scanning the area. Rastun estimated they had ten minutes before the last vestiges of sunlight vanished. Then it would be the lizard men's time.

There seemed little doubt the creatures were nocturnal. That meant superior night vision. How good were their other senses? How stealthily could they move?

Then came the question that worried him the most. How many lizard men were out there? That led to yet another troubling question. Who else was out there with an interest in the lizard men?

"There. Finished," Karen announced, then got on her sat phone. "Ops, this is Karen. Webcam Six is up. How does it look?"

There was a pause as the person back at the FUBI Operations Center answered. Karen nodded and looked down. "Jack, do me a favor and take a couple of steps back."

He did so.

"How does that look?" She paused, then moved the camera to the left. "Is that good?" She looked and gave Rastun a thumbs up. He waved to the camera.

Karen held the sat phone between her cheek and shoulder and pulled out her iPad. She tapped the screen a few times. "I can pick up all webcams on my iPad. We're looking good. You see anything that looks like a big reptile on two legs, give me a shout . . . Thanks, Kelsey. Bye."

She put away the phone and tablet and climbed down the tree, with Rastun helping her the last few feet.

"So I guess we're good with our camera picket?" asked Rastun.

"If there are any lizard men in this stretch of woods, we'll know about it."

"Good. Let's get back to Randy and the others."

"Before we do, I need to use the little boy's room." Geek started walking, then stopped. "Or I guess in this case, the little boy's tree."

"We'll wait here for you," said Rastun. "I wouldn't want to leave you in the dark, scary forest all alone."

Geek feigned a laugh. "I always did love officers who thought they were comedians. Please let me know when you're gonna open for Bill Engvall."

Rastun grinned as Geek set off for a copse of trees. He hadn't been an Army officer for two years.

Has it really been two years now?

From the time he'd been in high school, he figured he would make a career of the Army. Twenty years at least, maybe twenty-five. Probably get as high as bird colonel. Would General Rastun have been a possibility? Part of him had wanted to think so when he'd been in uniform. Another part didn't want any stars on his collar. One thing he learned in the Army was the farther up the ladder you went, the more removed you were from the field. Gone were the days of generals like Patton and Rommel riding into battle with their troops. These days, generals sat in air-conditioned command bunkers, watching the battle unfold on TV and computer screens, while the men fighting it were hundreds of miles away.

That wasn't him. He had to, *needed to*, be in the field, sharing the same dangers as privates and corporals and sergeants. Sitting in an office or bunker or any place with four walls every damn day would drive him insane. That's why working with the FUBI was perfect. Sure he was in the middle of the South Carolina woods with hostile cryptids and a crazed sniper roaming about, but this was where he belonged. Six years in the Army, five as a Ranger, he had the necessary skills to protect everyone in the expedition from monsters and madmen.

"I'm sorry." Karen interrupted his thoughts.

"Huh?"

"For earlier. The way I went off on Detective Blefary." She bit her lower lip for a moment. "It's just . . . when he hinted we might have something to do with those murders, after what happened last year . . ."

Rastun rested a hand on her shoulder. "Hey. You don't have to explain it to me. I understand."

He truly did, maybe better than anyone else. During the sea raptor expedition, evidence surfaced that suggested Karen was a mole planted by animal smuggler Norman Gunderson to help capture the creature. It turned out the mole had been Raleigh Pilka, whom Karen had an affair with in college, an affair that resulted in her becoming pregnant with Emily. It didn't surprise him that she'd get defensive when someone accused her of taking part in a crime.

Rastun averted his eyes from Karen. He, too, had believed she'd been the mole, despite the fact she had saved him twice from the sea raptor. Even though she had forgiven him, he'd never completely rid himself of the guilt he felt for believing the worst about her.

"Makes me wish I had your cool to deal with stuff like that," said Karen.

"My cool? If Sherlock hadn't been there, I might be in jail right now for assaulting a police officer."

Karen tilted her head, a thoughtful expression on her face. "Yeah, you did look like you were about to rip off Blefary's head." She smiled and tapped him on the shoulder. "Nice to know I got one of the last men in the world who still believes in chivalry."

"I thought all you modern, independent women could stand up for yourselves?" said Rastun.

"Oh, I can fight my own battles, but it's nice to know that I have a man who has my back."

"Always, babe." He wrapped an arm around Karen and pulled her close. She nestled her head against his shoulder.

"So I'm chivalrous, huh?"

"Absolutely," said Karen.

"So I guess that means I'll have to open the door for you more often."

"Yup."

"And lay down my coat over a mud puddle so you can walk over it."

"Uh-huh."

Rastun paused. "What about back rubs?"

"Oh yes."

"Foot rubs?"

"Yes again," replied Karen. "Along with taking me to a romantic movie at least once a month."

"Okay, so long as we balance it out with an action movie every month."

"I don't think bargaining has any place in chivalry."

"Hey, if I have to watch something like *The Notebook*, it's only fair you watch *Thor: The Dark World.*"

Karen chuckled, then gave Rastun a peck on the cheek.

"Jeez. I'm gone for two minutes and you guys are pawing each other." Geek strode up to them, a huge grin on his face.

"Thanks for killing the moment, Sergeant." Rastun gave him a faux glare.

"Any time, sir."

They set off, with Karen radioing Ehrenberg to let him know all the cameras were in place. They trekked three miles before rendezvousing with the rest of the expedition. Ehrenberg had them split up, with Rastun, Karen, Geek, Sherlock, and Petal going east, while the others continued south.

Rastun checked all around him, night vision goggles turning the landscape bright green. His eyes lingered on clumps of trees and bushes. Perfect hiding places for lizard men, or snipers.

Why? He didn't know how many times he'd wondered that. Why would someone want to kill Pam Mankowski? It had to be linked to the lizard men attacks. How, Rastun couldn't say. He hoped Blefary found some answers.

He scanned the trees around him. No sign of lizard men or snipers. He also noted the chirping of crickets. A couple of times he saw a rabbit scamper through the brush. That usually meant nothing big and nasty was nearby.

Rastun checked the ground for any sign of bent grass or footprints when he heard something buzz. He looked up to see Karen take out her sat phone.

"Hello . . . Yeah, Kelsey . . . When . . . You sure . . . which camera . . . Got it, thanks."

"What is it?" asked Petal.

"That was ops. Webcam Two just picked up three lizard men."

TWENTY

Tingles raced through Rastun, a mix of excitement and apprehension. There was the thrill of being so close to capturing a cryptid and proving its existence to the world. But it was tempered by the concern that these creatures could tear apart everyone on his team.

His gaze fell on Karen. He shuddered at the thought of her ending up like Welsh and Mankowski.

Rastun put all those thoughts out of his head. He had work to do. "Petal. Contact Randy and let him know about the lizard men."

"Okay."

"Geek. Tell Alana I want the Flapjack dispatched to the lizard men's last known position."

"Yes, sir."

"Also, cover our rear. I'll take point."

"Yes, sir."

"We need to move fast," said Rastun. "Stay together. Anyone sees a lizard man or anything suspicious, sing it out and sing it out loud. Got it?"

"Yes, sir," Geek and Sherlock responded.

Karen and Petal both said, "Okay."

They took off at a steady jog. Everyone kept up. No surprise to Rastun. Karen and Petal spent a lot of time in the field and kept themselves in good shape. Geek and Sherlock had done this countless times in the Rangers and had not grown soft in their post-Army lives.

Halfway to Webcam Two, something hummed overhead. Rastun spotted a round shape with small, blinking red lights. The Flapjack. He watched as it moved to the east, hoping it would pick up the lizard men.

They slowed as they neared Webcam Two. Rastun, Geek, and Sherlock all had their Aster 7 dart guns up. Rastun ignored the burning of his lungs and the heaviness in his legs. He'd been on much longer runs and felt worse discomfort in the Army. He swung his head, and weapon, left to right. No sign of the lizard men.

"Karen. Break out the -"

He stopped when he saw she was already scanning the area with the thermal imager.

"Way ahead of you, hon." She shot him a grin, then checked the screen. A minute passed before she shook her head. "I got nothing."

"I have something." Petal walked a few feet away and crouched. "Footprint."

Rastun and Karen went over to her.

"Definitely not a bear or a coyote," Petal told them.

Rastun examined the print while Karen photographed it.

"This looks like the one I saw in Phil Welsh's yard," he said.

"I have another print here." Sherlock pointed to the ground.

"There's also some bent grass here," Geek called out.

Rastun and Petal checked the prints and the grass while Karen took pictures. They moved east, finding more disturbed grass, bent branches, and footprints.

"Captain, it's Alana," she radioed Rastun.

"Go, Alana."

"Flapjack found them. Looks like they're taking a more southeasterly route."

"Stay on 'em." Rastun checked his Garmin Forerunner watch/GPS and read the coordinates to McClure, who was also assigned to the CP – command post – with Alana. "How far are we from our targets?"

"Standby." After a few seconds of silence, McClure answered, "Little over two-and-a-half miles."

"Copy that." He turned to the others. "Let's move."

They set off at a quicker pace.

"Jack." Karen caught up to him. "I've got the Flapjack feed on my iPad."

The screen showed three red and yellow blobs tramping through the woods. Definitely not bears. Bears didn't walk upright that long.

They encountered more bent grass and branches. The lizard men were leaving a heck of a trail to follow. Rastun radioed McClure for an update on the distance to their targets.

"Less than two miles. You're getting close."

Rastun fought the urge to order them to run faster. Their current pace was sufficient. Plus, running full-out for long stretches only worked in movies. As good as shape as they were all in, they'd tire out after sprinting a few hundred meters.

He called for another update. One mile away from the lizard men. Rastun ordered them to slow. Sucking down air, he scanned around him. The woods were pretty thick. He saw no sign of the lizard men through his NVGs.

Rastun drank from his CamelBak, then thought of something. "Rastun to McClure."

"McClure. Go."

"Go to Google Maps. Find out if there are any homes nearby."

"Standby."

Rastun and the others proceeded with caution through the woods. He signaled Karen to walk alongside him so he could check the Flapjack image on her iPad. The three lizard men continued on. Rastun wondered if the creatures had smelt or heard them. Probably not. If they had, they'd likely be running away or hiding.

Or attacking.

"McClure to Rastun."

"Rastun. Go."

"There's one home in your sector. I checked its location in relation to the lizard men's GPS coordinates. They're moving toward it."

Dread caused Rastun's muscles to tighten. "Get me a phone number for that house ASAP."

"Copy."

Rastun's group advanced a few yards before McClure contacted him.

"Got it. Homeowners are Charles and Wendy McMurtry." McClure gave him the phone number.

"Sherlock, take point." Rastun ordered as he pulled out his sat phone and dialed. They moved through the darkened woods as the McMurtrys' phone rang once, twice, three times, four times. The answering machine came on.

"Mister and Mrs. McMurtry, this is Jack Rastun from the FUBI. Are you home?"

No one answered.

"If you're home, please listen. We're currently in pursuit of creatures you probably know as the lizard men. They are approaching your house right now. This isn't a prank. You can call FUBI Headquarters and verify my sto-"

Someone picked up. "Travis, is that you? Cut the shit."

The voice sounded young. Probably not Mrs. McMurtry. Her daughter perhaps? "Who's this?"

A pause. "Travis?"

"I'm not Travis. I really am Jack Rastun from the FUBI."

"Seriously?"

"Very. Now who are you?"

"Um, um, Marissa."

"Okay, Marissa, are you alone in the house?" asked Rastun.

"No. Two of my friends are here."

Rastun nodded, then spoke into his radio. "Rastun to McClure, I want constant updates on those lizard men relative to the McMurtry house."

"Roger . . . four hundred meters and closing."

"Copy that. Pick it up, people," Rastun said to the others, then spoke into the sat phone. "Marissa, where are your parents?"

"Um, uh . . . are you really Jack Rastun?"

He fought to keep his frustration from flaring up. He couldn't blame Marissa for being hesitant. She was, what, a few years older than Emily, parents out, and some stranger calling out of the blue and asking her all sorts of questions. How did she know he wasn't some pervert freak looking to rape and kill her?

"Marissa." He softened his tone. "I know you have no reason to think I'm telling you the truth, but I am. There are three lizard men approaching your house-"

"Three hundred meters," McClure reported.

"Did Travis put you up to this?"

"Marissa, no one put me up to this. This is real. You have three hostile creatures headed your way. You need to take precautions."

"Yeah right." A pause. Marissa's voice sounded distant. "Oh, it's one of Travis's dumbass friends." She was probably talking to her two friends. "He's pretending to be Jack Rastun, says there are lizard men coming to get us."

The girls laughed.

Rastun swatted away a branch in front of him as he hurried through the woods. He wanted to be mad that Marissa thought this was a prank. But right now he was more worried than angry.

He ran faster, avoiding trees and bushes. He took a couple of deep breaths.

Marissa fake-panted. "See. I can do that heavy breathing shit, too."

"Two hundred meters and closing," reported McClure.

"Marissa, please," said Rastun. "You don't have a lot of time. Do you have a basement?"

"Yeah right. Everyone knows you don't go down in the basement in a horror movie."

"Jack!" blurted McClure. "These things just broke into a run. One hundred-fifty meters and closing."

"Jack, it's Randy." Ehrenberg broke in on the radio. "We're still too far out to help. You guys are on your own."

"Doc, call Nine-One-One. Get the cops rolling." Though they were much further away than Ehrenberg and the rest of the expedition.

"Hey, Jack Rastun." There was a new voice on the phone, another teen. "What are you wearing?"

"Becca, oh my gosh."

"What? If he is Jack Rastun I want him to save me from the big, bad monster."

The girls laughed.

Rastun clenched the Aster 7 with his other hand and closed his eyes. *Please, God, make them believe me.*

"One hundred meters and closing," said McClure.

"Get to the basement now!" ordered Rastun.

"Dude, knock off the shouting."

"Get to the basement, block the door with whatever you can."

"Fifty meters."

"Marissa, they're almost on top of you. I want you all in that basement, now!"

"Okay, this isn't funny anymore. Tell Travis he can-"

"They're at the house!" hollered McClure.

Rastun heard a thump over the phone. The girls screamed.

"Marissa!"

"What the hell are you doing?" the girl shouted.

"It's the lizard men. Get to the basement."

She didn't respond.

Fear swept through him. He imagined reaching the house and finding those three girls just like he found Phil Welsh.

"Oh my God!" Marissa's piercing shout nearly made Rastun wince. "Oh my God!"

"Basement! Now! Go! Go!"

"C'mon, c'mon!" Marissa sounded like she was yelling at her friends.

Rastun heard two sounds. Running feet and violent pounding.

"They're in," said McClure. "Lizard men have breached the house."

"Oh God, those poor girls." Petal's voice cracked. "Oh God, oh God."

"Hold it together," Rastun told her.

He heard a thump over the phone. A door slamming?

"Marissa? Marissa?"

"Yes?"

"Are you all in the basement?"

"Y-Yes?"

"Good," said Rastun. "Now barricade it."

"With what?"

"Anything you can. Just put it against the door. We're almost there."

"O-Okay." Marissa's voice broke.

Through the trees, Rastun saw lights. The McMurtry home.

"Karen." He twisted around and tossed her the phone. "Keep talking to her. Try to keep her calm."

"You got it." She put the sat phone to her ear. "Marissa? This is Karen Thatcher. I'm with the FUBI, too . . . We're coming, honey. We can see your house. You're gonna be fine."

Rastun and Sherlock cleared the woods. There was a twenty-yard expanse of lawn between them and the house. He saw the back door completely knocked down. He looked through the lighted windows. No sign of the lizard men. Did they see the girls go into the basement? Did they smell them?

Rastun pulled out his Glock. "Sherlock. Aim for the ground."

The marshal nodded and took out his Sig-Sauer pistol.

Rastun fired first, followed a split-second later by Sherlock. Nearly a dozen rounds impacted the lawn near the house. Rastun hoped the sound of gunfire would scare off the lizard men, or at the very least distract them.

The pair holstered their pistols just as they reached the back door, which led to the kitchen. The lights were on. Rastun pushed his NVGs onto his head and peeked inside, Aster 7 up. The door lay on the floor, broken in half.

"Clear." Rastun moved inside, Sherlock covering him.

They advanced past the refrigerator, past the stove. The dining room table lay ahead of Rastun. Beyond it was a dark hallway. He had a quick flashback to Iraq and Afghanistan and the raids his Rangers conducted on terrorist homes. Any moment some murdering scumbag could jump out behind a corner with a rifle, a grenade, or a bombvest hoping to take a few Americans with him to Paradise.

Here in this house in rural South Carolina, he didn't have to worry about guns and bombs. He had to worry about sharp teeth and claws.

Rastun slowed as he walked by the kitchen table. He saw no silhouettes in the hallway. He heard no thumping, no female screaming, no growling or hissing. Had the gunfire scared off the lizard men?

"Rastun to Alana," he whispered into his radio.

"Alana. Go."

"Did Flapjack see any lizard men exit the home?"

"Negative. Looks like they're still inside."

"Copy." Rastun's arms tensed, sweat dripping into his eyes. He tried to put the sound of his pounding heart out of his mind as he neared the archway.

Focus. Get to the basement. Make sure the girls are safe.

He stopped inches from the archway, then swung around it.

A large, dark green shape growled and leaped at him.

TWENTY-ONE

Rastun dodged right. The lizard man's leg rammed into his gut. He slammed into the wall. Pain exploded through his mid-section as he dropped to the floor. The Aster 7 tumbled out of his grasp.

Something sharp dug into his shoulder. Rastun groaned through clenched teeth, the jaws of the lizard man less than a foot from his face. Its harsh, stale breath washed over him, burning his nostrils.

Rastun punched the creature in the gut. It let out a deep grunt. Its mouth opened wider.

A muffled *pop* came from the kitchen. A needle with a blue feathery tail protruded from the lizard man's side. It unleashed a savage hiss.

Rastun punched the creature again. He glanced Sherlock in the kitchen with his dart gun.

"Captain." He hurried over, extending his hand. Rastun reached out for him.

The lizard man growled and backhanded Sherlock. He flew off his feet and slammed onto the kitchen floor.

The creature swung back to Rastun. He rolled on his side, pain lashing his ribs, and kicked it above the crotch. It let out a guttural, gargling snarl, reminding him of the sounds the crocodiles at the Philadelphia Zoo would make.

The lizard man ran down the hallway. Rastun chased after it, his shoulder burning. Sherlock groaned and began to rise.

Rastun pulled out his Glock as the beast turned down another hallway. He fired twice. Both 9mm rounds tore into the corner of the wall. Even with the tranquilizer coursing through its body, the lizard man's adrenaline and rage helped counteract it. It would probably be another five to ten minutes before the drug took full effect and knocked it out.

Rastun rounded the corner. The lizard man was about ten feet away. It threw itself against a door, smashing it open. Fear burst within Rastun.

The basement. Marissa and her friends were down there.

He now knew why the lizard man ran away. He'd fought back. So did Sherlock. Predators preferred easy prey, not ones that put up a fight.

Three teenage girls made for easier prey than two ex-Rangers.

He reached the doorframe and swung into the opening, pistol up.

The lizard man stood two steps below. It hissed and lashed out its arm. Rastun ducked. The blow missed by inches. He fired two shots into the creature's hip. A combination hiss and cry sprang from its throat. The lizard man began to fall backwards. It hooked its claws on the back of Rastun's shirt. A burning, tearing sensation went up his shoulder blades. He toppled forward.

The world flashed past him. Rastun caught glimpses of walls, stairs, and dark green skin. Sturdy wood pounded his body.

They hit the bottom, rolling into boxes and a folding chair scattered on the floor. Probably the makeshift barrier the girls made, knocked aside effortlessly by the lizard man.

Rastun rolled off the creature and clenched his right hand. The Glock was no longer there. He pushed himself to his knees. The lizard man also rose. Blood ran down its left leg. It let out a couple of grunts and wobbled.

Screams echoed through the basement. Rastun peered around the lizard man. Marissa and her two friends huddled together against the far wall.

The wounded creature turned to them. They screamed louder.

"Hey!" Rastun drew his M48 Commando Knife from its sheath.

The lizard man looked at him, then back at the girls.

"Hey!" He shouted louder.

The creature's head snapped toward him.

Rastun lowered himself to the floor, nearly curled into a ball. He wanted to appear the way all predators wanted their prey to be. Vulnerable.

The lizard man growled and took a shaky step toward him. He gripped his knife tighter. The creature loomed over him, claws raised, maw open.

Rastun pushed himself up and thrust the blade into the lizard man's right thigh. It let out a strangled, pain-wracked wail and dropped to its knees. The creature lunged at Rastun, jaws opened. He avoided its bite and rammed the knife into the lizard man's throat. Warm, sticky blood flowed over his hands. He gave the knife a twist. Blood poured out like water from a faucet.

"Cap'n! Cap'n"

"Jack!"

He ignored Geek and Karen's calls and pulled the knife from the lizard man's throat. The beast fell forward. Rastun scrambled out of the way. He leaned against the wall as Geek and Karen pounded down the stairs.

"Jack! Oh my God." Karen bounded past Geek and knelt beside him. Fear and worry filled her eyes. "Don't move. Just relax."

"I'm fine."

"Bullshit." Karen pulled off her pack and got on her hands-free radio. "Randy, it's Karen. Call an ambulance. Jack's hurt . . . Randy?" Her breaths quickened. "Randy, can you hear me? Dammit, I can't get him."

"The basement's probably interfering with the signal," Geek said as he looked over the lizard man. "Yeah, Cap'n, you did worse to it than it did to you."

"That's how I intended it."

"Everyone okay down there?" Sherlock called from the top of the stairs, grimacing and rubbing his chest.

"I'm alive at any rate," said Rastun.

"Call an ambulance." Karen whipped her head toward Sherlock. "Jack's hurt."

"You got it."

"Geek, Sherlock. Make sure the house is clear," ordered Rastun. "We've still got two lizard men unaccounted for."

"Not anymore," Geek informed him. "The Flapjack picked 'em up hightailing it from here."

Rastun breathed a sigh of relief, wondering why he hadn't heard that. He then realized his earpiece dangled around his shoulder, and the hands-free radio set attached to his right side was busted.

"Geek. Give me your knife." Karen held out her hand.

Geek handed her his blade, which she used to cut away Rastun's shirt at the shoulder. He saw four deep, bloody puncture wounds.

"Are you hurt anywhere else?" asked Karen.

"Yeah. My back." Rastun felt blood seeping through the gashes where the lizard man slashed him.

Karen coated his shoulder with Neosporin packets as Sherlock reappeared at the top of the stairs, Petal by his side. "The ambulance is on the way."

"Good," Rastun said as Karen bandaged his shoulder. "Now someone check on those girls."

"I'll do it." Petal jogged down the stairs and went over to the girls. "It's okay," she spoke in a soothing voice. "You're all right."

Rastun exhaled loudly. His heartbeat settled down. A sudden tiredness took hold. Probably his adrenaline wearing off. He stared at his shoulder. The blood loss might have something to do with it, too.

"Deja Vu, huh?" He said to Karen.

"What?"

"Didn't you get your Florence Nightingale on around this time last year?" He grinned, remembering how Karen gave him first aid after his bloody fight with the mercenary Andres Piet.

She managed a half-smile. She was clearly worried, but appeared convinced he was not in danger of dying.

"At least we're on dry land this time," said Geek. "Being on a sinking boat sucked."

Rastun nodded, then turned to the dead lizard man. "I wonder if this is proof enough for Blefary and the others."

TWENTY-TWO

For the second time in twenty-four hours, Rastun was at Lee County Memorial Hospital, this time as a patient. He sat on the table in an examination room, his shoulder and mid-section bandaged. Even though his wounds had been stitched up, a burning pain still lingered. Whatever. He'd felt worse, and he didn't wind up a pile of bloody meat like Welsh and Mankowski.

They also had a lizard man body, and this time no one or no thing would swipe it. Alana and McClure had tracked the other two creatures on the Flapjack after they exited the McMurtry home, until they got a low battery warning from the drone. Ehrenberg and the others wanted to pursue them, but the cops wouldn't allow it. "Too dangerous," they claimed.

Do they even know what we do for a living?

The sheriff's office took possession of the dead lizard man, labeling it possible evidence in the deaths of Welsh and Mankowski. Rastun hoped they would let the FUBI examine it.

Rastun heard footsteps approaching. He looked to the doorway, hoping it was Karen.

It wasn't. Lieutenant Blefary stepped inside.

"Lieutenant." Rastun winced as pain stabbed his two broken ribs.

"Mister Rastun." Blefary's mouth curled. He avoided eye contact with him. "You were right. These things are real." From the sagging expression on his face, it seemed like it pained him to admit that.

"Uh-huh." Rastun refrained from making some sarcastic, "I told you so," remark.

"Do you think the monster you killed was the same one that killed Phil Welsh and Len Mankowski?" Blefary took out his notebook.

"I can't say. We had three of them go into the house. It could've been any one of them. It could have been none of them. We have no idea how many lizard men are in this county."

Blefary asked for a rundown of events leading up to, and including, his fight with the lizard man. A couple of times he gave

Rastun skeptical looks. If not for his injuries, the detective would probably think the gun/claw/knife fight was a load of BS.

Minutes after Blefary wrapped up his interview, Karen showed up, along with the doctor, a tall man with receding dark hair.

"How are you doing?" she hugged Rastun, causing his shoulder to sting.

"I'm fine."

"Not entirely," said Dr. O'Brien. "I want you to rest for a few days, which means no running around the forest looking for monsters."

"How about we just make it a day, Doc?" Rastun countered. "I've been hurt a hell of a lot worse than this."

"Mister Rastun, you're not the first ex-soldier I've treated. You all think you're tough, but you have broken ribs, and I don't want to take the chance of your sutures opening and making you more susceptible to infection. So no monster hunting for the next three days at least."

"Look, Doc --"

"He said no monster hunting," snapped Karen. "So you're staying at the hotel, period."

From the harsh look on her face, Rastun knew he had no chance of winning this argument.

"The good news is, you're in remarkably good shape. That will help with your recovery, along with plenty of rest, and these." He handed Rastun a bottle of penicillin pills.

"Thanks."

O'Brien headed for the door, glancing over his shoulder at Karen. "Make sure he gets his rest."

"Oh, don't worry, I will." She turned to Rastun, arms folded and eyes narrowed.

Rastun slid off the table and walked over to his pack, lying on the chair. He pulled out his extra green-brown-black BDU t-shirt and pants, as well as fresh underwear and socks. Karen offered to help him into his shirt and pants, but Rastun shooed her away. That earned him an evil glare. Though it made his shoulder and ribs burn and throb, he managed to dress himself. He tried to keep from grimacing, and thought he'd been successful.

Judging by Karen's glare, he was not.

"You are going to take it easy for the next few days," she told him.

"Okay."

"That's not negotiable."

"I said okay."

"You do not want to try me on this one."

"*O-kay.* Jeez, if you're that concerned, why don't you just tie me down to the bed? On second thought, I might enjoy that."

Karen's lips tightened in a thin line.

Aw crap. Is she gonna yell?

Instead, she hugged him. "I love you." She kissed his lips, then his cheek.

Rastun hugged her tighter, not caring about the pulsating pain in his ribs. He stroked her hair and kissed her on the head. He thought back to the McMurtry house. *"Keep talking to her. Try to keep her calm."* That's what he'd told Karen when he handed her the sat phone. If things turned out differently, those would have been his last words to her. Not anything heartfelt, not anything about how much he meant to her. He would have spoken to her like he had privates or corporals or junior sergeants in the Army. Not as the most important woman in his life.

"I love you," he whispered in Karen's ear. "I love you so much."

Rastun gave her a long kiss and held her close. They stayed that way until a nurse opened the door and apologized for interrupting them.

He called a cab and headed for the front of the hospital. "Do me a favor?"

"What?" asked Karen.

"Let's not tell my parents about this." He knew Mom and Dad worried about him every time he went into the field, especially after the sea raptor expedition.

Karen gave him an incredulous look. "Seriously? What are you, seven?"

The taxi arrived ten minutes later. They'd barely gone a mile when the driver said, "When you two get back to your hotel, better make sure you lock your door. Maybe shove a couple of chairs against it."

"Excuse me?" asked Karen.

"You didn't hear about the Lizard Man attack? It's all over the news."

"No, we didn't hear about it." The cabbie apparently didn't recognize them, and Rastun wasn't about to tell him who they really were. He didn't feel like telling a complete stranger about his fight with the creature.

"Yeah, I thought it was a bunch of crap." The cabbie slowed as he approached a stop sign. "Even after what happened to those two guys outside'a town. But the news said those FUBI guys killed one of 'em. Unbelievable."

Believe it.

When they got back to their hotel room, they washed up and went to bed. Snarling lizard men dominated Rastun's dreams. Sometimes he managed to push away their jaws, other times they sank their teeth into his throat. A couple of times the monsters ripped apart Marissa and her friends while he stood frozen.

Music exploded in his dream. A harsh guitar, keyboards, a woman with an incredible operatic voice. Nightwish's "Dark Chest of Wonders." His ringtone.

Rastun's eyes snapped open. He rolled on his side and reached for the phone on the nightstand. An invisible vise crushed his ribs. He grimaced, picked up the phone, and stared at the screen.

"Crap." It was his mother.

"Hey, Mom," he said as Karen stirred next to him.

"Are you all right?"

"Let me guess. You saw my bout with the Lizard Man on the news."

"They said you were taken to the hospital. Are you all right?"

"I'm fine. I just needed some stitches and some antibiotics. In fact, I'm in my hotel room right now."

"Oh thank God." Mom let out a relieved breath. "They said you tranquilized it."

"You know as well as I do tranquilizers don't work instantly," said Rastun. "Especially when the animal's pissed off."

"Couldn't you have waited for it to take effect?"

"If I had, three teenage girls would be dead."

Mom paused. "Jack, will you please be careful. Please."

"I will."

"You don't have to go out in the field today, do you?"

"No, the doctor told me to take it easy for a few days."

"And you will, right?"

"Of course I will."

"Gimme that." Karen snatched the phone from Rastun's hand. "Joyce, it's Karen . . . I'm fine, and don't worry, I'll make damn sure he doesn't go anywhere near the woods until the doctor clears him . . . He's banged up, but he'll recover . . . I know, I worry about him, too." She gently rubbed Rastun's arm.

Next he spoke to his father. After expressing his concern and relief, Dad asked, "So what do you think? Could this lizard man be some evolutionary offshoot of dinosaurs? Some entirely new species?"

Rastun grinned. *My Dad, ever the zoologist.* "We don't have a clue yet. The Sheriff's Office has the body. We're hoping to get a look at it later. Hey, maybe it's an alien."

"You don't seriously believe that, do you?"

"No, because if it was an alien, it probably would have had a laser gun, and I would've been vaporized."

Dad gave a slight chuckle. He probably would have laughed more, but Rastun figured he was thinking about how close he came to losing his only son.

After he said good-bye to Dad, Karen called Emily to let her know they were both fine.

Or fine-*ish* in Rastun's case.

After that call, he went back to sleep. More nightmares tormented him. Not only of the Lizard Man, but the sea raptor. Rastun tried to shoot them, but his gun wouldn't fire. He hit the monsters, but couldn't feel the blows he landed. Teeth and claws tore into his flesh. Fear overwhelmed him. He was going to die.

Rastun awoke with a start, covered with sweat. He felt the bed under him, looked around at the curtains, the nightstand, the TV.

Calm down. It was just a dream.

He checked the alarm clock, which read one in the afternoon. Karen was nowhere around. Probably at the pre-mission brief. Or maybe Ehrenberg wanted them to get an early start in the field after last night's attack.

Rastun noticed energy bars, bagels, a fruit drink, and a bottled water on the table. He smiled. That had to be Karen's doing.

I've got one hell of a girlfriend.

After eating, Rastun wrote up his after-action report and emailed it to Colonel Lipeli. He flipped through the TV, but nothing caught his interest. He then fired up his laptop, went to YouTube, and called up a full-length Rush concert. Arms folded, he leaned back, enjoying the high-ranged vocals of Geddy Lee, the amazing guitar work of Alex Lifeson, and the masterful drumming of the man himself, Neil Peart.

Maybe this won't be so bad after all.

TWENTY-THREE

Cassian found it difficult to focus as he and his men trekked through Scape Ore Swamp. All he could think about was the stories he'd seen this morning on the news. Three lizard men attacked another home. Jack Rastun himself had killed one of the monsters, saving three girls from being ripped apart.

He'd read the story with much admiration. The man survived Iraq, Afghanistan, the sea raptor, and now humanoid reptiles. Rastun seemed invincible. Lansford might give him shit for his hero worship of the man.

"Aren't you a little too old for that?" he'd say.

Maybe, but Rastun deserved that worship. If he was half as good as him, those evil lizards would be on the verge of defeat by now.

Shock buried his awe when he read that Rastun had been wounded in the fight, suffering several lacerations.

"He's gonna turn into one of them," Smith had said. "You know that."

He did, dammit. He still found it hard to believe someone as good as Jack Rastun was on the way to becoming a hybrid. A servant of the greatest evil the world had ever known.

I guess he wasn't invincible enough. Cassian wanted him for an ally. Now, would he have to . . ?

He shut his eyes, stopping himself from finishing the thought.

Think about it later. The lizards might be out here somewhere.

They weren't. Several hours of searching had turned up zero trace of the enemy. Cassian wavered between anger and misery. He really wanted to take out one of those damn monsters today, get a measure of revenge for Jack Rastun.

They trudged back to the RV, where Cassian got a bottle of beer from the fridge. He got halfway through it when his cell rang. The screen showed a number, but no name. He had an idea who it was.

"Yeah? . . . Yeah, I heard about the attack. Heard Jack Rastun got hurt bad . . . You know what that means? . . . I've told you before, that's one way they create hybrids. Scratch 'em, bite 'em, their DNA will start to mutate them . . . Of course that's what happened to that woman . . . Yeah, I had to."

The person on the other end spoke in a hushed but angry voice.

"I told you this could happen. This is war, do you understand that? . . . You want me to kill these things, so let me do it my way. And don't worry, I didn't leave any evidence behind. They can't trace anything back to me or you."

"Does this mean you're going to . . . kill Jack Rastun?" The question was asked in a hesitant voice.

Cassian stiffened. "I don't know yet."

The conversation finished a minute later. Cassian gripped the neck of his beer bottle.

"Was that your special friend?" asked Lansford.

"Yeah, having a panic attack over the cop and the woman I capped." He bit his lip. "Also wanted to know if I planned to kill Jack Rastun."

"I know he's your hero and all, but he's gonna turn into one of them. Don't have much of a choice, man."

Cassian cast his gaze down. How many times had he imagined himself fighting alongside Jack Rastun as they cut a bloody path through those reptilian sons-of-bitches?

That wouldn't happen now. Rastun would be a mole inside the FUBI, an organization with the kind of personnel and resources to become the lizards' biggest threat. They had scored one hell of a victory turning Jack Rastun.

Turning Jack Rastun.

His head snapped up. "I got it."

"Got what?" asked Lansford.

"We don't have to kill Jack Rastun."

"Oh for God's sake." Lansford let out a frustrated breath. "It's time to get over your hero worship for the guy. He's a fucking hybrid now."

"I know, and we can use it to our advantage."

"What are you talking about?" Proly gave him a puzzled look.

"What if we made him a double agent?"

Lansford shot him a doubtful look, but said nothing.

"I think it's an awesome idea," Smith declared. Proly nodded a second later.

"We've never tried anything like this before," Lansford pointed out. "What if it doesn't work?"

"How does the saying go?" said Cassian. "'Nothing ventured, nothing gained.' Shit, the lizards have infiltrated the government, law enforcement, the media, everything. It's time we do the same to them. Imagine how much we can hurt them if we had our own spy.

Jack Rastun might be able to get the evidence we need to prove to the world what the lizards are really up to. We've gotta do this."

Lansford folded his arms and stared at the wall. He let out a long breath. "I guess it's worth a shot."

"You're damn right it is."

"Now you just have to find a way to meet him," said Lansford. "Not that your first attempt went so well."

"Don't worry," Cassian answered in a confident tone. "One way or another, I'm going to get face time with him."

***

Rastun got through his first day on the sidelines well enough. Day two, however, was another matter. He'd grown sick of being cooped up in the hotel room. He didn't want to watch TV or YouTube or Netflix any more. The only upside was he and Karen had a hotel room all to themselves. But when he suggested a romp between the sheets, she hadn't been keen on it. Not at all.

"I'll be damned if I'm going to explain to the doctor that you popped your stitches because we were having sex."

He lay on the bed, watching reporters on ESPN picking their most disappointing baseball teams of the first half of the season, toying with the idea of bribing his doctor to clear him to go back into the field. *Or threaten him. Whichever works.*

His phone rang. It was Colonel Lipeli.

"Jack, how goes the recovery?"

"Wonderful, sir. I love watching TV and staring at the same four walls all damn day."

Lipeli chuckled. "You make one lousy couch potato."

"I consider that a compliment."

"Well, maybe I can spring you for a while."

Rastun sat up. "Am I going back in the field?"

"Not yet."

Rastun grunted.

"Try not to sound disappointed," Lipeli told him. "I do have a job for you."

"What is it?"

"I take it you've been watching the news of late?"

"Actually, I've been avoiding it. I'm sure most of it is about the lizard men, and ninety percent of what the reporters and talking heads are saying is bullshit."

"Gotcha. But here's something that's not bullshit. These lizard men attacks have people all over Lee County scared."

"That I can believe," said Rastun.

"Some people are also questioning the FUBI's ability to capture or kill the other lizard men."

Rastun sneered. "Of course. If we don't find these monsters five minutes into our expedition, we're failures."

"Director Lynch and I are coordinating with Mayor McAllister and Councilman Sawyer to put on a town hall meeting tonight, so you can reassure everyone we're doing our damnedest to find the lizard men. We want you to be part of it."

"Okay."

"We're also going to have Karen and Doctor Ehrenberg join you."

"Why them? They're more good to us in the field."

"You three are the faces of the FUBI," Lipeli explained. "Director Lynch feels people will be more inclined to listen to you. Like it or not, you have star power. We might as well put it to good use."

"Yes, sir."

Lipeli said he would call back in an hour with more details. Rastun propped himself against the headboard, leaving the TV on mute. He wasn't thrilled to speak at a meeting where his job was to pipe sunshine up people's asses.

Better that than being cooped up here.

He wondered if his doctor would be okay with it, then dismissed the concern. It was a town hall meeting. What the hell could he possibly do to injure himself at some gabfest?

TWENTY-FOUR

To his surprise, Rastun looked forward to the town hall as he climbed into the SUV with Karen and Ehrenberg. Anything to get him out of that damn hotel room and doing something productive.

Pain clamped down on his ribcage as he put on his seatbelt. He groaned and grimaced.

"You all right?" asked Karen, sitting in the driver's seat.

"I'm fine." Rastun spoke through clenched teeth. Damn, he hated broken ribs.

He glanced at Karen. Her thin eyebrows knitted together in a look of concern.

"I'm fine," Rastun repeated.

Lips pressed into a thin line, Karen sighed. He guessed she didn't believe him. She gave a slight shake of the head and started the engine. They headed out of Bishopville, Karen turning on the headlights as night set in.

They neared the site of the town hall, a church outside of town. The parking lot completely filled, with other vehicles parked on the grass or along the road. Rastun picked out a number of vans and cars with TV and radio logos.

"Looks like we'll be playing to a sold out crowd," quipped Ehrenberg.

Karen parked behind one of the news vans. The trio got out and walked toward the church, a one-story beige building with a slanted roof and a steeple in front. Beside it was a plain rectangular building, the community center, where the town hall would take place.

"Well, well, well." Ehrenberg halted next to an SUV, staring at the decal on the door. "This could make things interesting. Don't know if it'll be in a good way or a bad way."

"What?" Rastun stared at the decal. It showed the stoic portrait of a blond, angular-faced man. TRUTH TALK WITH DARREN STAUB. It showed links to his radio show, podcast, and best-selling books.

"This guy supposed to be famous?" He nodded at the decal.

"In certain circles," replied Ehrenberg. "Staub's made a name for himself linking cryptids to all kinds of conspiracies. I was actually on his radio show a few years ago."

"How did it go?" asked Karen.

"He spent most of the time trying to convince me Sasquatch come from another dimension. He got annoyed when I told him I didn't believe it."

"Aren't you the one who always says to keep an open mind about cryptids?" Karen pointed out.

"Okay, yeah." Ehrenberg gave an innocent shrug. "But let's just say on my list of theories as to the origin of Sasquatch, inter-dimensional being is waaaaay down at the bottom."

Rastun eyed Staub's image, then looked at Ehrenberg. "Would it be wishful thinking to hope this loony tune doesn't ask a question tonight?"

"*Very* wishful thinking."

***

Cassian made sure to get to the church community center an hour before the town hall began and stood near the entrance. He didn't want to take the chance on missing Jack Rastun.

People filed in, a few when he first arrived, more as it got closer to seven o'clock. Many cast glances his way, eyebrows raised or foreheads wrinkled in disapproving looks. It made him look over his hand-me-down shirt and pants, and become more aware of his thick beard and the mess of hair that came down to his shoulders.

Maybe I should have cleaned up before I came here. But Cassian caught news of the town hall when he and the others returned from searching the local swamps late in the afternoon. No time for a shave and haircut, or to go out and get a decent-looking shirt.

He started regretting that decision when some of the local bigwigs arrived. The county council chairman, Sawyer, turned up his nose at the sight of him. Mayor McAllister gave him a prolonged look. Neither politician said anything to him, instead heading for the stage, talking to people along the way.

Nerves clenched Cassian's stomach when Sheriff Haddix arrived. The big man ran a suspicious gaze up and down him, but the sheriff did nothing more.

No law against looking like a bum.

Many of the rows of folding chairs were full, dozens of separate conversations reverberating through the auditorium. Cassian remained near the entrance, glancing outside, where reporters lined the walkway. He checked his watch. Fifteen minutes before the town hall began. He bounced a bit on the balls of his feet, anxious. Jack Rastun should be here soon.

Keep your head, Alex. He had to be careful about this. Rastun was turning into a hybrid.

Excited voices rose from outside. The reporters blurted out questions.

"Any progress on the hunt for the lizard men?"

"Do you expect them to attack again?"

"Do you know where these things come from?"

A bearded man in a Hawaiian shirt held up his hands. Cassian straightened and sucked down a breath when he recognized Dr. Randy Ehrenberg.

Jack Rastun shouldn't be too far behind.

Ehrenberg raised his hands. "Folks, the questions you're asking are the same ones the people at this town hall are probably going to ask anyway. And that's where I'll answer them. So just be patient, and I'll provide you with as much information as I can."

He grinned at the reporters and headed inside.

A slender, athletic woman with shoulder-length light brown hair followed. Karen Thatcher. Damn, but she was hot. Rastun was a lucky man to bang something like that every night.

Then came the man himself. Jack Rastun. War hero. Killer of the sea raptor.

Cassian pressed his fists against his legs, trying not to let his excitement overwhelm him. He tried to focus on exactly what he wanted to say to Rastun. *Please don't let me say anything stupid.* Too much was at stake to blow this opportunity.

Rastun walked through the door. Cassian was taken aback for a moment. Rastun was a bit shorter than he expected. Around his height of 5'10. Not muscular, but lean and trim. Hell, he looked rather ordinary.

Cassian knew better. He'd read Rastun's book. The man was anything but ordinary.

He took a breath to settle himself. "Excuse me, Captain Rastun?"

The ex-Ranger turned to him. "Yes?"

"I know you're busy, sir, but I really need to talk to you."

"I'm sorry, but this town hall is going to get started soon. Hopefully we'll be able to address any questions you have. If not, then see me after the meeting."

Cassian's jaw stiffened. He thought about blocking his path, pressing him for a one-on-one meeting. But that would draw too much attention, something he didn't need right now, especially with the sheriff here.

"Yes, sir. I'll do that."

Rastun nodded to him and headed toward the stage.

Cassian leaned against the wall, satisfaction building. Rastun told him to see him after the meeting. He could let him know the truth, how he'd eventually become a hybrid, how he could get revenge by becoming a double-agent.

Cassian smiled. By the end of the night, Jack Rastun would be on his side.

TWENTY-FIVE

Rastun glanced back at the scruffy-looking man who'd wanted to talk to him, who'd called him captain. Not many people called him by his former rank these days. He also noted the man's tone, like it was urgent he speak to him.

I wonder what his deal is.

"Doctor Ehrenberg." A man near the front row got up from his seat and waved. It took a second for Rastun to recognize him. Darren Staub.

"Darren." Ehrenberg gave the conspiracy theorist a forced smile and shook his hand. "How are you doing?"

"I'm fine. You?"

"Fine as well. Busy, obviously." Ehrenberg looked around the auditorium.

"Oh, I'm sure," said Staub. "Bishopville's the center of the cryptid universe right now. That's why I came down here from Charlotte. No way I'm covering this from a studio. I want to be right on the front lines for this. Say . . ." He put a hand on Ehrenberg's shoulder. "Why don't you come on my show? I've been wanting to have you back on. Did you get the emails I sent you since your first appearance?"

"I did. Sorry I didn't respond. Sometimes life gets a little hectic and you forget." Ehrenberg gave him an innocent shrug.

Translation, thought Rastun. *I'm not wasting my time with a crackpot like you.*

"Well, now that I've got you here, what do you say?" Staub gave Ehrenberg a large, used car salesman grin. "I've got a special podcast lined up for tomorrow night. I'd love to have you on, especially after you've seen one of these lizards up close."

"Sorry, but tomorrow I'll be in the field looking for more lizard men."

"Then you can call in," said Staub. "A special report from the field with the world's foremost cryptozoologist."

"Jeez, this guy's persistent," Karen whispered to Rastun.

"More like pain in the ass," he whispered back.

"Like I said," Ehrenberg said to Staub. "I'll be in the field tomorrow. But thanks for the invitation, anyway. Good luck with your podcast."

He made for the stage before Staub could press him further.

Rastun and Karen followed. They'd only managed a few steps when Staub called out, "The invitation applies to you two, as well. My audience would love to hear from the heroes of the sea raptor hunt."

Staub's mouth opened wider as he held up a finger. "Even better. You come on my show, *and* . . . I invite you to TruthCon."

Karen's face scrunched. "To what?"

"TruthCon. It's a convention I put on every August in Charlotte. We cover cryptozoology, UFOs, paranormal phenomenon, government cover-ups." He put on the used car salesman smile again. "I'll even sweeten the pot for you. All expenses paid. Travel. Hotel. Meals . . . for five days. The convention's only two days, so you two get a mini-vacation out of the deal. What do you say?"

Rastun and Karen looked at one another for a couple of seconds. The slight frown on her lips told him what she thought of the deal.

"Thank you, Mister Staub," she said. "But August . . . I need to start getting clothes and supplies for my daughter for school, and she's also involved in youth soccer. It's just hard for me to get away."

"I understand. Mister Rastun, how about flying solo?"

"Thanks, but I think I have to help my mother make ice that week."

Rastun strode toward the stage before Staub could respond.

Karen's eyebrows knitted together. "'Help my mother make ice'? Really?"

"Hey, I didn't tell the guy to go piss up a rope."

She shook her head as they walked onto the stage. Rastun gazed out at the auditorium. All the chairs had been taken. More people stood along the walls, some behind video cameras mounted on tripods. A cluster of microphones seemed to grow out of the lectern.

He chatted with the local officials while Karen occasionally snapped pictures of the crowd to put up on the FUBI website later. More people filed into the community center. Rastun wondered if the place had ever seen a crowd like this.

He spotted the man who'd called him "Captain." He stood with his back to the wall, arms folded, glancing left to right, looking impatient. There seemed something off about the guy. Maybe he was some obsessed fan. Maybe he was something worse. Rastun made a note to keep an eye on him.

At seven o'clock on the dot, Sheriff Haddix began the meeting. He didn't bother with the usual icebreaker. That didn't surprise Rastun. This wasn't an icebreaker kind of meeting.

"I know you have a lot of questions and concerns," Haddix addressed the crowd. "I know what's happening here is . . . a unique situation. But we will conduct this meeting in an orderly fashion. No shouting out questions. No interrupting. Raise your hand and I'll call on you. If I can't answer your question, I'll defer to one of the other people here on stage."

A few in the audience nodded.

"Now, first question?"

Over half the people in the room raised their hands.

This could be a long night, thought Rastun.

Haddix pointed to a bearded, overweight man, who asked, "What are you doing to find these monsters?"

"We're searching the area where the attacks occurred. Along with the FUBI, my deputies and Sheriff's Office volunteers, and the Bishopville Police Department, the Highway Patrol and the State Department of Natural Resources have committed personnel to the search."

"Then how come you haven't found 'em yet?" blurted another man. "The county ain't that big?"

"Lee County is 411 square miles in size," Haddix answered, "and a lot of it is forests and swamps. That's a lot of ground to cover. We're doing our best to search it all."

A thin brunette in her early thirties raised her hand. "So are these things, like, aliens?"

"I've got this one, Sheriff." Ehrenberg walked up to the lectern. "I did help examine the body of the lizard man Jack killed. It has a heart, two lungs, stomach, two kidneys, male sexual organs. Its respiratory, circulatory, and digestive systems all indicate the creature is terrestrial in origin."

Rastun noticed the scruffy man in the back shaking his head.

Another man raised his hand. "I heard someone say they're intelligent dinosaurs. Is that true?"

"Not intelligent dinosaurs," Ehrenberg answered. "They might be some evolutionary offshoot of dinosaurs, but we don't know for sure. We do know the creature's brain is larger, much larger than that of a crocodile, but smaller than a human's. It could have intelligence on the level of a chimpanzee or an orangutan. Honestly, folks, we've only just started collecting information on the lizard men."

"Is this the same monster that killed those two men?" a woman asked.

Sheriff Haddix took this question. "That has not been determined yet. More examination still needs to be done."

"Excuse me?" An attractive Asian woman in the back called out. "Felicia Chang, ABC Columbia. We still have yet to hear from Jack Rastun about what happened when he killed that lizard man and saved those girls."

"Jack's been recuperating from his injuries," Ehrenberg responded. "Besides, this town hall is meant to address the concerns of the people of Lee County. I'm sure we can arrange an interview afterward."

"Maybe Mister Rastun's actions can give people some ideas what to do if attacked by a lizard man."

Many in the audience nodded, some saying, "Yeah, yeah."

Ehrenberg turned to Rastun and shrugged.

"Great," he sighed.

Karen patted him on the leg. "You'll be fine."

Rastun walked to the lectern and briefly surveyed the people before him. "As for what happened at the McMurtry residence, we spotted three lizard men breaking into the house and went to help the people inside. I engaged one lizard man and killed it, the other two got away. Now, to answer your second question on what to do when attacked by a lizard man . . ."

"Just how many of these things are out there?" a man in the middle of the room blurted out.

Rastun glared at him. "If you have a question, raise your hand." He spoke the last three words in a slow, deliberate tone. That sort of interruption would have never occurred during a briefing in the Army. It also shouldn't occur in the civilian world. Didn't courtesy and protocol mean anything?

The man who interrupted him lowered his head.

Rastun looked around the room. No one raised their hands. "We have no estimate on the number of lizard men. So let's stick with the facts, the main one being there is a newly discovered species in this county that killed one, possibly two people. These animals are hostile, they appear to be two, maybe three times stronger than a man, and trust me on this one, their claws are razor sharp."

Rastun saw many audience members stiffen, fear registering on their faces. He also noticed the stubbly-faced man in the back listening to him with rapt attention.

He continued. "Now, Ms. Chang suggested that I can give you some ideas on how to protect yourself from a lizard man. First thing, fortify your home. Get security bars for your doors and windows. If you have lumber, board up your windows. So far every attack has occurred at night, so when the sun goes down, stay inside."

One man raised his hand. "What if they still get inside?"

"Designate a secure room beforehand, probably a basement, or any room with a strong door, and barricade it with furniture."

"What if we have a gun?" asked a stout, middle-aged man.

"Then be prepared to use it."

"And if we don't have a gun?" asked a young woman.

"Improvise. Get a baseball bat or a golf club. Hell, Duct tape a knife to a broomstick. Just have a weapon handy, but remember, fighting these animals is an absolute last resort. If one breaks into your home, get out if possible, or get to a safe room."

"You killed one," said a redheaded teenage boy. "I say we just shoot 'em if we see 'em."

A few others nodded.

"Yes, I killed a lizard man," said Rastun. "Through luck and skill. I put two slugs from a Glock into its side and it still put up a fight. Then I took a tumble with it down some steps, and it still wanted a piece of me. I had to knife it in the throat to finally put it down. So before you put 'shooting it' at the top of your list, just remember, if you hit it and it keeps coming, or if you miss it, you're dead."

Silence consumed the room. All eyes locked on him. A few people swallowed. Couples clutched hands.

A mousy woman with glasses hesitantly put her hand in the air. "M-Mister Rastun?"

"Yes, ma'am."

"I-I . . . I don't think that was necessary. You're scaring these people."

Rastun gritted his teeth, holding back a groan. *God save us from overly sensitive snowflakes.* "There are an unknown number of dangerous animals attacking homes in this county. That's something people need to be scared of. I'm here to give you advice on what to do if the worst happens, so you don't allow fear to overwhelm you and freeze up, because if you let that happen, you're dead."

He scanned the auditorium. No one else raised their hand.

Figuring he was finished, he took his seat next to Karen.

"So how was that?" he whispered to her.

"Very direct."

"And this surprises you?"

"I would have been surprised if you'd done it any other way."

Rastun grinned, then spotted Stubbly-Face in the back. The man nearly stood at attention. He had to be ex-military. Probably why he'd called him "Captain" instead of "Mister."

One of the reporters raised his hand. "Along with search parties, what else are you doing to locate the lizard men?"

"I can take that." Karen went over to the lectern. "We've set up a perimeter of camera traps and webcams toward the east, the projected path of these creatures. You can think of it as an early warning system. We also have a small drone with an infrared camera."

A few people in the audience spoke softly to one another.

"You're not using it to spy on us?" one man asked.

"Why would we do that?" asked Karen.

"You're with the government. What if you're using this as a smokescreen to gather information on us?"

Karen took a slow breath. Rastun knew she was trying to settle herself before answering. "The FUBI is not a government agency."

"Aren't you with the Department of Agriculture?" asked a middle-aged man.

"We only take money from them as part of our public-private partnership, but we run ourselves, and we are not using our drone, or anything else, to spy on people. The only thing we care about is finding the lizard men and preventing them from killing anyone else."

"Miss Thatcher." Staub stood, holding a phone. "Darren Staub, host of Truth Talk and best selling author."

Rastun groaned. What did this moron want?

"I want to go back to Doctor Ehrenberg's statements about the body of the supposed lizard man you recovered."

Supposed? Rastun furrowed his brow at that.

Ehrenberg took over at the lectern for Karen. "What is it you'd like to know, Mister Staub."

"Have you disclosed everything about your examination of the body?"

"Of course I did."

"Then how can you tell these people that the 'Lizard Man'," Staub made quotation marks with his fingers, "is terrestrial in origin?"

"Because their anatomy is similar to that of known reptile species."

"Or maybe that's what they want you to think."

Ehrenberg glanced to the side for a moment, then looked back at Staub. "And who is *they?*"

"The Reptilians."

Several members of the audience scrunched their faces or looked to one another in puzzlement.

Karen leaned close to Rastun. "I think we're about to take a detour into the *Twilight Zone.*"

"I think we're about to take a detour into an insane asylum."

Staub faced the audience, moving his phone right to left, no doubt recording everything. "For centuries, these otherworldly beings have secretly lorded over our world. They have disguised themselves as humans, used their DNA to create human/Reptilian hybrids. These lizard men, you call them, are their foot soldiers, and the fact they've made themselves known to the world could mean the beginning of a dark age for the human race."

All eyes were on Staub. Most faces showed disbelief. Some shook their heads and rolled their eyes. Mayor McAllister lowered his head, looking embarrassed.

The scruffy guy in the back nodded.

Ehrenberg gripped the sides of the lectern, shoulders lowering in a low, calming breath. "Mister Staub, I don't think this is the time --"

"I think this is the perfect time. We finally have a body of one of these aliens." Lines etched across Staub's forehead. "You still have the body, right?"

"Yes. The county coroner has it."

"Do you know that he still has it? The Reptilians took that body Phil Welsh had. They may have taken it from the coroner so we don't learn their secrets and find a way to defeat them."

Staub moved into the aisle. The scruffy man stared at him with rapt attention. Even Councilman Sawyer moved near the edge of his seat, gaze locked on Staub.

Don't tell me he's taking this shit seriously, thought Rastun.

"Humans have an innate fear of reptiles," said Staub. "This goes back to Biblical times. In science fiction, many bad aliens are reptilian in nature. Some of the most terrifying cryptids are reptiles.

The Flatwoods Monster, the Dover Demon, dragons. This is to condition us to fear reptiles, that way when the Reptilians finally reveal themselves, we'll be too scared to fight them."

"All right." Sheriff Haddix strode to the lectern, face tight in annoyance. "If you want to ramble about alien reptiles on your show, fine. But we're having a serious discussion here."

"Why are you trying to shut me down, Sheriff?" Staub moved closer to the stage. "Do you just want people to stay ignorant, or are you with them?"

"Siddown, ya whackjob," said one lady in the audience.

"What if he's telling the truth?" a man said.

Rastun slapped his palm over his forehead. Fucking wonderful. The town hall had degenerated into a conspiracy theory convention. More than anything, he wanted to grab this Staub shithead by the collar and put his fist through –

A sharp *bang* echoed through the room. Everyone turned to the back with a start.

Another *bang.* The doors buckled.

Rastun jumped out of his chair. He went for his Glock.

The doors crashed open. Screams rang out.

Two lizard men pushed aside the wrecked doors.

TWENTY-SIX

An explosion of noise filled the community room. Screams of terror. Metal chairs scratching the floor or clanging together. The gurgling bellow of the lizard men.

The mass of people rushed the stage, knocking over chairs and each other. Sawyer gaped at the chaotic scene, face pale. Rastun aimed his Glock at the creatures. There were too many people in the way for a clear shot.

"Move!" He herded Karen and Ehrenberg to the side of the stage. One of the lizard men slashed Felicia Chang's back. The reporter threw out her arms and fell.

Sawyer bolted from his chair, stumbling as he ran for the rear exit.

A dozen people leapt onto the stage, then two dozen more after them. Sheriff Haddix tried to guide them to the exit while speaking on his cell. Mayor McAllister also waved people to safety.

Rastun pressed his back against the wall, as did Karen and Ehrenberg. He caught Haddix saying, "I need all available --"

Three people crashed into him, knocking him to the floor. Two others tripped over him. Several more rushed through the rear exits. Others ran to the back of the stage, banging against walls or pulling back curtains, desperately looking for a way out.

Screaming people fled past Rastun. He glanced at Karen and Ehrenberg, making sure they didn't get swept away in the human wave. His mind raced to come up with a way to control the situation, restore order.

He came up blank. Frustration boiled inside him. He had to do something. But what could one man do against a panicked mob?

Gunshots cracked from the front of the room. The scruffy man fired a pistol into the back of a lizard man. It growled and staggered. The man shot it again and again. The creature trembled and collapsed.

The other lizard man turned and hissed. The man ejected his spent clip and reached for another one.

Glass shattered. Another lizard man burst through the window.

Two more shots echoed through the room. The scruffy man sprinted through the front doorway.

"Help me! Help me!"

An elderly man crawled on the floor, pushing away chairs. A lizard man stalked toward him. Rastun brought up his Glock. People ran in front of him, denying him a clear shot.

The creature leaped on the old man. It buried its jaws into his neck. Rivers of blood flowed onto the floor.

"Oh my God." Karen pressed a hand over her heart.

Another scream went up. An elderly woman lay on the floor, her walker a few feet away. The second lizard man pounced on her. Its jaws dug into her throat, then snapped to the left. Bloody chunks of flesh dangled from its mouth.

Rage filled Rastun's soul. Rage and loathing. Two people had died right in front of him and he hadn't been able to do a damn thing to save them.

The crowd thinned. Sheriff Haddix and the mousy woman who had scolded Rastun for scaring people lay on the stage, bloody, bruised, and half-conscious. He dashed over to them, followed by Karen and Ehrenberg.

"Help 'em up," Rastun ordered. "I'll cover you."

Karen grabbed the woman by the shoulders and lifted her to her feet. Ehrenberg strained as he tried to raise the Sheriff.

"C'mon, big guy. Help me out here."

Haddix groaned and struggled to stand.

Something growled nearby. The lizard man who'd busted through the window locked its red eyes on Rastun. It snorted and charged.

Rastun fired. Three red holes sprouted on the lizard man's torso. Four. Five. Six. Seven. The creature faltered, its breaths coming in short bursts.

Rastun put three rounds into its head. The monster collapsed.

The remaining lizard man unleashed a prolonged growl, like a combination of grief and anger. It stood over the savaged, bloody body of the old man, snarling at Rastun.

He glanced at Karen and Ehrenberg. They hurried toward the exit with the injured woman and Haddix.

The lizard man knocked aside a couple of chairs and loped toward him.

Rastun emptied his Glock. Blood poured from the creature's torso and shoulder. It roared in pain, but kept coming.

Rastun ejected the empty clip and inserted a new one. The lizard man was only fifteen feet away.

The pistol cracked four times. Blood spurted from the beast's throat and snout. It let out a choked-off gargle and fell on its back.

Rastun checked over his shoulder. Ehrenberg, Karen, and the wounded made it through the exit.

More growls came from the front. Three more lizard men entered the community room.

TWENTY-SEVEN

Rastun fired three times. One lizard man jerked and snarled. He probably grazed the monster.

He ran into the hallway after Karen and Ehrenberg. They made slow progress from carrying the listless woman and Sheriff Haddix.

"Go! Go!" Rastun urged them on, checking over his shoulder. They didn't have long before the lizard men caught up with them.

Ten people were jammed against the rear door, pushing and clawing, trying to get outside.

"One at a time!" Rastun shouted.

They ignored him. Two people shoved their way outside, followed by two more. The others stumbled through the door.

A large, dark shape tackled someone. Screams erupted. People ran faster.

A second large shape appeared in the doorway. Another lizard man.

Rastun spotted a door to his left. He kicked it open and herded the others inside.

The lizard man snorted and entered the hallway.

Rastun fired. The monster hissed and stumbled back, two bloody holes around its right shoulder.

He rushed into the room, slammed the door shut, and locked it. The room turned out to be a kitchen, with five other people taking shelter. Mayor McAllister, Darren Staub, and three women, two middle-aged, the other a dark-haired teen.

Rastun checked the door. It was wood, maybe two inches thick. No way would it hold up against the lizard men. He hurried over to a large, silver refrigerator. "Move this against the door!"

He grabbed the side and pushed, aided by Ehrenberg and Karen. McAllister joined them, along with the women. High pitched scratches came from the bottom of the fridge as they shoved it across the floor.

Staub stood near the far corner of the kitchen, shaking.

"Get your ass over here and help us!" yelled Karen.

Swallowing, Staub made his way over. They pushed the refrigerator in front of the door.

119

A harsh *bang* sent tremors through the fridge, pushing it back a couple of inches.

Staub screamed and jumped back.

Through the opening, Rastun saw a lizard man back up, then fling itself against the door. The refrigerator tipped over. Everyone strained and grunted to keep it upright. Except Staub, who stood to the side, hyperventilating.

Rastun fired through the opening. The lizard man wailed and drew back. He grabbed the refrigerator and helped the others shove it against the door.

"Everyone brace it!" He reloaded his pistol, pressing his shoulder against the fridge.

Something slammed against it. The tremor went through the refrigerator, and his fractured ribs. Rastun gritted his teeth, trying to block out the pain.

"Hold the line!" he growled. "Do not let them through!"

The fridge took another vicious blow. The teen and one of the middle-aged women cried out and jumped back.

"Get up against this fridge!" Rastun ordered.

The two hesitated, then pressed themselves against it.

The lizard men crashed against it again. Rastun feared the fridge would cave in.

It held. Ten seconds passed without another assault. Thirty seconds. A minute.

"They stopped." The brown-haired middle-aged woman closed her eyes. "Thank God, they stopped."

"Don't get complacent," said Rastun. "They may try again."

He walked over to the mousy woman, who lay in a fetal position near the stove. A quick examination revealed several bruises and cuts, including a nasty one on the ear. Sheriff Haddix also appeared in rough shape, but remained alert.

"Did you tell your deputies what's happening here?" asked Rastun.

Haddix groaned before answering. "I just got on the phone when the crowd knocked me over. I dropped it."

Rastun handed his phone to the Sheriff.

"Thanks." Haddix dialed, while McAllister went through the draws until he pulled out a large carving knife.

"What are we gonna do?" Staub's voice trembled. His head whipped from left to right. "There's no way out of here. We're trapped. They're gonna get us and --"

"Hey!" Rastun pointed at him. "Either say something useful or shut up!"

Staub pressed himself against the corner, lowering his gaze to the floor.

Rastun checked around the kitchen. He didn't like what he saw. There were no other doors. The window above the sink was rectangular and not very big.

"Dammit." He'd just put himself, and the others, into the worst defensive situation possible. An enclosed space with no exit.

Rastun gripped his pistol tighter. He'd just inserted his last magazine. Seventeen rounds. There were at least five lizard men on the other side of the door, maybe four if the one he'd shot died. With their strength and resilience, he'd need a lot more than seventeen rounds to put down all of them.

Just have to hold out and –

A heavy blow struck the refrigerator. Screams and gasps came from the people pressed against it. Rastun slid over the island table and added his weight to the fridge when the next blow came. The big appliance jerked forward. Rastun and the others pushed back. The lizard men pounded the refrigerator again. The teen bawled, but held her ground. They all did.

The next blow rocked the fridge back. A green, scaly arm slipped through the opening of the door. McAllister let out an enraged cry and brought down his knife. The blade drove deep into the lizard man's arm. It let out something between a wail and a hiss. McAllister tried to stab it again, but the creature drew back its arm.

They pushed the fridge back against the door. Rastun braced himself for another strike.

It didn't come.

He turned to Haddix. "How long before your deputies get here?"

"Could be anywhere from five to ten minutes."

The fridge took another hit. Karen and the others shoved it back against the door.

"We may not have five minutes, definitely not ten."

Another lizard man rammed the fridge. With everyone pushing back, it barely moved. Sweat drenched all their faces. Karen and Ehrenberg held up well. Both kept themselves in good shape. Of the four civilian adults, only Staub looked like he kept himself in decent shape. The teen was a twig. She couldn't have much strength. How long before they gave out? How long before the lizard men got inside?

"We're gonna have to get out of here," said Rastun.

"How?" asked McAllister.

"There's the window," said the dark-haired middle-aged woman. "But none of us can fit through it."

Karen stared at it. "I can, not that it does the rest of you any good."

The refrigerator got hit again. A lizard man snarled. The teen and the brown-haired middle-aged woman strained to hold back the assault, sobbing.

"This is a kitchen." Rastun headed toward the cabinets. "There's gotta be cooking oil and soap in here."

"So?" blurted Staub.

"So I break out the window, grease the sides, and slide out."

"You're gonna leave us?" the teen whimpered.

"No. I'm going to get our car and bring it around here."

"Then what?" Staub threw up his arms. "How the hell are *we* supposed to get out of here?"

"I plan on making a new door."

"You're never going to fit through that window." Karen jabbed a hand at it.

"I have to try." Rastun's face stiffened with resolve.

"It won't work! Greased up or not, you won't make it. And if you get stuck, we're done for."

"We don't have another choice."

"We do. I'll go." Karen's face blazed with determination.

Rastun stopped breathing. A cold, penetrating fear took hold. "There's no way I can let you --"

"We don't have a choice. If I don't get to our car, we're finished."

"Our SUV doesn't even have enough room for everyone," said Ehrenberg.

"I-I have a pick-up," the teen said in a shaky voice.

A lizard man pounded the fridge. They held it at bay.

"Good. Gimme the keys." Karen grabbed Rastun's wrist, her voice softening. "Jack, you know this is our only chance."

He did. That was the bitch of it. Karen was the only one who could make it through that window and outside.

Where he had no doubt more lizard men lurked.

Fear coiled around his soul. He'd ordered men he considered brothers to risk their lives. But could he do the same with the woman he loved?

Karen's been through this before. She survived several encounters with the sea raptor. She knew how to handle herself in dangerous situations.

It didn't make the decision any easier.

The refrigerator shook from another hit.

"Jack!" Karen hollered.

"All right." He handed her his Glock.

She grimaced. "You know I'm not comfortable with guns."

Rastun snorted. Karen had never fired a gun in her life. If she had to use one now, she'd likely miss. "You're not going out there unarmed."

"I've got mace and an asp."

"You need to be better armed." Rastun opened one of the closets and found a mop leaning against the wall. He grabbed the handle and kicked the bottom, breaking it off.

The fridge took another hit, shoving it over an inch. A lizard man pushed its snout through the opening and snarled.

Rastun fired two shots. Both hit the doorframe, driving back the beast. Ehrenberg and the others pushed the fridge against the door. All of them panted. The teen and middle-aged woman slumped against the door.

How much longer could they hold up?

Rastun threw open drawers until he found what he needed, kitchen knives and Duct tape. He taped a knife to each end of the mop pole, then busted out the window with the butt of his Glock.

He faced Karen, a chill sweeping through him. Could he ever forgive himself if anything happened to her? My God, what would he tell Emily?

"I love you," he said.

Karen kissed him hard and fast. "I love you, too."

Rastun helped her through the window. When she had her feet on the ground, he handed her the mop-turned-spear. With one last look, she ran off into the night.

Please, God, keep her safe.

TWENTY-EIGHT

Karen hurried along the side of the community center, scanning all around her. Light from the windows illuminated some of the church grounds. Beyond it lay darkness. She tried to make out any sort of movement in the shadows, but couldn't.

She kept moving, clenching her makeshift spear. Her heart hammered in her chest. Images of what the lizard men did to the two old people in the auditorium played through her mind. What if one of those monsters leapt out of the darkness and did the same to her?

Get a grip. Karen thought of Jack and Randy, and all the others back in the kitchen. She couldn't allow fear and panic to take control, otherwise she was dead. So were the others.

So was Jack.

She kept him in her thoughts, summoning the courage that had gotten her through all those terrifying situations along the Jersey Shore.

Karen made it to the edge of the community center and peered around the corner. Nothing.

Letting out a sigh of relief, she gazed at five vehicles sitting on an expanse of grass forty yards away. One had t-boned another, probably in a frantic attempt to escape. The other three were undamaged, including the dark full-cab pickup that belonged to the teen, Kelly.

Karen tensed. Realistically, the distance was nothing. But in the dark with large, reptilian monsters around, those forty yards felt like forty miles.

Karen's muscles coiled. She prepared to run.

A sound came from behind. A soft *thump* on the grass. Another followed a moment later.

She spun around. Her mouth hung open in shock and terror.

The lizard man bellowed and charged. She tried to jump out of the way. It tackled her, knocking her to the ground. The air blasted from her lungs. Pain tore through every bone and muscle in her body. The spear fell from her grip.

The creature crouched above her, glowing, blood red eyes aimed at her. Its jaws opened, revealing rows of sharp teeth. A throaty growl reverberated in its mouth.

Karen pulled in her legs and rolled away as the lizard man lunged. Its jaws snapped shut inches from her. She scrambled to her feet, digging through her pocket.

Hissing, the creature turned and slashed at her. Karen twisted away.

Claws ripped into her thigh. White hot pain shot up her leg. Karen cried out and dropped to her side. She stared up at the reptilian maw, her skin cold with fear. She thought about Dr. Malakov, who'd been devoured by the sea raptor, how horrifying the sight had been.

No. That's not going to happen to me.

The lizard man brought down its jaws.

Karen nailed it in the side of the snout with a palm strike. Something stung the base of her hand. The creature turned back to her with an enraged hiss.

She tried to pull her hand out of her pocket. It got stuck. Her body tightened in panic.

The lizard man lunged at her again. She jammed her forearm under its jaws. The creature pushed forward. Karen strained. No use. The thing was stronger, pushing her arm down, its teeth barely a foot away.

She yanked her hand out of her pocket, gripping her pepper-spray. She shot a stream into the lizard man's red eyes. It bellowed and drew back. Karen redirected the stream into its mouth for good measure. The creature toppled over and pawed at its face.

Karen scurried over the grass on all fours, blades of pain tearing at her right leg and left hand. She grabbed her fallen spear and turned around. The lizard man hissed and gurgled, staggering to its feet.

Teeth bared, Karen thrust the spear into the monster's chest. Its jaws hung open, no noise coming from its throat. Shoulders tensed, she pushed the tip deeper inside the beast. The red glow faded from its eyes. Its body went limp and sagged to the side.

Karen pulled out the spear and sat on the grass, panting, overwhelmed with relief. She was alive. She would see Jack and Emily again.

She wanted to sit for a minute or two, collect herself.

But Jack and the others didn't have a minute or two. She had to get to that pickup, now!

Karen pushed herself to her feet and ran. Her right leg throbbed with each step. The side of her pants was wet and sticky. She clenched her teeth and kept running. She couldn't stop. Too many people depended on her. Jack depended on her.

Karen pulled the keys from her pocket as she neared the pickup and heard the faint *click* of the door unlocking. She threw open the door and put the spear between the driver's and passenger's seat, wanting it nearby just in case.

Putting on the seatbelt, Karen swung the big pickup around and drove along the rear of the church grounds. She kept the headlights off. Many animals were attracted to light. She didn't know if that included lizard men, but she wasn't about to find out the hard way.

Karen took out her phone and called Jack. *Please be all right.*

One ring. Two rings. Three rings. Her throat tightened in dread.

"Karen!" Jack's voice burst through her phone.

"Jack! Are you okay?"

"We won't be for long. These damn things really want our asses."

"I'm coming. Just hang on."

She tossed the phone onto the passenger seat and looked for the small window she'd crawled out of. There! She lined up the truck with the wall of the kitchen, then glanced at the large hood. It looked pretty sturdy. It should hold up.

It better hold up.

Karen floored it. The pickup wobbled as its rear wheels tore up grass and dirt. The vehicle shot forward. The wall loomed in the windshield. She hit the brakes just before impact.

The wall shattered in an explosion of metal, wood, and plaster. A quake rocked the pickup, and Karen. The airbag burst open. She took a breath, her body shaking. She pressed down on the airbag, trying to make it collapse faster. The windshield was spiderwebbed, the hood crumpled.

Please work.

Karen put the pickup into reverse and stepped on the gas. The engine responded and the truck backed out of the large hole in the wall.

Staub started for the wall, but McAllister grabbed him by the arm, stopping him. Kelly sprinted for the pickup, followed by the other two women. Randy picked up the mousy woman and carried her outside.

That left Jack, Sheriff Haddix, Mayor McAllister, and Staub. Karen gasped when she saw the refrigerator tilt. The four held it upright.

C'mon, c'mon, c'mon.

Jack waved them to the truck. He waited until they were near the hole before letting go of the fridge.

It tipped over. Three lizard men rushed through the door into the kitchen.

"Jack!"

He fired his pistol on the run. The first lizard man jerked backwards. Jack leaped over what looked to be the remains of the kitchen sink. He opened the door and jumped into the cab.

"Go! Go! Go!"

Karen stomped on the accelerator. Two lizard men chased after the truck. She cut the wheel and threw the gearshift into drive. The truck sped across the church grounds. Karen checked the rear-view mirror. She couldn't see the lizard men. No way were they going to catch them now.

The truck bounced onto the road. She headed east, toward Bishopville. They needed to get Sheriff Haddix and the mousy woman to the hospital.

Karen felt the blood soaking her left hand and the steering wheel, then glanced at the dark stain on the side of her leg. She needed to get to the hospital, too.

She reached over to Jack, clenching his leg, as though to reassure herself he was there, that they'd both survived.

"Oh my God." Jack stared at her leg. "You're bleeding."

"I got jumped by a lizard man. I'll be fine."

"Pull over."

"I said I'll be fine."

"Half your leg is covered with blood," Jack said in a sharp tone. "Now pull over."

She glanced at him. His face scrunched in determination and concern. Karen eyed the dark stain saturating her pants, felt the blood on the steering wheel. It'd take at least ten or fifteen minutes to reach the hospital. How much blood would she lose before then? Enough to pass out behind the wheel?

She pulled to the side of the road and spun in her seat, pain stabbing her leg as she stretched it out onto the passenger seat. Jack turned on the dome light. He searched the glove compartment for a first aid kit, but found none. Next he rummaged through the mess on the floorboard and came up with a paper bag from a fast food restaurant, which contained a lot of napkins.

"Why the hell are we stopping?" Staub spoke through the open rear window, his voice cracking.

"Karen's hurt," Jack told him. "I need to bandage her."

"Those fucking things may still be after us. We need to get out of here."

"I need to make sure my girlfriend doesn't bleed out." Jack glared at the talk show host.

Staub winced, then moved to the far end of the pickup's bed.

Jack used his shoelaces to tie the napkins around her leg and hand.

"Keep pressure on that leg wound." He jumped out the passenger side door and ran around the front. Karen slid over so he could get behind the wheel. Seconds later, they were speeding toward Bishopville.

"I don't believe it," she heard McAllister through the rear window. The mayor shook his head and continued. "This wasn't like any animal attack I've ever heard about. This was like . . . a full-on assault." His eyes widened. "An invasion."

Karen turned to him, forehead wrinkled, while she pressed down on her wound. An invasion? Jeez, he was sounding like that nutjob Staub.

"I don't know if invasion is the right word for this," said Ehrenberg.

"Then what would you call it?" asked McAllister.

"This is the fourth lizard man attack we've had." Ehrenberg held up his phone. "When you look at a map of Lee County, you'll see that every attack has ranged further east. These aren't isolated incidents. I think the lizard men are expanding their territory."

Karen tensed. "Which means if they keep going east, they're going to wind up in downtown Bishopville."

TWENTY-NINE

Rastun lowered himself into a sofa in the hospital's lobby, with new sutures in his left shoulder and back. The old ones had popped open during the lizard men attack. As luck would have it, the doctor who treated him earlier in the week stitched him up again, then scolded him for going back to work without medical clearance.

"It was just a town hall meeting," Rastun pleaded his case. "All I was supposed to do was talk. I didn't expect an army of lizard men to show up."

He pushed himself deeper into the sofa, grimacing as twisting pain shot through his mid-section. Leaning against the refrigerator while bloodthirsty monsters pounded it hadn't helped his injured ribs.

Whatever. I'm alive. So was Karen. She needed stitches and antibiotics, but had suffered no life-threatening injuries. Neither had Sheriff Haddix or the mousy woman.

The two senior citizens and the man who tried to escape out the back, however, were beyond help.

Dammit. How far away had he been from them? He recalled the chaotic scene in the community center over and over again. What could he have done different?

"Excuse me, Jack Rastun?"

A tall man with a paunch approached. He wore a casual dress shirt and slacks, but had an air of authority.

"Yes?" Rastun rose, his ribs torturing him. He clenched his teeth.

"Are you all right?"

"Don't worry. Nothing serious. Can I help you?"

"I'm Commander Umbarger, Sheriff Haddix's second-in-command."

"Commander." Rastun shook his hand. "How's the Sheriff doing?"

"I just came from his room. He has a concussion, a couple of broken fingers, and some bruises. Nothing that'll keep him down for long."

"That's good to hear."

"The Sheriff told me what you did back at the community center," said Umbarger. "Good work. You saved a lot of people."

Rastun nodded. "Do you have a final tally on the casualties?"

Umbarger cast his eyes down. "Eight dead."

"Eight?" That was double the number Rastun had seen during the attack. He figured the lizard men picked off the others as they ran from the church.

"We also have over thirty injured," said Umbarger. "Most of them minor, thank God. I wanted to talk to you about the attack, along with Karen Thatcher and Doctor Ehrenberg. Do you know where they are?"

"Karen's still being treated. Doctor Ehrenberg went back into the field to rejoin the rest of our team."

Umbarger waved him to the sofa, taking out a notebook and a small tape recorder. Rastun ran down what happened at the community center. He just got to the part where the lizard men tried to break into the kitchen when Karen appeared, her left hand bandaged. She also wore bland white pajama bottoms in place of her ripped and bloodied pants.

"You okay?" He hugged her tight, kissing the side of her head.

"I'm fine."

Rastun released her and introduced her to Umbarger. After taking her statement, the commander turned back to him. "Mister Rastun, I want to talk to you about the shots you fired inside the community center."

"What do you want to know?"

"Where were you when you fired at the lizard men?"

Umbarger had asked that before, but Rastun knew from Sherlock that cops usually asked the same questions multiple times to make sure someone was telling the truth. Most people found it difficult to keep details straight when they were lying.

"I was on the stage, then later in the kitchen."

"Let's stick to the main room. All the shots you took were from the stage?"

"Correct."

Umbarger handed him his notebook. "Could you draw me a diagram of the community center and where your shots went?"

Rastun drew a circle for the stage, three stick figures representing himself, Karen, and Ehrenberg, and blob-like images with J-shaped heads that were supposed to be lizard men. He made a half-frown at the crude rendering. He'd never been much of an artist.

Rastun drew lines showing where his shots went and handed the notebook back to Umbarger. He pointed to the lines going to the front of the building.

"When did you fire these shots?"

"When the three lizard men came in, right before we retreated to the kitchen."

Umbarger gave a slight nod. "Were there any people around there at the time?"

"No. I made sure I had a clear line of fire."

"What about the other civilian who was shooting? Where was he?"

"He stood at the back of the room the entire time."

"And he got out before those three lizard men entered?"

"That's correct. What's this all about, anyway?"

"It's about that reporter, Felicia Chang," said Umbarger. "She was one of those killed in the attack."

Rastun nodded. "I saw her go down when one of the lizard men took a swipe at her."

"That's not what killed her."

"What do you mean?" Rastun tilted his head, puzzled.

"I spoke to one of our detectives before I came here. The lacerations on her back appeared superficial. They wouldn't have been fatal."

"Then how did she die?"

Umbarger took a breath. "She was shot in the head."

THIRTY

Rastun and Karen didn't leave the hospital until after midnight. Umbarger had more questions for him about the scruffy-looking man who shot the one lizard man, and most likely Felicia Chang. They also had to wait for a sketch artist to come so they could give him their description of the suspect.

Why did he kill her? And why did he want to talk to me? Rastun wondered if the man had anything to do with the murders of Pam Mankowski and the deputy.

After giving the descriptions of the feral man and Felicia Chang's killer to a sketch artist, he and Karen walked out of the hospital and into a mob of reporters. Both refrained from answering questions as they got into a cab. Rastun called Ehrenberg to let him know they would join them in the field.

"Forget it," the cryptozoologist said in an unusually firm voice. "You two are injured."

"Doc, we can --"

"No. Both of you. Hotel. Recover. Now. Bye."

Rastun snorted, staring at his phone. "All of a sudden, I feel like a six-year-old." He looked down at Karen's bandaged hand. "You okay?"

"I'm fine," she snapped, clearly annoyed at the question.

"Now you know how I feel when you keep asking, 'Are you okay?'"

Karen shot him a scathing look, then tacked on a smile. Rastun put an arm around her and drew her against him. He rested his cheek on Karen's hair, relishing its softness.

Had things gone differently tonight . . .

The cab dropped them off at their hotel. Rastun opened the door for Karen, then followed her inside. She stood near the bed, hugging herself, staring down at the floor. He'd seen a fair number of soldiers do the same thing in Iraq and Afghanistan after combat. Just standing in silence, thinking about being so close to death, yet coming out alive.

Rastun continued staring at her. The sea raptor expedition bubbled up in his mind, all the close calls Karen had. All the terror he'd felt seeing that beast bearing down on her.

Now she'd had another close call with the lizard men. If she hadn't kept her wits about her, if she hadn't been as tough as she was . . .

His throat clenched. He did not want to think about a life without Karen.

Their gazes locked. Her eyes glowed with relief, the relief of someone who had survived something horrific.

Rastun wrapped Karen in his arms and kissed her. They tightened their embrace, their mouths hungry for each other. Clothing was yanked off and flung in all directions. Karen took both his wrists and pulled him onto the bed. Rastun kissed her breasts, her shoulders, her neck. She gasped and wrapped her firm, slender legs around him.

He entered her, each thrust harder than the last. Karen's moans became gasps that grew louder and louder until climaxing in a cry of passion.

They lay next to each other, panting, sweating. Rastun stroked Karen's hair and cheek. She closed her eyes and smiled.

"I love you," she said.

Rastun grinned. "I love you, too."

***

Rastun drifted off to sleep. He found himself back at the community center, standing in the middle of the stage. People ran past, screaming. By some miracle, no one knocked him over.

The lizard men stalked through the room, growling, heads swiveling, searching for victims. One broke from the pack and went after the old woman with the walker.

Get your gun. Shoot it.

His body would not obey his brain. Rastun continued to stand there, unmoving, as the lizard man jumped on the woman.

"Help me!" she yelled. "Help me!"

The monster tore into the woman's throat. Her mouth and eyes opened wide and blood cascaded over her body.

The lizard men took down more people. Rastun tensed, trying to move. He couldn't.

Do something!

He heard a crack in the distance. The stubbly-faced man walked along the back of the room, casually shooting people.

Why can't I stop this?

The lizard men turned to Rastun, snarling. His fear and anger built up. He couldn't fight, couldn't run. He couldn't do anything except watch these monsters get closer and closer.

Rastun jerked awake. His heart beat a machine gun pace. He sat up on the bed, taking deep breaths. It took a minute for his heartbeat to settle down.

He pushed himself to his feet, running his hands through his hair, damp with sweat. He walked about the room, memories of the attack on the community center playing in his mind's eye. Could he have done more?

Hell yes I could have.

Instead, he just stood there, while chaos churned around him. People died because of his inaction.

Rastun slammed his fist on the door.

"Jack?"

He turned around. Karen propped herself up on her elbow. Despite the dark of the room, Rastun could see the concern on her face.

"Sorry." He leaned against the door.

"What's wrong?" Karen slid off the bed and walked over to him.

"I'm fine."

"Then why are you pounding on the door?"

Rastun looked away from her.

"Jack." Karen cupped his cheek and turned his head so he faced her. "What is it?"

He let out a loud, slow breath. "Just thinking about what happened at the community center."

"Well that's not surprising. It was pretty intense."

"That's not it. When the lizard men came in, everyone was running, I was trying to think of something to do." He shook his head. "My mind went blank. I just stood there. People were getting knocked over, stomped on, some of them died. And I just stood there."

"What do you think you could have done? It was chaos."

"That's what I was trained to do, that's what I did in Iraq and Afghanistan. Combat is chaos, and it was my job to make sure the men around me kept their heads and did what they had to do when the whole fucking world was exploding around them."

"But you were all soldiers," said Karen. "You were trained to deal with that kind of stuff. Most of the people in the audience weren't. You were one man with more than a hundred scared, panicked people running for their lives. What do you think you could have done to calm them down?"

"I don't know," Rastun replied. "Something."

"Well you did do something."

"What's that?"

"You got me and Randy out. You kept us safe. And what about Sheriff Haddix and Mayor McAllister and the people in the kitchen? Do you think any of them would still be alive if it weren't for you?" Karen inhaled slowly before speaking. "Do you think I'd still be alive if you hadn't made me that spear? A spear made out of a mop, kitchen knives, and Duct Tape. How many other people would have thought to do that?"

She rested a hand against his bare chest. "You did everything you could. I feel so bad for the people who died. But think of all the people who survived, all the people *you* saved."

Rastun cast his eyes to the floor. He found it hard to argue with Karen's logic. They'd gotten Haddix and the mousy woman to safety. How many others would have left them and saved their own skin? He thought of the lizard men he'd shot. How many people would they have killed if he hadn't have put them down?

It still bothered him that he hadn't done more to gain control of the situation, but he had to think of the people he'd gotten to safety, including Karen and Ehrenberg. And with everything going on in this crazy expedition, he didn't have time to beat himself up.

He let out a humorless chuckle. "What I wouldn't give for this to be like the Skunk Ape expedition."

"You mean no monsters trying to kill us and no psychos shooting reporters?"

"Yeah. Well, hopefully the cops will find the guy who shot Felicia Chang. I thought the sketch artist did a good job."

"I thought so, too. Still, a photo is better than . . ." Karen's mouth hung open for several seconds. She then shut her eyes and smacked her forehead. "Shit. Stupid!"

"What?"

"I can't believe I forgot about it." She strode over to the dresser and pulled out a flannel shirt. "I was taking pictures of the audience for our photo gallery. The guy has to be in one of them."

She slipped on the shirt, then got her camera and laptop. Rastun put on a pair of boxers and sat next to her at the table as she downloaded the photos. There were a total of twelve shots of the audience.

"Concentrate on the back of the room," he said, "to the left of the doors. He was there the whole time."

Karen moved the cursor to one of the pictures, highlighted the upper half and enlarged it. Rastun leaned closer, scanning the photo.

"That's him." He pointed. "Shit, he's looking away."

"Let's try another one." Karen selected a second photo and blew it up.

This time the scruffy-looking killer looked straight at the camera.

"You got him." Rastun clamped his hands on Karen's shoulders and kissed the side of her head.

"Just give me a second." She highlighted the man's head and shoulders and enlarged it, giving them a perfect mug shot.

"Great. Send a copy to Sherlock." Rastun searched the floor for his phone, finding it next to his discarded pants.

"Captain," Sherlock answered.

"You still in the field?"

"Negative. I'm helping the SO interview the folks who were at the community center during the attack."

"Good. Karen found Felicia Chang's killer in one of her photos. She's sending you a head shot of the guy."

"He should have it now," Karen called out.

"Did you hear that?"

"I did. Hang on . . . I got it. I'll forward it to the Sheriff's Office and run it through NCIC."

"Check it against DoD records, too." Rastun referred to the Department of Defense.

"You think our suspect is ex-military?"

"I don't think, I know."

THIRTY-ONE

A knock at the door woke Rastun. He glanced at the alarm clock on the nightstand. It was a little before nine in the morning.

He threw off the covers. Karen mumbled something and buried her face in the pillow. Rastun went to the door and stared through the peephole. Geek, Sherlock, and Ehrenberg stood on the other side. He opened the door halfway. "Hey. What is it?"

"Facial recognition got a hit on our man," said Sherlock. "You were right. He did serve. DoD sent me his service record."

That news brought Rastun fully awake. "Give us a minute to get dressed."

He and Karen threw on t-shirts and shorts before letting in their three friends. Sherlock set up his laptop on the table.

"This is our man. Alex Cassian."

The man in the photo had no beard or long hair. He was clean-shaven and unsmiling, as one would expect in an official military photograph.

"This guy's not your dime-a-dozen nutcase," said Geek. "Cassian did three years in the Marine Corps. Force Recon."

Rastun nodded. "That explains why he stood and fought and didn't run like the other civilians."

"What's Force Recon?" asked Karen.

"They're the Marines' version of the Rangers," answered Rastun.

"Except we're just a little bit better," Geek chimed in.

Rastun couldn't help but grin before continuing. "They do deep reconnaissance, airborne and heliborne insertions, direct action, VIP security. Those guys are beyond damn good."

He leaned closer, checking out Cassian's file. "One tour in Afghanistan, airborne qualified, SERE graduate." He used the acronym for Survival, Evasion, Resistance, and Escape. "Rifle sharpshooter and pistol marksman badges."

"The crime techs estimate Pam Mankowski and Deputy Spillman were shot from a distance of between one hundred and one hundred-fifty yards," Sherlock stated. "Easy shots for a man like Cassian."

Rastun nodded, reading further. "This guy never even made corporal. Heck, he got busted from lance corporal to private first class."

"Yeah," said Geek. "Turns out Cassian had his share of fuck-ups. Got nailed for drunk and disorderly a couple of times, had some write-ups for mouthing off to his superiors and threatening to fight some of his platoon mates."

"Sounds like he was a head case."

"It gets better," said Sherlock. "Cassian went out drinking one night, picked up a girl, and was driving back to her place when he clipped another car at a stop sign. Thankfully, the girl and the other driver suffered minor injuries, but Cassian was arrested for DUI and endangerment. That was the last straw for the Marine Corps. They let him go with an Other Than Honorable Discharge."

"Mm-hmm." That didn't come to the level of a Bad Conduct or Dishonorable Discharge. Still, anyone who got an OTH could never re-enlist, never qualify for the GI Bill, and in a lot of cases, lost their VA benefits.

"So what happened after he got booted out of the Marines?" asked Rastun.

"His last known address was an apartment here in town," Sherlock answered. "That was two years ago. After that, nothing. It looks like he became a transient."

"Does he have any family?" asked Karen.

Sherlock shook his head. "Both of his parents died when he was six. He stayed in a few foster homes until he enlisted."

"What happened to his parents?" Rastun folded his arms across his chest.

"The Sheriff's Office says they were murdered while camping at Lee State Park. They found a lot of blood at the campsite, but no bodies, and they never did find who was responsible. I did call the lead detective in the case. He's retired now." Sherlock bit his lip for a moment. "This is where it gets interesting."

"Interesting how?" asked Karen.

"Some deputies found Cassian a mile or so from the crime scene, curled up under some bushes. When the detective talked to him, he went on about dinosaur people with red eyes."

Rastun straightened, eyes widening. "You're telling me that Cassian's parents were killed by lizard men?"

Sherlock nodded. "Possibly. Of course, at the time, all the investigators thought the kid was scared out of his mind."

"And now that we know these creatures exist," said Ehrenberg, "maybe he was telling the truth."

"But we still have no idea why he would kill the reporter." Karen extended her arms out. "Or Pam Mankowski and the deputy. Or why he wanted to talk to you, Jack." She swallowed. "You . . . You think he wanted to kill you, too?"

"I don't know." He shrugged. "He seemed like he really wanted to talk to me for some reason."

"Well, I'm going to talk to some of the men in his unit," said Sherlock. "See what else I can learn. The Sheriff's Office sent Cassian's picture to every news organization and law enforcement agency throughout the Southeast. Someone is bound to spot him."

"And we're about to head back into the field to try and track down the lizard men who survived the community center attack," added Ehrenberg.

Rastun sighed and leaned back in his chair. "So I guess Karen and I are stuck in here doing nothing."

Sherlock glanced at Ehrenberg, then back to him. "Actually, there is a way you can help us."

"How?" Rastun slid forward a couple of inches in his seat.

"We figured this shouldn't be too strenuous for you two. While I'm interviewing Cassian's platoon mates, I want you to talk to his former foster parents."

THIRTY-TWO

When are these assholes gonna leave?

Lansford sat on a bench, watching the hotel across the street. Over a dozen reporters milled around the front, waiting for Jack Rastun to pop his head outside. Actually, he was waiting for that himself. But his interest in the former Ranger went far beyond some stupid celebrity sighting.

He still had doubts about this mission. As he had told Cassian, it would be easier just to kill Rastun.

"We do that, and there goes our one chance to have a spy within the Reptilians' ranks," Cassian had countered.

After what happened last night, Lansford had to admit Cassian may have a point. According to the news, Rastun killed at least three Reptilians. Why would he do that if he'd already been turned? Maybe the damn monsters hadn't indoctrinated him yet.

Now if only he could find a way to get to Rastun without those damn reporters noticing.

He continued sitting and watching. He glanced at the hand-written cardboard sign propped up next to him on the bench. "Out of work. Anything will help. God Bless."

Lansford felt a surge of pride. He knew he'd picked the right disguise. He couldn't spend hours just sitting on a bench reading a newspaper or a book. That might look suspicious. Heck, most people these days didn't read newspapers, or anything else for that matter. But pretend to be a homeless guy with a sign begging for spare change, he was practically invisible. Lansford had worried the cops might give him shit, but the two police cars that had driven by kept going. It might have been different had he been bugging everyone on the sidewalk for money. But just sitting here, not bothering anyone, the cops apparently didn't care.

And he'd already made a couple of bucks. Not a bad bonus for sitting on his ass and staring at a hotel.

His patience was eventually rewarded. A little after ten, Jack Rastun and his mega-hot photographer girlfriend, Karen Thatcher, left the hotel. The reporters followed them, but the monster hunters ignored them on their way to the parking lot.

"Fuck," Lansford muttered under his breath. There were too many people around for him to make a move. He watched Rastun and Karen Thatcher get into an SUV and drive off.

Part of him felt relieved he didn't have to confront Rastun. The man was a combat veteran, an Army Ranger. He even went one-on-one with a sea raptor and lived.

He shut his eyes, trying to rid himself of his worry. He didn't want to sound like Cassian, who thought Jack Rastun was some damn superman. So the guy was a Ranger? How many of them bought it in Iraq and Afghanistan?

Lansford pressed his hand against his waist, feeling the pistol beneath his shirt. Sooner or later, he'd have his chance to grab Rastun. If he didn't come peacefully, well, Ranger or not, he'd like to see him survive a bullet to the brain.

THIRTY-THREE

Karen looked back at the old one-story brick house with its faded, peeling roof, shaking her head. This was the second set of Cassian's foster parents she and Jack had visited, and she'd been less than impressed. The house was a mess, the two kids they cared for couldn't stop being loud or running around for more than a minute, and she could boil down the couple's assessment of the then eight-year-old Cassian to, "He was a brat," and "He was crazy, talking about monsters."

Not very helpful.

She opened the passenger side door to their SUV, taking one last look at the house before sliding in. She clenched her teeth as her leg throbbed.

"I can't help it."

"Help what?" asked Jack as he started the engine.

"Seeing what those foster parents were like, I feel bad for Cassian."

Jack grunted and pulled into the street.

"They don't give a shit about their kids." She scowled over her shoulder, her mind conjuring an image of Emily living in that damn house. It made her cringe. "They just probably want their check from the government. And how long have they been getting away with this? What if most of Cassian's foster parents were like that? How could he not be screwed up? Poor guy."

"Yeah, it sucks what happened to the guy's parents, but there are plenty of people who've had crap childhoods and don't become murderers. He made his choice. Maybe I feel bad for him as a kid. As an adult, not so much."

Karen stared at Jack as they continued through the residential neighborhood. Yes, what Cassian did to Felicia Chang, and maybe Mrs. Mankowski and Deputy Spillman, was horrible. He had to be punished. Still, she couldn't help feeling some sympathy. Maybe if Cassian's parents hadn't been killed, or if he had better foster parents, he could have turned out normal.

What if something happened to me, or Jack? What would happen to Emily? Would her parents take her in? They had been estranged for years, but Emily was their granddaughter. They couldn't ignore her. At least she had her aunt and uncle in Tampa. They'd taken care of her during her freelance days, when the job made it impossible for her to take her daughter along.

She'd be fine. She wouldn't turn out like Cassian. I just know it.

Karen shifted in her seat. She couldn't wait to finish visiting Cassian's foster parents so she could call Emily.

Jack's phone rang. She picked it up and checked the screen. It was Geek. Thumbing the speaker icon, she held it between her and Jack.

"So, how goes *Law and Order* with Jack and Karen?"

"Could be better," she replied. "The last foster parents we visited were absolute jokes."

"Actually, they were useless ass-hats who I wouldn't trust to take care of a goldfish." Jack's grip on the steering wheel tightened.

"Damn. Sounds like Cassian was doomed from the start," said Geek. "Anyway, got some news I thought you'd want to hear."

"What is it?" Jack slowed as they approached a red light.

"Sawyer called an emergency session of the county council this morning. They voted to ask the Governor to bring in the National Guard. Looks like we're about to get a crap ton of reinforcements."

"Good." Jack nodded. "What do you know? That dipshit's actually good for something."

A slight frown creased Karen's lips. She didn't think much of Sawyer either, but Jack could have said it in a more diplomatic way. One thing about him, he did not suffer fools, and more often than not was not shy about saying so. She worried that could get him, or the whole FUBI, in trouble one day. She'd tried to smooth out those rougher aspects of his personality, but it was a work in progress.

"Well," said Geek. "Allow me to piss all over your newfound faith in Sawyer. The guy went on TV this morning, ripping our asses, practically blaming us for last night's attack."

"What?" Jack blurted. "How does that dumbfuck figure that?"

"He said we refused extra manpower, that we cared more about capturing the lizard men alive than protecting the public."

"Oh he's full of shit." Karen's eyebrows scrunched together, her anger burning. She glanced at Jack, deciding she wouldn't encourage him to be tactful when it came to talking about Sawyer. The man was a dumbfuck.

"Wait, it gets better," said Geek. "He's offering a five thousand dollar bounty to anyone who shoots and kills a lizard man."

"Oh great." Jack thumped the steering wheel. "That's all we need. A lot of panicky, greedy people with guns running around the county."

"The county council actually agreed to this?" Karen asked in an incredulous tone.

"Actually, he's doing this as a private citizen."

"Where's he getting the money for the reward?"

"Sawyer owns an engineering consulting business. I'm assuming it's pretty successful if he's willing to pony up 5-K of his own money."

Karen fell back against her seat, closing her eyes. Concern built up. The people who went out hoping to claim that reward were more likely to shoot each other than a lizard man.

"Thanks for the info, Geek," said Jack. "Tell everyone to keep an extra eye out for dumbasses with guns."

"I already did."

"I figured you would."

When the call ended, Jack shook his head, muttering. "Like we don't have enough crap to worry about."

Minutes later, they arrived at the home of another set of foster parents. The Tudors had Cassian when he was ten years old, and according to the father, the boy had been a handful.

"Always getting in fights at school, wouldn't do homework, never did what we told him to do." Mr. Tudor shook his head. "That was one kid I was glad to see go."

Karen clasped her hands together, squeezing tight, trying not to make a face or say something she'd regret. Had Tudor and his wife done all they could to help Cassian, or did they just say, "Screw this," and dump him on someone else?

Again, she couldn't help but think if one set of foster parents had really cared about Cassian, would he be in this situation?

After finishing their interview with the Tudors, they drove to Sumter, twenty miles south of Bishopville. The next couple on their list, Molinaros, lived in an upscale neighborhood of large brick homes with angular roofs and dormers and a two-car garage.

"Well this is definitely the nicest house we've visited," Jack said.

"Yeah." Karen nodded. "Let's hope the people inside are just as nice." Maybe Cassian's time in foster care hadn't been all bad.

Jack rang the doorbell. A portly, dark-skinned teenage girl, phone in hand, answered.

"Hi. Can I help you?"

"Hello. I'm Jack Rastun. This is Karen Thatcher. We're with the FUBI." They both took out their IDs.

"No way." The girl's eyes and mouth went wide. "Oh my gosh. You guys are, like, famous. You're awesome."

"Thank you." Karen smiled. "And you are . . .?"

"Oh. I'm Vanessa."

"It's nice to meet you, Vanessa." Karen shook her hand. "We're here to see Nancy and Wayne Molinaro. Are they home?"

"Wayne isn't, but Nancy is." Vanessa walked across the foyer and called into the kitchen. "Nancy. Nancy, come here. You won't believe this. Jack Rastun and Karen Thatcher are here."

A round woman with curly brown-gray hair and glasses appeared. Just like Vanessa, her eyes went wide, too.

"Oh my goodness. Well . . . well this is a surprise." Nancy Molinaro pumped their hands, smiling wide and invited them in. "I saw you on the news with that whole sea monster thing last year, and with the lizard men in Bishopville. That must have been scary."

That's an understatement. Karen stiffened, thinking about the creature standing over her last night, its jaws inches away, ready to rip her to pieces.

"So why are you here?" Nancy asked.

"It's about one of your former foster kids," Jack answered. "Alex Cassian."

The cheery disposition vanished. Nancy ceased smiling and looked at the wall. Her shoulders sagged. "I can't say I'm surprised someone came by to ask me about him. I saw on the news what he did."

"Can we talk to you about him, ma'am?" asked Jack.

"Um, yeah. Sure. Vanessa, dear, would you mind going upstairs while we talk?"

"Um, sure. No prob." The girl started to turn, then said. "Um, Miss Thatcher? Mister Rastun?"

"What is it?" Karen replied.

"Could I get a picture with you guys before you leave?"

"Sure." Karen smiled. "We'd be happy to."

"You bet." Jack also smiled, not a forced one.

While their celebrity status could get on his nerves, Karen had never seen him go out of his way to be rude to autograph or photograph seekers. As he explained to her one time, "So long as they're polite, I have no problem with it."

145

That attitude endeared her to him, and made him a good role model for Emily. Her stomach fluttered, thinking how lucky she was to have a man as good as Jack in her life. Hers and Emily's.

Vanessa thanked them and headed upstairs. Nancy led them to the kitchen. The hallway was spacious, with a few nest tables and glass cabinets lining the walls. Some held framed photos, others had decorative plates or colorful porcelain flowers. The large kitchen featured chestnut-colored cabinets, counters, and an island.

"You have a lovely home, Mrs. Molinaro."

"Thank you, and please, it's Nancy." Hands on her hips, she surveyed the kitchen, grinning. "Honestly, Wayne and I never thought we'd live in a house like this. We lucked out when we won the lottery."

"Really?" Jack nodded. "Congratulations."

"Thank you. It wasn't one of those mega-multi-million dollar ones you see on the news, but we won a good amount. Would you care for something to drink? Coffee? Iced Tea? Lemonade?"

Karen and Jack agreed to iced tea.

"So you're still taking in foster children?" Karen perched on one of the island seats.

"Oh yes. There are a lot of kids out there in need of a good home, even if it's for a little while. We weren't going to stop doing that because Wayne and I suddenly struck it rich. In fact, it was a blessing. A house this size, we can take in three children."

Warmth swelled in Karen's chest. They'd barely been here for two minutes, and already Nancy was her favorite foster parent of the bunch. "Where are the other two?"

"Daryl is at a nature camp." Nancy took two glasses from a cabinet. "My husband took Jacob to a movie."

She poured out the iced tea and took the glasses over to them. "If you'll forgive me, why are you here to talk about Alex? I thought it would be the police, not monster hunters."

"We think Cassian might have some connection to the lizard men."

Nancy let out a long breath, shaking her head, as she poured herself a glass. "I know Alex had his issues, his parents being murdered when he was so young, but this . . ."

"Actually, Mrs. Molin . . ." Jack paused. "Er, Nancy. Alex's parents may not have been murdered."

She turned to him, face scrunched. "What do you mean? That's what the police said."

"Our liaison with the Sheriff's Office found some new information. When the police found him after his parents were killed, he claimed that dinosaur people did it. We think he might have been talking about lizard men."

"My God," Nancy said in a hushed breath, a hand over her heart. "He never mentioned that to us."

Karen thought it strange, especially since Cassian had told the story to his other foster parents. "When did you have Alex?"

"His senior year in high school. We were actually his last foster parents."

Karen nodded, gently clutching her glass. That could explain it. So many foster parents not believing him, probably other foster children making fun of him over it. By the time he was seventeen or eighteen, he may have decided it was best to shut up about the whole thing.

"We talked to some of Cassian's other foster parents." Jack rested his arms on the table. "They said he got into a lot of fights, could be disruptive, argued a lot. Was he like that with you and your husband?"

"No. Not at all." Nancy emphatically shook her head. "If anything, he was on the quiet side. Sure, we had meetings with teachers about him not doing homework, we caught him drinking a couple of times. Other than that, he really wasn't a bad kid. He talked a lot about joining the Marines. Wayne thought it was a good idea, that it would give him some structure, stability. I was scared they'd send him to Iraq or Afghanistan."

"Did he keep in touch after he joined the Marines?" asked Karen.

"A few times. The last we heard from him was an email saying they were sending him to Afghanistan." Nancy closed her eyes tight for a few moments. "When we didn't get any more messages, I thought . . . I thought the worst." She looked at Jack. "You were in the Army, right? Could the war have done something to him? Make him . . . Make him kill that reporter?"

"Maybe. War affects everyone differently. Some people can cope with what they saw and did over there. Others . . ." His jaw stiffened. "I really can't say about Cassian."

He stared at his glass, not moving, not picking it up, not saying anything else. Karen's throat constricted, sympathy filling her. She imagined him thinking of friends and former colleagues dealing with PTSD, and the ones who couldn't and took their own lives. She knew Jack had his demons from Iraq and Afghanistan. They may not have consumed him, but he'd woken up in the middle of the night from nightmares on more than one occasion.

She gave his arm a supportive squeeze. He smiled at her.

"So what was Alex like in school?" asked Karen. "Did he have a lot of friends? Did he play sports or anything?"

"He had a few friends. I don't think they were that close. He mainly kept to himself. We tried to get him to join sports teams or other clubs. We try and keep our foster kids involved in all sorts of activities. But Alex wasn't interested in any of it." Nancy sighed. "I wish he found some club he liked at school. He needed to do something else beside listen to those weird radio shows and go on those weird websites."

Karen tilted her head. "What radio show and websites?"

Nancy's eyes bulged. "Oh my God. If he thought those monsters killed his parents, maybe that's why he liked them so much."

"Why did he like them?" Karen leaned forward.

"Like I said. It was weird stuff. Crackpot stuff, like Bigfoot . . . well, before we all knew he was real. And then aliens, secret groups, strange experiments. And that one guy on the radio. He had a show on late at night. Alex would stay up and listen to him. A few times I had to tell him to turn down the radio because we were trying to sleep. I looked him up online and . . ."

Nancy let out a humorless laugh. "He believes in the craziest stuff. Earthquake machines, chemtrails, time travel experiments. He even thinks George Bush and the Queen of England are alien lizards in disguise."

Karen straightened and turned to Jack. Their gazes met. From the look in his eyes, he was thinking the same thing as her.

"Nancy," she looked back at the woman. "The guy on the radio. Do you remember his name?"

Lines etched in Nancy's fleshy face as she concentrated. "Um . . . yeah. Yeah, I do. Darren Staub."

THIRTY-FOUR

"How about reptoids?" Ehrenberg turned to Geek as they tramped through the forest with the rest of the team.

The ex-Ranger bobbed his head from side-to-side. "Eeeeh . . . I don't know. Sounds kinda ordinary."

"Petal?" He looked over his shoulder at her. "How about you?"

"Keep trying, Randy."

"Dan?"

The young investigator-in-training tensed. "Um . . . it sounds okay to me." Hesitation laced his voice. Ehrenberg figured he gave his approval for fear of pissing off his boss.

His leg brushed some tall grass, which crackled. He grimaced. The whole forest was dry. One little spark and Lee County could turn into an inferno.

He checked to the front of the group. Herrera scouted ten yards ahead of them, while the other field security specialist, Norgay, brought up the rear. Alana and McClure stayed behind at the command post, recharging the Flapjack. He hoped it was almost ready to fly. It would be nice to have some advanced warning if any lizard men were in the area, especially after last night.

The memory of the attack sent a chill through him.

"What about caimanoids?"

Geek scrunched his face, perplexed. "Where the heck did you get that one from?"

"Caimans are part of the Alligatoridae family, and there are a few similarities between alligators and lizard men."

Geek shrugged. "It's better than reptoids."

"Keep trying, Randy." Petal grinned.

He let out a faux sigh. Naming a newly found species could be so hard. That name would be with it forever, so it had to be good. Look at platypus. Whoever came up with that one was more lazy than creative.

The mental exercise also helped keep his mind off last night's attack on the community center, and all the people who died.

And last year's sea raptor attack on *Epic Venture*, and watching Lauren get devoured.

Ehrenberg slowed his pace, staring at his boots. He never imagined searching for cryptids could be so dangerous, that it would result in so many nightmares. In the weeks following the sea raptor hunt, he had seriously considered quitting the FUBI. But he wavered. He finally had his dream job, searching for cryptids full time. But did he want to risk another deadly encounter like he had with the sea raptor? Did he want to see more friends and colleagues killed like Lauren and the crew of the *Epic Venture?*

He had gone to see a therapist a few times. That helped. The main thing he took away from her was he had to learn to deal with his trauma, otherwise it would consume him.

Ehrenberg felt he had done that. Also, the lure of discovering new creatures, of showing all those "respected" scientists who dismissed cryptozoology how wrong they were, was too great to just walk away from.

"What about lizaroids?"

"Um, I think it's good," Plank said, again in a hesitant tone.

"Ugh." Petal scrunched her nose. "Terrible."

"I gotta agree with the other doc, Doc," said Geek. "Lizaroids rhymes with hemorrhoids, and both of them are unpleasant."

Ehrenberg lifted his hands in defeat. "I guess it's back to the mental drawing board."

Herrera halted and snapped up his fist. Everyone stopped.

"What is it, Herrera?" Geek whispered in his radio.

"I thought I heard branches snap. Someone, or something, is out there. I'm gonna check it out."

"Copy. I'll cover you."

Pistol out, Geek headed over to Herrera.

Ehrenberg's heart sped up. He took deep breaths, trying to calm himself. Herrera could have heard a deer, or a wild pig.

Or a lizard man.

Herrera moved past some bushes and up to a tree. Ehrenberg looked around. The vegetation was too thick to see through.

Herrera moved away from the tree.

A gunshot shattered the forest air. Ehrenberg jumped. Herrera fell on his back.

"Everyone down!" Geek shouted, charging ahead.

Ehrenberg, Petal, and Plank dropped to their stomachs. Norgay vanished in the brush. Geek knelt next to Herrera.

Chest tightened from worry, Ehrenberg stared with unblinking eyes at the fallen ex-soldier. How bad was he hurt? Fear threatened to root him to the spot, but he was expedition leader. That made Herrera his responsibility.

Sucking down a deep breath, he crawled toward the man.

"Drop your guns!" he heard Norgay holler. "Drop your guns or you die!"

Geek sprang to his feet, pistol up. "Drop those damn guns now."

Ehrenberg made it to Herrera. The ex-soldier bared his teeth, blood covering his left shoulder.

"I got him, Geek." Ehrenberg reached into his back for the first aid kit.

The big man nodded and hurried deeper into the forest, probably after whoever shot Herrera. Who in the hell would do that? Could it be that Alex Cassian wacko?

Ehrenberg took out a wad of gauze and pressed it against Herrera's shoulder. He noticed the man's right hand clenched his rifle.

"Alfonso, let go of your gun."

"No way. Some asshole fucking shot me. I'm not letting go of my weapon till I know Geek and Norgay got 'em."

With a frustrated sigh, Ehrenberg kept pressure on the wound. All the while he heard Geek and Norgay yelling. No more gunshots came. He took that as a good sign.

Petal joined him, taping the gauze to Herrera's shoulder. He clenched his teeth and groaned, but didn't cry out. Nor did he let go of his rifle. Ehrenberg couldn't help but be amazed. Then again, being around men like Jack and Geek for over a year, he knew Army Rangers had a high threshold for pain.

Dry grass crackled under heavy footsteps. Ehrenberg looked up to see Geek return.

"How is he?" The big man nodded to Herrera.

"Shoulder wound. He was lucky. A few inches to the right and he would have been hit dead in the chest."

"Did you find who shot him?" asked Petal. "Why did they do it?"

"Three hunters. They were after that fucking five thousand dollar reward that jackass Sawyer put out on the lizard men." Geek's face grew redder with each word. "One of those dumbasses thought Herrera was a monster and shot him."

"How the hell did they do that?" Herrera spoke through clenched teeth. "I'm way better looking than some fucking swamp monster."

Ehrenberg grinned, but only for a moment. He looked at Herrera's wound, thinking about his earlier words. Another few inches to the right and the bullet would have gone through his chest. He'd have another dead friend and colleague to mourn. Not because of a monster, but because of human stupidity.

He had Plank call 911, though this far into the woods they'd have to carry Herrera to meet the paramedics.

After making sure his wound was securely bandaged, Geek helped Herrera to his feet.

"What about the hunters?" asked Petal.

"Me and Norgay Duct taped their wrists and feet. They can stay here until someone from the Sheriff's Office finds them." He glowered at the vegetation, probably in the hunters' direction. "Or they can just stay out here till they decompose. I don't give a shit."

Ehrenberg followed Geek's angry gaze, his own fury mixing with his concern for Herrera. He pulled out his satellite phone and dialed the number for the county administration building.

"This is Doctor Randy Ehrenberg of the Foundation for Undocumented Biological Investigation. Please put me through to the Councilman Sawyer."

Less than a minute later, Sawyer's secretary picked up.

"I'm sorry, sir, Councilman Sawyer is out at the moment. Can I leave a message for him?"

"Yes. Can you tell him to meet us at the hospital?"

"The hospital?" The secretary sounded confused. "May I ask why?"

"I thought he'd like to apologize to one of our field security specialists."

The secretary paused. "I don't understand, sir. What does Councilman Sawyer need to apologize for?"

"Because thanks to that bounty he put out on the lizard men, one of my people just got shot."

THIRTY-FIVE

"Change of plans," Rastun said as he and Karen exited the Molinaros' house. "We're going back to Bishopville to talk with Darren Staub."

"You think he might actually know Cassian?"

"Maybe. That TruthCon of his is in Charlotte. It's not that far a drive from here. At the very least, maybe we can learn more about this Reptilian conspiracy of his. See what makes Cassian's mind tick. I know when Staub was doing his spiel last night, Cassian looked to be hanging on his every word." He took out his phone as he opened the door to his SUV. "I'll give Sherlock a call. Maybe he can track him down."

"Or there might be another way." Karen slid into the vehicle, then held up her phone. "A guy like Staub is probably all over social media."

She played with her phone for a minute, then said, "Jackpot. Found him on Instagram. He's set up outside the Lee County Library interviewing people about last night's attack. Looks like he'll be there for another hour."

"Great. To the library, then." Rastun got in and started the engine. "I think we make pretty good amateur sleuths."

"I think you're right." Karen smiled and pocketed her phone. "Now all we need is a groovy green van and a talking dog."

"And maybe you can top it off by dyeing your hair red." He winked at her before pulling out of the driveway.

"If I have to dye my hair red, you have to wear an orange ascot."

"Like hell. Ascots aren't manly."

"Oh come on. Fred was manly."

"Bullcrap," said Rastun. "All Fred ever did was tell people where to go and what to do. Let's be honest. Velma did all the grunt work. Without her, the Scooby Doo gang wouldn't be able to solve a crossword puzzle."

"So maybe I should dress in a frumpy sweater and wear Coke bottle glasses instead," said Karen.

"You'd still look hot." Rastun waggled his eyebrows at her.

When they returned to Bishopville, they found Staub's vehicle parked on Main Street, a block from the old red brick building that housed the county library. The show host stood at the corner with a thin bearded man holding a video camera. Rastun and Karen exited their SUV, trading the cool interior for the hot, muggy air.

"Jack Rastun and Karen Thatcher." Staub extended his arms to the side, greeting them with a huge smile as they approached. "So you did decide on an interview? Great. This is my producer and videographer Elliott." He pointed to the younger man. "If we can have you stand --"

"Actually, Mister Staub," Rastun cut him off, "We'll be the ones asking questions."

Staub's face scrunched. "Okay. About what?"

"Alex Cassian."

"The guy who shot that reporter at the town hall? What does he have to do with me?"

"He was a fan of your show," said Karen.

"I have millions of fans all over the country. Obviously I don't know them all, and I certainly can't be held responsible for what they do."

"Are you sure you don't know Cassian?" asked Rastun.

Staub let out an incredulous snort. "How the hell would I know him?"

"Because Charlotte is, what, a two-hour drive from here? That's where you have your TruthCon thing. As big a fan as Alex Cassian is of yours, I wouldn't be surprised if he's gone there. Maybe you've run into him there, talked to him."

"I meet and talk to a lot of people at TruthCon."

Rastun took out his phone and showed Staub two pictures of Cassian, the unkempt version from the town hall and the clean cut version in his Marine dress blues. "He look familiar to you?"

"No." Annoyance crept into Staub's tone. "Again, I meet a lot of people at TruthCon. I don't remember them all."

Eyebrows bunched together, Staub took a step back. "Are you trying to shut me down?"

"What?" Rastun drew his head back.

"The world is this close to learning the truth about those lizard men and the Reptilians are one and the same. Are you really serving them?   You   and   the   whole   FUBI?"
Rastun blinked slowly, barely able to believe someone could say something that insane. "Yeah, I'm working for the Reptilians. That's why I shot a bunch of them last night."

"Maybe you're not directly involved with them. You and the FUBI could be influenced by some politician or corporate entity tied to them. Maybe they want you to try and link me to Cassian murdering the reporter. Try to ruin my reputation. It's not going to work." Staub wagged a finger. "You can't stop me from spreading the truth."

Rastun turned to Karen, who rolled her eyes. He decided they hit a dead end with Staub, the craziest dead end ever.

"Thanks for your time. I'm sure there are a few psychologists in this town. Maybe you should make an appointment with one."

He started back to the SUV with Karen.

"People like you," Staub called to him. "You think you know how the world works. You can't see you're being manipulated by powerful forces. Forces not even of this world. They're the ones who sent you to the Middle East, told you to kill people for their oil and to eradicate their religion. You're not free, Jack. Neither are you, Karen. You're both tools. We're all tools. But I had the courage to break away. You don't."

"Oh my God." Karen shook her head. "Does Cassian actually believe all that crap?"

"If he does, that makes him a highly trained combat veteran and a nutcase. Not a good combination."

Rastun just started the engine when his cell rang.

"Jack, where are you?" asked Ehrenberg.

"Main Street near the library. We just got done talking to Staub. The guy's an entire bag of fries short of a Happy Meal."

"Uh-huh." Ehrenberg's voice sounded flat.

"Something wrong, Doc?"

"Yeah. We came across some hunters who took up Sawyer on his five thousand dollar reward. Herrera got shot. We're on the way to the hospital now."

***

Rastun and Karen beat the others to the hospital by ten minutes. The paramedics wheeled in Herrera on a gurney, his shoulder heavily bandaged.

"How are you?"

"I'll live, sir," Herrera said through clenched teeth.

"The round hit him just above the armpit," one of the paramedics told Rastun. "He's lost quite a bit of blood, but the wound isn't life threatening."

All his muscles loosened in relief. He'd lost enough men during his time in the Army. Thank God he wouldn't lose one on this mission.

"Hang in there, Herrera."

He gave Rastun a thumbs up. "Just need some stitches and I'll be back in the field with you guys."

Rastun knew that wouldn't be the case. Herrera was done for this mission.

And now I'm down a security specialist because of that dumbfuck Sawyer.

The paramedics wheeled Herrera through the swinging double doors, probably to one of the surgical rooms.

Rastun looked over his shoulder. Ehrenberg and the others entered the emergency room lobby. He spun around and strode toward them.

"How did it happen?"

Ehrenberg ran down the incident. Every sentence stoked Rastun's anger at the hunters. It sounded like they hadn't even confirmed their target before shooting, something he feared would happen when Sawyer announced his stupid bounty.

And it happened to one of his men!

The lobby doors slid open. Commander Umbarger entered, followed by Detective Blefary.

"We heard about your man," said Umbarger. "Is he going to be okay?"

"Yeah," Rastun answered. "He got hit in the shoulder. Non-life threatening."

"Good." Umbarger shook his head. "I had a bad feeling something like this would happen. And there are probably more hunters out there hoping to get that five thousand dollars. We need to stop this before they shoot more people, maybe fatally."

Blefary took statements from Ehrenberg and the others. He actually sounded somewhat civil with his questioning, until Geek told him how they left the hunters in the woods, tied up with Duct tape.

"You couldn't bring them with you?" the detective snapped.

"We could have. I just didn't feel like it."

Blefary clenched his notebook. "It's ninety-five degrees out, you tied them up, and there are monsters running around the woods. What if they dehydrate? What if a lizard man finds them? Their families could sue you, sue the county."

"Those assholes shot one of my men," Geek replied sharply. "Be lucky I didn't work 'em over."

"You better believe you're lucky, because if you did, I would lock your ass up."

"I doubt it. Because I would have said they all tripped and fell, and everyone on my team would back me up."

Blefary glared at Geek, a hard stare that probably would have withered your average street punk. Geek, however, didn't flinch.

"Let's dial it back a notch or two, Sergeant." Rastun tried to defuse the situation.

"Yes, sir."

Both men settled down, and Blefary resumed his questioning.

Rastun's phone rang. Sherlock was on the other end.

"I thought I'd let you know I talked to some of the men in Alex Cassian's old Force Recon platoon."

"What did you find out?"

"His former CO called him a pretty competent Marine, and did a good job during his tour in Afghanistan."

Rastun nodded. Not a bad evaluation, but not exactly glowing. "I sense a 'but' coming."

"You sense correctly," replied Sherlock. "From what Cassian's CO and platoon sergeant said, he was one of those men who thrived in a combat environment. When he was stateside, however . . ."

"That's where you get the drunk and disorderlies and DUIs."

"Correct. Some of the more interesting information on Cassian came from his former squadmates."

That didn't surprise Rastun. As a former platoon leader himself, he knew it wasn't the commanding officers that knew their grunts best, but the privates and corporals they were around nearly every waking moment. "What did they have to say?"

"Most got along with him well enough, but when they started talking about Cassian's hobbies and interests, that really caught my attention."

"Let me guess. He talked a lot about cryptozoology and crazy-ass conspiracy theories?"

"Yeah. I take it you learned that talking to his former foster parents?"

"I did, and guess who one of his favorite conspiracy theory whackos is? Darren Staub."

"A couple of Cassian's squadmates mentioned his name, too," said Sherlock. "One told me of an incident at Camp Lejeune where he saw Cassian on Staub's website and asked what it was. Cassian went on about Reptilians, other dimensions, aliens and Nazis working together. The other Marine made fun of him. Cassian got incensed and punched him. He spent thirty days in the brig and was demoted."

Rastun gave a short huff of disbelief. "What a dumb shit."

"Actually, it gives us some insight into his mind. Cassian believes all these conspiracies are real, and he has little to no tolerance for people who think otherwise. He's also willing to resort to violence to make his point."

"I think he's also obsessed with Staub. That's the feeling I got from one of his foster parents, Nancy Molinaro. I know when Staub went on his rant at the town hall, it was like Cassian was hanging on his every word."

"He came to the meeting armed, shot a lizard man and that reporter. Maybe he's not just listening to Staub. Maybe he believes he's being given instructions by him to protect the world from Reptilians."

"Then why shoot Chang?"

"There's a lot of distrust of the media these days. A lot of people think they're working with powerful politicians or corporations. What if he thinks they're colluding with the Reptilians?"

"I only got a taste of Staub's delusions," said Rastun. "If Cassian's been listening to his crap for years, who knows what that lunatic believes."

Sherlock paused. "I wonder if they've crossed paths before last night. Maybe at that TruthCon Staub puts on."

"Karen and I talked to him about an hour ago. He said he didn't know Cassian."

"Do you believe him?"

Rastun let out a long breath, staring at his shoes. "I don't know. The guy said he meets a lot of fans at TruthCon, said he can't remember all of them. Hell, if you asked me to remember everyone I ever met at my book signings, I sure as hell couldn't do it."

"That sounds reasonable. Still, it might be worth doing some more digging into Staub."

Rastun told Sherlock the other information he learned from Cassian's foster parents, explaining how he and Karen had a few more to question.

That's when Sawyer entered the hospital lobby.

"Sherlock." Rastun's eyes narrowed at the county councilman. "I'll call you back."

He put away his phone. Everyone in the room turned to Sawyer, the anger in their faces evident. Ehrenberg took a deep inhale, his lips tight, like he was holding back an explosion. Rastun couldn't remember ever seeing the good-natured scientist so angry.

Having one of your men almost killed because of someone else's stupidity would do that.

Rastun sidled over to Geek. "Do me a favor. Hold me back so I don't beat the shit out of this guy."

"Okay, Cap'n, but who's gonna hold me back?"

"How's your man?" asked Sawyer.

"He'll live," Ehrenberg spoke in a deliberate tone.

Sawyer exhaled loudly and sagged to the left. "Thank God for that."

"I'm sure you're relieved." Anger bubbled under the surface of Ehrenberg's words. "Considering you were responsible for this."

Sawyer gaped, blinking repeatedly. "Wh-What? How the hell is this my fault? I didn't shoot your man."

"No, but you encouraged who knows how many people to go out in the woods, ready to shoot anything that even remotely resembles a lizard man."

"That's ridiculous."

"No it isn't." Umbarger walked in front of Sawyer. "The people in the woods hoping to get rich quick by shooting a lizard man are putting the public in danger, and possibly interfering with a law enforcement investigation. I'm going to instruct my deputies that if they come across anyone looking for that five thousand dollar lizard man bounty, they will be ordered to leave the woods immediately. If they do not comply, or if they return, they'll be arrested for endangerment and obstruction of justice."

"You can't do that." Sawyer threw out his arms. "You're not the sheriff."

"I'll bet anything Sheriff Haddix will back me up."

Sawyer gaped. His gaze swept over the entire FUBI contingent. "I thought you'd appreciate the extra help. I told you you needed more people to hunt down these monsters, but you just brushed me off. And look at what's happened. Eight people dead and dozens more injured at the town hall. You think I'm responsible for your man getting shot? If you would have listened to me from the beginning, last night's attack never would have happened."

"You really believe that?" asked Ruud.

Sawyer's nostrils flared. "That's what I'm going to tell the press."

THIRTY-SIX

Rastun stayed at the hospital until the doctors finished operating on Herrera. He'd need some rehab on his left arm, but the doctors expected him to make a full recovery.

With the rest of the team heading back into the field, Rastun suggested they finish interviewing Cassian's other foster parents.

"Can we get something to eat first?" said Karen. "I'm starving."

He found it hard to argue. With the exception of some granola bars from a hospital vending machine, neither had eaten anything since breakfast. His stomach had become an empty hole.

They drove to The Good Ol' Café two blocks from their hotel. His eyes swept over the roofs of the nearby buildings, searching for silhouettes poking out from behind ramparts. He saw none. The parking lot and the nearby sidewalks were also devoid of anyone suspicious. Rastun pressed a hand against the inside-the-pants holster containing his Glock for reassurance. He was probably being paranoid, but with a cold-blooded killer who believed intelligent lizards ruled the Earth, and who really wanted to talk to him, no way would he let his guard down.

The hostess greeted them and led them to a table in the middle of the dining area. Good. He did not want to sit by a window, where they'd be easy targets for a sniper.

Rastun scanned the restaurant again. It was a quarter full. A few people stared at him, but none looked suspicious. Just surprised to have – in their minds – a celebrity in their midst.

Price of fame. He opened the menu, hoping the police arrested Cassian soon. Trying to find the lizard men was hard enough without having to worry about a lunatic blowing his head off.

***

It's them. Holy shit, it's them.

Sitting at the counter, Lansford took another glance over his shoulder. Both Jack Rastun and Karen Thatcher sat at a table in the middle of the dining area.

He turned back around, clutching his coffee mug, the black liquid inside now lukewarm. His heart pumped harder. He'd sat outside the hotel all day in this damn heat waiting for those two to return. Lansford continued to wait into the evening, but they never showed. After updating Cassian, the ex-Marine told him he'd have Proly or Smith relieve him. Cassian couldn't stakeout the hotel himself, not with his face all over the news.

Lansford clenched a fist. Infected or not, Cassian never should have shot that reporter. Now the cops were hell-bent on finding him, especially the ones who were secretly hybrids. Cassian couldn't go anywhere in public without the risk of someone identifying him. If he did get arrested, it would be only a matter of time before he gave up the rest of the group. Cassian had told him even the toughest men had their breaking point when being tortured, and the Reptilians probably had methods he couldn't imagine.

Their entire operation was at risk, right when the slimy monsters were making their biggest move ever. If he and the others got killed, what chance would the people of Bishopville, maybe even the world, have?

Lansford glanced at Rastun and Thatcher again. They could be their only chance of stopping the attack on this city, of revealing to the entire world the depth to which the Reptilians infiltrated human society.

His stomach clenched. Sweat ran from every pore in his body. Could he do this?

He's just a man. He's not indestructible.

He's done a hell of a lot more than you ever did in the Army.

So what? The fucking asshole instructors at Infantry School made a mistake cutting him. He was meant to be a warrior. He would have been if they'd given him half-a-chance.

Lansford pressed a fist against the counter. He breathed deep, summoning every ounce of courage and confidence he possessed. He could do this. For the sake of humanity, he *had* to do this.

He reached under his sweatshirt for the small Taurus .380 pistol tucked into his waistband, trying to get his breathing under control. Two men sat a few stools away from him at the counter. Four other couples sat at tables or booths. Could he pull out the pistol without attracting attention?

He decided not to chance it and headed for the restroom. He looked over at Rastun and Thatcher, who gave their orders to a waitress.

No one was in the restroom. Lansford stared at himself in the mirror. Sweat glistened on his brow. His breaths came rapidly. He thought of Rastun's medals, his battle on that FUBI ship with the sea raptor and those mercenaries. Did he, an ex-Army cook, really stand a chance against him?

You can do this. Cassian had given him a lot of combat training since they first met. He had the gun, he had the element of surprise.

He took out the little pistol and pulled his shirtsleeve over it. With one last deep breath, he exited the restroom.

Rastun and Thatcher chatted casually. Damn, but Karen Thatcher was hot. None of the women he'd ever been with could match her looks, not by a longshot.

Muscles tensed, Lansford strode across the dining area. Thatcher glanced up at him as he neared. He grabbed a chair from an unoccupied table and plopped it down in front of their table. Both turned to him as he sat, wearing shocked expressions.

"Excuse me," said Thatcher.

"Something we can do for you?" Rastun sounded annoyed.

Lansford squared his shoulders. "Yeah. Don't do anything stupid or you're dead."

THIRTY-SEVEN

Rastun narrowed his eyes at the stocky man in hand-me-down clothes. "What the hell are you ta-?"

"I've got a gun pointed at your gut," the man cut him off. "Check for yourself if you don't believe me." He emphasized the point by nodding toward his lap.

Rastun leaned back in his chair and glanced down. The man's right hand rested on his leg. He drew back the sleeve, revealing a small, compact pistol.

Shit! He thought he'd been so careful, so alert, and yet this shitkicker got the drop on him.

The man pushed his sleeve back over the gun. "Ditch your gun and phone. Don't try anything funny or I'll shoot you, then her," he jerked his head toward Karen, "then I'll shoot some other customers for the hell of it."

Anger boiled within Rastun. He pushed it aside. If he and Karen were going to get out of this alive, he needed to keep a clear head.

He removed his Glock, then his phone. "Where do you want me to put them?"

The man's wide eyes locked on Rastun, showing indecision.

This guy isn't a pro. But he still had the gun, and from this distance, even a total schmuck couldn't miss.

"Um, just put 'em on the floor. Cover 'em with a napkin or something."

Rastun unfolded a napkin, wrapped the Glock and phone with it, and laid them under the table. The man had Karen do the same with her phone and pepper spray.

"Now get up and keep your hands where I can see them."

"Where are we going?" asked Karen.

"You'll see." The man stood and backed away, his covered gunhand at his side. "Now let's go."

Rastun looked over at Karen, her face stiffened in a mask of determination. He gave her a slight nod. *We're gonna get through this.*

They rose, hands at their sides. The man walked behind them as they made for the door.

"Leaving so soon?" asked the hostess at the front desk.

"Yeah. Something came up." Rastun didn't look at her, just kept walking. He wanted to get out of the restaurant and away from so many civilians before making any kind of move.

"Where to now?" Karen asked when they were outside.

"Go left."

They obeyed, with Rastun walking between Karen and their kidnapper. He glanced at the large windows of the restaurant, checking their distorted reflections. The man was roughly seven or eight feet behind him. He had a bit of a cushion to get a shot off before Rastun could lay a hand on him.

"So did Cassian send you?" he asked.

"W-What?"

That one word gave Rastun encouragement. If he kept talking, he could get this fuckwit off his game. "I know he wanted to talk to me at the town hall, but we got interrupted by those lizard men. I guess with the cops looking for him, he had to send a flunky to get me."

"Shut up," the man snapped.

"I didn't even know Cassian had flunkies. How many of you are there?"

"Just keep walking, okay?" Agitation filled the man's voice.

Rastun was thinking of what to say next when he heard laughter up ahead. Two women in their mid-twenties stumbled out of a bar. They leaned against the wall, cackling louder.

He had an idea, but could he really risk the lives of two innocents?

The women were just ten feet away. He had to decide now.

Karen passed the two, who continued laughing. As Rastun neared them, his focus was on the closest one, who had short black hair, jeans shorts, and a pair of shapely legs. He shifted his direction slightly.

I'm so sorry about this. He was about to brush past the woman when he grabbed her ass. She gasped and spun around, mouth agape.

"What the fuck, asshole!" The woman slapped his chest.

"I'm sorry, ma'am." Rastun glanced at the kidnapper. He'd frozen in his tracks, gaze shifting between him and the enraged woman, unsure what to do.

"I apologize for -" Rastun slid to the left and brought up his elbow. The point cracked against the kidnapper's mouth.

He sent a sidekick into the man's gut. Rastun barely heard the women from the bar scream as he grabbed the kidnapper's wrist. He drove his knee up and into the man's forearm. A sickening *crack* followed. The man wailed. His gun clattered on the sidewalk.

Rastun chopped the kidnapper in the throat. He let out a wheezing gasp, his good hand clasped around his neck. Rastun kneed him in the gut again. The man doubled over, mouth open wide. He emitted a clicking, grating noise as he tried to suck in oxygen. Blood dripped from his busted lips.

Rastun swept the man's legs out from under him. He crashed to the sidewalk. Rastun stomped on his stomach twice, then picked up the little pistol.

"Don't move!"

The man responded with weak groans.

"Karen, you okay?" Rastun shouted over his shoulder.

"I'm good."

He nodded as the kidnapper started to regain his breath.

"Ma'am," Rastun called out. "I'm sorry about what I did. I had to distract this guy, and that was the only thing I could think of."

"Uh . . . Uh-huh." The woman sounded in a daze.

"Call the police."

"Um, okay."

Rastun took a couple of steps back, still covering the kidnapper. "On your feet. You do anything I don't like and you're dead."

The man slowly rose, wheezing and grimacing. Rastun marched him past the two women. Both looked on in shock, while the brunette in the jeans shorts had a phone to her ear.

Two buildings past the bar was an alley. It stank of mold, piss, and vomit. Rastun saw a puddle of fresh puke by the wall. Probably someone from the bar who couldn't hold their beer.

"Have a seat." He nodded to the nasty-looking beige puddle. The kidnapper looked at him in disbelief, teeth bared in obvious pain.

"What are you waiting for?" He aimed the pistol at the man's heart.

Wincing, the kidnapper lowered himself into the vomit.

"Gross," muttered Karen, who stood next to Rastun. He would admit, it was gross. But one of the rules to interrogation was to make the prisoner as uncomfortable as possible.

"Okay, let's start off with something simple," he said. "Name?"
The man's face contorted, attempting defiance while fighting off pain, and probably fear.

"Name!"

"T-Todd. Todd Lansford. Aaah, my arm." He grabbed his injured forearm, gritting his teeth.

"Fuck your arm. Just be glad you're still breathing, though that might change if you don't answer my questions."

Lansford shivered.

"Did Alex Cassian send you?"

Lansford took a couple of deep breaths. He closed his eyes and looked away.

Rastun drove his heel into Lansford's forearm. He let out a piercing cry.

"Did Alex Cassian send you?"

"Yes!"

"Why does he want to kill me?"

"He doesn't."

Rastun advanced on him.

"It's the truth, I swear it!" Lansford yelled. "He wants you on our side."

"What the hell is that supposed to mean?" asked Karen.

Lansford's gaze switched from Rastun to Karen, then back to Rastun. "You were both attacked by Reptilians. Their DNA is in you. You're turning into hybrids. Cassian wanted to recruit you," he nodded at Rastun, "as a double-agent."

Rastun's brow crinkled. "Double-agent? What the hell are you talking about?"

"Like you don't know. I was watching your hotel all day. Where did you go? To meet with some Reptilians? Did they already indoctrinate you? Are you gonna feed 'em info about the FUBI?"

"Are you serious?" Karen drew her head back in disbelief.

"Don't play stupid with me." Lansford sat up straighter, looking bolder. "You're the ones who are trying to convince everyone the Reptilians around here are just some new kind of animal. Well you're not fooling me. I know what you really are, what you're really planning. There are more people like me and Alex out there, a lot more. We'll stop you. You won't win. You hear me? You won't win!"

"What a nutcase," Karen muttered.

The wail of sirens carried across the night. The police were close by.

Looks like this interrogation's over. At least he learned that Cassian wasn't working alone. Maybe he didn't have an army of followers like Lansford claimed, but he figured he had a handful.

And if they were anything like Lansford, they were all delusional, and dangerous.

THIRTY-EIGHT

"Lucky me," Rastun muttered as a deputy led him and Karen to Lieutenant Blefary's desk. The detective's scowl deepened as they approached.

"Killing monsters isn't enough for you?" grumbled Blefary. "Now you're putting people in the hospital?"

"The asshole was holding us at gunpoint. I didn't think asking nicely to let us go would work."

Blefary glared at him, then jabbed his hand at a pair of chairs. "Sit." He jerked his head to the deputy who'd driven Rastun and Karen to the Sheriff's Office headquarters. He left without a word.

The detective pulled out a notebook and recorder from a desk drawer and took their statements about their brief kidnapping. When Rastun explained how he'd distracted Lansford, shock blazed in Blefary's eyes.

"You actually grabbed that woman's ass?"

"Yes." Rastun nodded.

"Terrific." Blefary slapped a hand on his desk. "She'll probably file a sex assault charge against you."

"I needed a way to distract Lansford, give me an opening to take him down."

"Take him down? You put him in the hospital."

Rastun shrugged. "Hopefully that'll teach him not to pull guns on people."

Blefary leaned forward, eyes narrowed. "You think this is a joke? Do you have any idea how this could reflect on our department?"

"I don't work for you."

"But you're assisting us, and now you just admitted you groped a woman and broke a suspect's arm. The damn press loves any kind of story with a hint of inappropriate behavior by the police, or anyone associated with us."

Rastun leaned back in his chair, fighting to keep any trace of annoyance off his face. "Maybe we should stop worrying what other people think and concentrate on what's important, that we have a friend of Alex Cassian's in custody."

Fleshy creases spread across Blefary's face, deepening the angrier he got. He snorted and straightened in his seat, continuing the interview.

When Rastun ran down his interrogation of Lansford, Blefary bounced his pen off the desk. "Are you fucking kidding me? You questioned him at gunpoint?"

"I wanted to make sure he didn't bolt," said Rastun, "or attack us."

"Any half-assed lawyer can argue you got the information out of him through coercion and get it thrown out of court."

"Well, I'm not a cop."

"It doesn't matter! You held a gun on someone while you were questioning him. If this fucks up our investigation, I'm gonna nail your ass to the wall."

"I guess you'd be happier if we let that asshole take us to Cassian?" said Karen. "He might have shot us both, but at least it wouldn't screw up your investigation."

Blefary's gaze shifted to her. "You are really trying my patience."

"Uh-huh." Karen folded her arms and stared back at him, not the slightest bit intimidated.

Rastun couldn't keep the smile off his face. *Damn, I love her.*

Blefary started to open his mouth when another, deeper voice carried through the office. "I thought I'd find you up here."

Sherlock rounded one of the dividers and strode over to them, a folder under his arm.

"I'm in the middle of an interview, Marshal," said Blefary.

"About Todd Lansford? If so, I can help you." Sherlock placed the folder on Blefary's desk.

"What's this?" The detective nodded at it.

"DoD emailed me copies of Lansford's records. He served four years in the Army, MOS Ninety-Two Golf."

"What?" Karen's face scrunched in confusion.

"Military Occupation Specialty Ninety-Two-G," answered Rastun. "Food service specialist. The guy was a cook." He shook his head. "I knew that jackass wasn't a pro."

"What the hell's an Army cook doing running around pretending he's Rambo?" Blefary wondered aloud. "And how the hell would he know Cassian if they were in different branches?"

"They probably met after they were both out of the service," said Sherlock. "We'll have to do some digging on that."

"I'd start with Staub's TruthCon," Rastun suggested. "Seems like a great place for Cassian, Lansford, and who knows how many other nutbars to hook up."

"Good point." Sherlock nodded.

Blefary scanned through the folder. "Looks like Lansford failed infantry school. Evaluations range from average to below average. I think this dumbass is out of his league as a lizard man hunter, at least I guess that's how he thinks of himself." He looked back up at Rastun. "Anything else about Lansford that sticks out to you?"

"It seemed like he had a plan for getting us out of the restaurant. I wouldn't be surprised if he got some tips, maybe even a little training, from Cassian. But whenever something unexpected came up, like when I grabbed that girl's ass or when I asked him where to drop my gun, he froze up, couldn't make snap decisions under pressure. Like I said, the guy wasn't a pro."

Blefary asked a few more questions before wrapping up the interview.

"If that's all, we'll be taking off." Rastun started to get up, Karen following suit.

"Wait." Blefary held up a hand.

"Wait what?" Karen's face scrunched in puzzlement. "I thought we were done?"

"You are, but Commander Umbarger wants you two to stay here until further notice."

"What?" Rastun blurted. "When did he decide this?"

"He called before you got here. One of Alex Cassian's friends tried to kidnap you two. Who knows if he has other dipshits out there looking for you. Next time you may not have some girl's ass to squeeze to save you."

Rastun's mouth pressed into a thin line. "Sherlock . . ."

"Sorry, Captain. I have to agree with Lieutenant Blefary on this one."

The skin between Rastun's eyebrows wrinkled. "I can take care of myself."

"Commander's orders," Blefary said in a gruff tone. "You and Miss Thatcher stay here until further notice, and if that means putting you in a holding cell, then so be it."

For the first time Rastun could remember, he saw Blefary smile. Just a hint of one, but a smile nonetheless. He sucked down a deep breath, trying to hold back his rising anger. "Then how about this?" He planted his palms on the desk and leaned forward. The detective stared back at him, eyes simmering.

It didn't intimidate Rastun. "Cassian's out there looking for me, fine. Use me as bait and let's draw the bastard out."

"I don't care if the press does think you're a hero after what happened at the town hall. You're still a civilian."

"A civilian who knows what to do when shit goes down."

Blefary bared his teeth. He appeared seconds from another meltdown.

Rastun didn't budge an inch.

Sherlock laid a hand on his shoulder. "How about I pass your idea along to Commander Umbarger?"

He wanted to say, "How about I tell Umbarger myself," but dismissed that idea. Sherlock could approach this from a more levelheaded standpoint than he could. When something threatened Rastun and people he cared about, his response was direct action, not hiding behind four walls. He'd probably go into any meeting with Umbarger pissed off. Sherlock wouldn't.

"Thanks, buddy." He slapped Sherlock on the arm, then looked back at Blefary. "So, since we're your less-than-willing guests, what do you want us to do?"

"Do whatever you want, just do it somewhere else. I have work to do."

"And suddenly I feel unwanted." A sarcastic half-smile formed on Karen's lips.

Blefary glared at her, then shifted his gaze back to the computer.

Arms folded, Rastun wondered how to kill time here, instead of doing something useful, like finding Cassian, or tracking down that pack of killer lizard men.

An emptiness grew in his stomach. His dinner had gotten interrupted by that kidnapping. "You have a cafeteria here?"

"There's a vending machine in the lobby," Blefary replied without looking up.

That didn't sound appealing. Rastun needed more than potato chips and a Snickers bar.

I could always order a pizza. Rastun reached for his phone, then realized it, and his Glock, were still being held by the police as evidence.

Sherlock offered him his phone. Rastun found the number for a nearby pizza place and called in his order.

"I'll take a large cheese pizza and -"

"Actually," Karen jumped in, "make it half-cheese and half-black olives and peppers."

Rastun stared at her, grimacing. "On second thought, make that a large half-cheese, half-black olives and peppers, and a liter of Sprite."

He handed the phone back to Sherlock and headed for the lobby to wait for the delivery guy.

"Don't leave the building," Blefary called out.

"Yes, Dad." Even though Rastun had his back to him, he sensed the detective shooting him a nasty look.

As he and Karen entered the stairwell, he turned to her, face scrunched in disgust.

"What?" she asked.

"I can't believe you'd deface a perfectly good pizza with olives and peppers."

"I can't believe you're fine with plain old cheese pizza. Booorring."

When they reached the lobby, they plopped down on a bland, beige sofa that had seen better days. Rastun put an arm around Karen's shoulder. She leaned into him.

"You okay?" he asked.

"I'm fine." She took a slow breath. "What does it say when I'm starting to get used to having guns pointed at me?"

"That you lead a hell of an interesting life."

Karen chuckled. "I feel so blessed."

Rastun ran his hand up and down her arm. "Well, we could always quit, live off the royalties from our book sales and treat every day like a vacation."

"Mm, that would be nice . . . for about a week. Then we'd be bored out of our minds."

Rastun smiled and kissed the top of Karen's head. He truly had found a woman after his own heart. Lounging around day after day did not suit him. He liked being active. He *needed* to be active. Karen was the same way. Dangerous though their jobs may be, what they did was satisfying, important. They helped discover new animals, and protected them. Unless they proved violent, then they protected people from them.

He closed his eyes, relishing the softness of Karen's hair against his cheek. Thoughts of lizard men, Alex Cassian, and their kidnapping faded from his mind. The only thing in his world was Karen, the feel of her body against his.

The long day and lack of food finally caught up to him. Rastun fell asleep.

***

"Excuse me, Mister Rastun."

Rastun's eyes snapped open. All his muscles coiled, ready for action. A portly, mustached man stood over him. The desk sergeant.

"Sorry to wake you, sir. Your pizza's here."

Rubbing his hands over his face, Rastun turned to the front doors. A gangly, acne-riddled teen stood in the foyer, holding a pizza box and a plastic bag.

Rastun got to his feet. Karen pushed herself off the sofa moments later.

"Thanks," he paid the kid, adding a generous tip.

"You're welcome, sir." The kid handed him the pizza and soda. "Hey, are you really Jack Rastun and Karen Thatcher?"

"That's us." Karen grinned.

"Oh cool." The kid, Brandon according to his nametag, had all his attention on Karen. "Um, say, you don't mind if I get a picture with you, huh?"

Rastun stared at the pizza box, the tangy smell of cheese and tomato sauce filling his nostrils. To hell with a picture. He wanted to eat. But Brandon seemed like an okay kid, and he had called him sir.

"Sure. No problem."

Brandon stood between them while the desk sergeant snapped the picture. He thanked them and headed out.

Rastun's stomach grumbled as he opened the pizza box. He inhaled the scent again, smiling as he gazed at the melted cheese and bright red sauce on one side, then winced at the other half.

"Black olives and peppers." He shook his head.

"Oh, just enjoy your half while I enjoy mine." Karen tore out a slice and bit into it.

Rastun shook his head. *To each his own.* He reached for a slice of pizza.

"Captain."

He looked down the hallway and saw Sherlock approaching.

"We need you back upstairs," said the marshal.

"What is it?"

"It looks like we have a lead on Alex Cassian."

Box in one hand and slice in the other, Rastun followed Sherlock to the stairwell entrance. "Did you find out where he is? And I hope you don't mind if I eat while you talk. Actually, even if you do mind, I'm still gonna eat." He emphasized the point by taking a large bite of his pizza.

"Not a problem." Sherlock held the door open for them. "We went through Lansford's phone records. There was one number that came up quite a bit over the past week, including three calls today. It belongs to a Paul Green."

"Who's that?" Rastun asked after swallowing. He slowed his pace when the realization hit. "Lemme guess. An alias for Alex Cassian."

"That's what I figure, considering Green's address is a cemetery in Winston-Salem, North Carolina, and Paul Green is the name of a three-year-old boy buried there back in 1901."

Rastun took another bite of his pizza before they reached the Detective Bureau on the second floor. Blefary stood over another desk, where a thin woman with her dark hair in a ponytail sat. A laptop was set up in front of her.

"So what's the plan?" asked Rastun.

"We want you to call Cassian," said Sherlock.

"Me?"

"Lansford said Cassian wanted to talk to you. My hope is hearing from you will keep him on the line for a good amount of time."

Rastun's eyes shifted to the woman with the laptop. "And you're going to trace the call?"

The woman nodded.

"Miss Osborn is with the Sheriff's Office technical support unit," said Sherlock.

Rastun finished his slice, staring at Blefary. The skin along the right side of his nose wrinkled. He did not seem keen on this plan.

"All right." Rastun nodded. "Let's do this."

Blefary gave him the cell phone. Before Rastun hit the number, he turned to Sherlock. "Anything specific you want me to say to him?"

"Cassian called you Captain Rastun the first time he met you, right?"

"Yeah."

"Try talking to him like you're both still in the service. That should resonate with him."

"You got it." Rastun stared at the phone, then back at Sherlock. "Wish me luck."

He hit send. The person on the other end picked up after the second ring.

"About time, Todd. Where the hell are you?"

"PFC Cassian," Rastun spoke in his best commanding officer tone.

A pause. "Who's this?"

"This is Captain Jack Rastun. Your friend Specialist Lansford said you wanted to talk to me. So talk."

THIRTY-NINE

Rastun waited for a reply. There was nothing but silence on the other end. Would Cassian hang up? Would they miss the opportunity to catch him?

"Where's Lansford?" asked Cassian.

"He's fine. Well, he's breathing at any rate, which makes him damn lucky."

"What did you do to him?"

"Let me put it to you this way, it's never a good idea to send an ex-Army cook after an ex-Army Ranger."

Another long pause from Cassian. Again, Rastun feared he'd hang up.

"Your man's alive," he reassured Cassian.

"How do I know that's true?"

"Are you doubting my word, Private?"

"Um, uh, no, I'm not."

"'No I'm not' what?"

"Um, no I'm not, sir."

Rastun looked over at Sherlock, who listened to the conversation on a pair of headphones. The marshal nodded to him. Sherlock had been right. Cassian was receptive to being spoken to like he was still a grunt.

"Now," said Rastun. "What did you want to talk to me about?"

"Um . . . I saw on the news about you and Karen Thatcher. You were attacked by Reptilians."

"That's right."

Cassian paused. "You know what that means, sir?"

Rastun had an idea what Cassian meant and played along. "Yeah, I do."

"I'm sorry to tell you this, sir, but there's no way to reverse it. Once you're bitten or scratched, you're a hybrid forever."

"I see." *Jeez, he really believes this shit.* "So is that why you sent Lansford after me and Karen, to kill us?"

"No. No, no, no." The words came out rapidly. "No, sir. I don't want to kill you. I want to use you."

Rastun's forehead wrinkled. "Explain, Private."

"The Reptilians, they've infiltrated everywhere. I think it's time we infiltrate them."

"How so?" Rastun eyed the tech, Osborn, who remained focused on her screen. It appeared she was still working to trace the call.

"I want you to spy on the Reptilians."

Rastun stood still, thinking of a response. He never expected to hear something like that. Then again, how could he anticipate anything from a man who believed lizard men were trying to take over the world?

"Sir?" said Cassian.

"Yeah, I'm here. It's just a lot to digest."

"I know I'm asking a lot, but this could be our one chance to have someone on the inside. This could mean the difference between us winning or losing."

"Why me?" asked Rastun.

"You've just been converted. You haven't completely lost your humanity."

"The same was true of that reporter you shot. And what about Pam Mankowski and the deputy? You could have asked the same of them, instead of killing them."

Another pause by Cassian. "I didn't want to kill them, but the women were converted. I had to assume the same with the deputy."

Rastun's face twisted. Three people were dead because of this SOB's delusions. What he wouldn't give to gut Cassian and strangle him with his own intestines.

He looked over at Osborn and her computer. They had Cassian on tape admitting to murdering three people, including a cop. He was as good as convicted.

Unless the police don't take him alive. Rastun would not be upset if that happened.

"I didn't know their backgrounds," Cassian rambled. "I didn't know if they had what it took to infiltrate the Reptilians. You do. You're a war hero. You're an ex-Army Ranger. You can do this."

Out the corner of his eye, Rastun saw Sherlock wave to him. Osborn gave him a thumbs up and mouthed, "We got him."

Sherlock made circles with both hands. "Keep him talking," he mouthed.

Rastun nodded. "What about Karen? You know I'd never let anything happen to her."

He waited for an answer. Cassian stayed silent as Blefary strode past him, cell phone to his ear. Rastun figured he was calling in Cassian's location, maybe heading there himself.

"She can help, too," Cassian finally replied. "Two spies are better than one."

"Good thinking, Private."

"Thank you, sir." Cassian's voice shot up with enthusiasm.

"So what exactly do you want us to find out about the Reptilians?" asked Rastun.

"First, their plans for Bishopville. I think they intend to turn as much of the population as possible into hybrids. We need to find out how they'll go about it, then stop it."

"Got it. I figure they'll want me to give them information on what the FUBI is doing, given its interest in creatures like them. What about feeding them false information about our operations?"

"Yeah, yeah, that's a great idea." Cassian even offered him a few suggestions, like providing them with fake documents and phone recordings.

Keep talking, asshole. Rastun sensed Cassian felt at ease talking to him. His guard was down. He wouldn't know anything was up until the cops surrounded him.

"We need to set up a meet," said Cassian. "Make arrangements on how we can contact one another to -"

Rastun heard a distant voice over the phone. "Alex! The cops are coming!"

"What? How did they . . ." Cassian fell silent. Moments later, he exploded at Rastun. "You! You led them to us! You bastard! You fucking bastard! You sold us out! I'll kill you! I'll fucking kill you!"

The line went dead.

Rastun stared at the phone, a grin slowly forming. "We got your ass."

FORTY

"Mother fucker!" Cassian slammed his fist on the dashboard. "Mother fucker!"

"Stop yelling and get us the hell outta here," Smith shouted from the back.

Cassian glanced at his side mirror. Two cop cars sped through the parking lot of the suburban shopping center, lights flashing. He started the engine and stomped on the gas. Tires screeched as the RV shot forward, buildings and parked vehicles flashing past. His hands crushed the steering wheel, his focus narrowed to the lot's exit.

Red and blue strobes to the right caught his attention. A police car raced into view and skidded to a stop, blocking the exit.

"Shit!"

Cassian cut the wheel left. The RV bounced onto the curb. A *thud* rattled the vehicle as it struck a thin tree. Cassian bucked in his seat as the RV hit another curb and rumbled onto the street. Horns blared. More tires screeched. He glanced out the window. An SUV swerved out of the way, missing him by barely a foot.

Cassian twisted the wheel right. The RV took off down the street. He veered around a car, drifting into the oncoming lane. A pair of headlights blazed in front of him. Cassian held his breath and cut the wheel right. The oncoming car just missed him. The RV clipped the side of another car. Cassian clenched his teeth, and the steering wheel, fighting to keep the vehicle straight. The other car angled toward the sidewalk. Brakes squealed.

Too late. The car smashed into one of the oak trees lining the sidewalk. The hood crumpled.

Cassian glanced at the side mirror. Three cop cars raced after him.

"Fuck, fuck, fuck." He should have known something was up when he couldn't get hold of Lansford. Even when he saw the police not far from Rastun's hotel, he still drove around downtown Beloit looking for his friend. Cassian knew he'd taken a big risk, but one thing they drilled into him in The Corps was you never left a man behind.

Now that loyalty may cost him.

"Dude, they're catching up to us," Proly cried out.

"I know!" Cassian hollered back. He swerved around a car, gas pedal mashed to the floor.

"C'mon. C'mon!" He urged the RV to go faster. A check in the side mirror showed the red and blue flashing lights getting closer.

"Shit!" He banged the steering wheel with his fist. Cassian had no idea if they were real cops or hybrids. Not that it mattered. If they served the Reptilians, they'd kill him and his men as soon as they caught them. If they were human cops, they'd take them to jail, where the lizards would find some way to kill them in their cells.

Rows of headlights moved east and west ahead of him. I-20. Would the cops already have the exits to the roadway blocked off?

He cut the wheel, tearing down a road bordered by farmland and woods. The cops stayed on his six, closing the distance between them.

Cassian clenched his teeth. RVs weren't built for speed. But he had prepared for this situation.

"Smith. Proly. Deploy pursuit counter-measures."

"Cool," said Smith.

A rattling came from the RV's rear. Cassian glanced over his shoulder. Smith and Proly had pulled cardboard boxes out of a storage compartment. Each contained an assortment of rocks, nails, and broken glass.

"Ready?" Smith said to Proly.

Cassian heard the rear door swing open. The sound of wind and engines blasted through the RV. Smith chucked out his box. Proly did the same a second later.

Cassian checked the side mirror. Two of the cop cars veered away from the debris. One of them bounced on its right side. Maybe it hit one of the rocks.

The police car spun a full 360 and smashed into a tree. The second cop car also skidded out of control and off the road, sending up a huge cloud of dust.

The third police car pulled to the curb and stopped, probably to check on his buddies.

Smith and Proly cheered as they closed the rear door.

"Good job, guys." Cassian pumped his fist, his eyes still on the road. He checked for more cops. They'd be coming after him in force now.

His elation over taking out the police cars vanished. What the hell was he going to do now? Could he get out of Bishopville before more cops showed up? Were they putting up roadblocks?

Cassian hung a left onto County Road 29. He saw no cars, and more importantly, no flashing lights. Just more trees and fields.

How did they know where to find me?

The answer came a second later. The phone. The damn phone. He'd been so psyched actually talking to Jack Rastun he'd stayed on long enough for the cops to trace his signal.

Stupid. I shoulda known better.

Cassian snatched his cell phone from the cup holder and tossed it out the window.

"Son of a bitch!" His rage toward Rastun took hold again. It hadn't even been a week since his conversion and already he'd gone completely over to the Reptilians. Some fucking hero.

He'll pay. I'll make him pay. He imagined himself plunging his knife into Rastun's fucking gut. He'd slice him all the way up to his chest and start carving out his organs. Then for good measure, he'd piss on his worthless body. That's what fucking traitors like him deserved.

He continued down the darkened, deserted rural road. He didn't relax, didn't stop scanning around him. The police had to have a description of his RV by now. He'd have to ditch it.

Dammit. This wasn't just a vehicle. This was his home. What would he do now?

Deal with it later. Right now he had to concentrate on getting away, on survival. Everything else was –

Something flickered in his side mirror. Something red and blue. Cassian shifted his eyes left.

"Shit."

A cop car was after them.

He sped down the darkened country road. Only now did he notice just one of the RV's headlights worked. Had the other been busted when he hit that tree?

He approached a bend in the road and swung the RV to the right. It came up on two wheels. Fear flashed through Cassian. Would it tip over?

The RV settled back down. How far did this road go? Where did it end up?

Cassian checked the side mirror. No sign of the cop. That would probably change soon. He refocused ahead of him.

Just beyond the lone headlight he saw the silhouette of a car parked to the side. A shadowy figure sprang out from behind the hood. It rolled something long and flat across the road.

"Oh shit!"

Cassian twisted the wheel left. Every muscle tensed when he realized he wouldn't avoid the spike strip.

FORTY-ONE

The RV shuddered and dipped to the left as Cassian drove off the roadway. Sweat drenched his hands as he jerked the wheel right. A dull drumbeat echoed through the interior. His chest tightened. The tires were going flat.

He tried to straighten the RV, but it fishtailed. He cried out and stomped on the brake. The RV shook with a crunch and thud. The mini-quake flung Cassian from side to side, his seatbelt keeping him from being thrown to the floor.

Everything went still. The only noise came from his pounding heart. He took a shaky breath, tremors going through his arms. Swallowing, he turned around, wincing. Pain squeezed the muscles in his neck.

Proly and Smith lay on the floor near the back of the RV.

"Web. Doug. You guys okay?" He undid his seatbelt and started to get up.

Smith slowly pushed himself up, then pressed a hand against the back of his head. Proly sat up, teeth bared. He let out a high-pitched moan and grabbed his ankle.

Cassian looked to his left. The side of the RV had caved in. They must have hit a tree after they –

"You in the van," a loudspeaker blared outside. "Come out with your hands up."

"Shit." Cassian turned around. His jaw clenched as painful needles pierced his back. He checked out the driver's side window.

Two police cars were stopped about twenty feet away.

"Come out of the van with your hands up now," an officer ordered.

Cassian's breathing quickened. Was this it? Would they be captured?

No. Marines don't surrender.

I *won't surrender.*

"Get up." He hurried over to Smith and Proly. "Get up."

"My ankle." Proly looked like he was about to cry as he rubbed his ankle.

"Fuck your ankle. If the cops get us, we're dead."

Cassian threw open a storage trunk. Inside were four compact P415 semi-auto rifles and several 30-round magazines. He handed two to Smith and Proly. "Here. Keep those cops pinned down."

"What are you gonna do?" Smith flicked off the safety of his rifle.

"Something to cover our escape." Cassian gave them extra mags. "Now go."

Smith nodded. He stood at the rear door, drew a slow breath, then flung it open. He let out a yell and opened fire. Proly let loose several bursts from his rifle.

Cassian reached into the compartment, pulled out a road flare, and stuck it in his belt. He grabbed a gasoline can. Gunshots cracked non-stop outside.

He poured gas onto the walls, the floor, the counters, even on his bed. His lips pressed into a thin line as he stared at the mattress, thinking of his trophies beneath it. He hated to leave them behind.

But if he wanted to stay free, he had no choice.

Cassian bolted toward the front. The stale-sweet, overpowering smell of gasoline clung to the air. He coughed and pushed open the passenger side door. Both Smith and Proly fired around the corner of the RV.

"Go! Into the woods!" ordered Cassian.

Smith ran for the trees. Proly limped after him, grabbing his laptop along the way.

Cassian removed the plastic cap on the flare. He held it away from his body and ran the striking surface on the bottom of the cap over the flare. A bright orange flame sprang from the top. He threw the flare through the open door and ran.

A muffled *whoosh* sounded behind him. He turned, painful twinges shooting through his neck. An orange glow poured from the RV. It illuminated the woods around him.

Cassian kept running. Ahead of him Smith had his arm around Proly's shoulder, helping him along.

"Go! Go! Go!" Cassian yelled.

They dodged trees. A couple of times Cassian glanced at the ground. They were doing nothing to cover their trail.

Just keep running. Priority one was to get as far away –

A *crump* went up behind them. A tower of flame rose from the RV. Fire spread across the dry grass along the side of the road. It wouldn't be long before the trees caught fire. With the drought turning the forests into tinderboxes, Cassian doubted the cops would pursue them and risk getting deep fried.

We might get deep fried if we don't move faster.

The three kept going. Proly's injured ankle slowed their progress. Cassian tried to keep his frustration from overflowing as he constantly checked over his shoulder. No sign of the cops. Through the trees he saw the orange glow of the fire increase.

A hole opened in the bottom of Cassian's stomach. He thought about his Coachmen RV. Sure it was old and not very big, but it had been his home, the only home he could truly call his own. A place without foster parents who either didn't give a damn or tried to control his life. A place without other Marines who snored and farted while he tried to sleep.

Now his home was in flames. *And I'm the one who burned it up.* But if it helped them get away from the police, it would be worth it.

Cassian grimaced as his eyes stayed locked on the flames. Maybe one day, he could truly accept that.

The trio hurried deeper into the dark woods. Cassian's sense of loss was replaced by worry. They had lost their transportation and base of operations. They'd lost their supplies. They'd even lost Lansford. Every cop in the area, probably the entire state, would be after them.

How the hell are we supposed to stop the Reptilians now?

FORTY-TWO

Blefary had just left the Bishopville city limits and could already see the evil, orange glow in the woods.

Crazy son-of-a-bitch. The deputies on scene radioed that Cassian had blown his RV's gas tank to cover his escape. The flames spread to the nearby trees. Now they were faced with the possibility of a major forest fire *and* searching for a cop killer.

He ground his teeth and pushed down on the gas. The car shot down the road. The glow from the forest fire intensified. Was the fire department getting a handle on it?

Maybe we should let it burn. Maybe Cassian would get barbecued. Blefary didn't have a problem with that. That fucker had killed three people, including a deputy sheriff. Served him right.

Too bad they couldn't do that. As dry as the forest was, they had to jump on any fire before it grew to the point it threatened Bishopville.

Blefary saw flashing lights up ahead. Lee County Sheriff's cars. He pulled to the side of the road and got out.

"Sorry, Lieutenant," said one of the deputies. "The fire department told us to block off the road. That fire's spreading fast."

Blefary started to open his mouth, then looked past the deputy. A large, orange aura hung over the forest. He had no desire to be in the middle of a forest fire. Plus, Cassian and his two accomplices would no doubt be heading away from the fire.

He strode back to his car, pulled out a road map, and spread it out on the hood. Flicking on a mini-Maglite, he played the beam over the map. There was another road about two miles to the south, and I-20 roughly two miles beyond that.

Blefary stared hard at the map, trying to guess how far Cassian and his pals might have gotten. *Dark forest. They'd have to be careful. But they're trying to get away. I wouldn't be surprised if they tripped and fell a few times. I'd give 'em a mile head start, tops.*

Blefary got on the radio. "Dispatch, this is David Two."

"Go, Two."

"I need all available units to meet me at the 29/173 intersection. We're gonna try to cut off our fugitives."

"Affirmative, Two."

Blefary got back in his car and sped to the intersection. He pulled to the side and retrieved a Remington 870 Magpul shotgun and his Kevlar vest from the trunk. He just finished putting on his armor when the first patrol car pulled up. It was Deputy Wills. Less than a minute later two more cars arrived. Deputies Clay and Lamont. Another minute passed before a fourth patrol car rolled up, this one driven by Deputy Johnson.

"All right." Blefary gathered the deputies around his car. "My guess is Cassian and his friends are still in the forest, running away from the fire. They're probably coming right toward us as we speak. We're gonna go into the forest and try to head them off, except you, Lamont. I want you to patrol up and down this road in case they slip past us."

"Um, Lieutenant." Clay raised a hand. "There's a forest fire going on. Do we really want to go in there right now?"

"I'll be in touch with the fire department. They'll update us on the fire's progress. If it gets too close to us, we'll get out of there. Remember, Alex Cassian is likely the one who killed Deputy Spillman. We're gonna get this little fuck. Got it?"

The faces of all four deputies stiffened with resolve.

"Remember," Blefary said. "These men are packing semi-automatic rifles, and Cassian is a former Marine, Force Recon. The guy knows how to kill. Don't take any chances with him."

The deputies nodded.

"Let's go."

Blefary headed into the forest, followed by three of the deputies. Wills also had a shotgun, while Clay and Johnson carried AR-15 rifles. They switched on the flashlights under the barrels. Beams swept over darkened trees as they penetrated the forest.

"Clay, take point," Blefary ordered.

"Yes, sir."

The deputy jogged past him. Clay was an avid hunter, had been since the age of fourteen. The guy knew how to track, a hell of a lot better than him. Blefary had never been much for the outdoors. He'd never seen the appeal of freezing his ass off in a deer blind or using a bush for a bathroom.

They trekked deeper into the forest. Blefary swung his shotgun left to right. The flashlight beam swept over trees, branches, and dirt paths. He saw no sign of the fugitives.

His stomach quivered the further they went. Even with their flashlights, there were too many shadows around them. Too many places for Cassian to hide. Could he be tracking them with a rifle? Blefary shuddered at the thought of a round blowing out his brains.

Still he pressed on, teeth clenched, flashlight playing over the forest. *Where are you, you son-of-a-bitch? Where are –*

His beam swung left. Something leaned out from behind a tree.

"There." Blefary went to a knee and racked the shotgun.

The figure didn't move.

"Po-" He cut himself off when he saw the shape wasn't a man leaning out from behind the tree. It was just a round growth of bark protruding from the trunk.

"Fuck," he spat, groaning as he rose to his feet. He looked at the other deputies. All of them avoided his gaze.

"C'mon." Blefary stomped down a dirt path. He couldn't believe that happened. Fooled by a damn lump of bark. Now he looked like some panicky, pants-pissing rookie in front of all these deputies.

"Lieutenant Blefary's sure brave against a big, bad tree," he imagined them saying to their buddies later.

He glared at the deputies. If he ever learned one of them actually said something like that, he'd rip off their nuts and shove them down their throat.

Focus.

Blefary took a breath, scanning the forest with his shotgun's flashlight. Nothing. Every so often he glanced at Clay in front of him. The deputy also found no sign of Cassian and his pals.

Blefary checked in with the fire department's battalion chief. The fire was still spreading, but wasn't close to his position. He and the deputies pressed on.

The light fell on another shape against a nearby tree. Blefary tensed, but said nothing. The shape didn't move. Probably just another growth of bark. He wasn't going to look like a fool again.

The rustle of branches caught his attention.

"You hear that?" asked Wills.

"Yeah," replied Blefary, glad someone else heard the noise.

Branches rustled again, to the left.

"Take cover," ordered Blefary.

The four hurried behind trees, then aimed their flashlights in the direction of the rustling.

"Anyone see anything?" asked Blefary.

The deputies all responded, "No."

The beams washed over the woods. Blefary strained his ears to pick up any sound out of the ordinary. All he heard was the thumping of his heart.

Something dashed out from behind a tree and into the darkness.

"What was that?" blurted Clay.

"Lee County Sheriff's Office!" yelled Blefary. "Show yourself."

No response.

"Come out with your hands up!" Blefary's finger kissed the shotgun's trigger. He stared into the flashlight beams, waiting, hoping, someone would appear.

Or maybe they'll start shooting.

More branches crackled . . . from behind them.

Blefary swung around, sucking down a brief, panicked breath.

"Shit, what the hell now?" said Johnson, a slight quiver in his voice.

Blefary stayed silent, trying to see something moving within the flashlight beams.

The branches rustled again. Another sound followed. A prolonged, guttural growl.

Blefary held his breath. That couldn't be Cassian, or any other human being.

"Oh shit," stammered Johnson. "Shit, shit, shit, no way."

"Button it, Johnson," snapped Blefary. "All right, everyone. We're going to get up and get out of here, nice and slow. Don't startle these things. Got it?"

The deputies nodded and said softly, "Yes."

Blefary put a hand on the ground and pushed himself up. Tremors went through his legs. He backed up, scanning the forest.

Another growl came from the darkness.

He reached for his radio. "Lamont. You read me?"

"Affirmative, Lieutenant."

"We're heading back your way. We've got -"

"Shit!"

Blefary snapped his head left. Clay swung around his rifle. A large, dark figure slammed into the deputy. He screamed as a clawed hand arced down and tore into his face.

Wills fired his shotgun. The figure attacking Clay flinched. The shotgun boomed again.

Another large shape tackled Wills. Blefary's chest tightened when he saw the lizard-like head.

A shadow moved to his right. Blefary turned.

A lizard man charged him.

He fired from the hip. The monster staggered. Blefary racked the shotgun and fired again. The lizard man let out a strangled cry. Blefary racked the shotgun a third time.

The beast jumped at him. A mass of muscle crashed into Blefary. All the air shot out of his lungs. He hit the ground, the monster crushing him. Fire sliced through his ribs. The shotgun fell from his hand.

The lizard man drew back, snarling. The stale, rank smell of its breath burned Blefary's nostrils. He punched it in the throat. Sharp teeth clamped down on his forearm.

Blefary cried out. The teeth sank deeper into his flesh, into his bones. He pawed for his holster, his fingers wrapping around the grip of his Glock.

Blood cascaded from his forearm. A crushing, blazing pain seared his left arm. He let out another cry and pulled out his pistol, jamming it into the lizard man's gut and fired. Muffled crump after muffled crump sounded. The monster bellowed, then trembled. It collapsed on top of Blefary.

He shoved a hand into the monster's bloody gut and pushed with all his strength. The body rolled off.

Blefary got to his knees, staring down at his left arm, covered with blood. Pain hammered every inch of his forearm.

He closed his eyes and gritted his teeth. Groaning, he started to stand.

Something scuffed the dirt behind him.

Blefary turned, bringing up his pistol.

The rough, scaly hand cracked against his temple. The world went out of focus. He fell on his side.

The lizard man growled and pounced on him. Sharp teeth dug into Blefary's throat. He opened his mouth, gurgling, as the world grew darker, darker . . .

FORTY-THREE

"Sir."

The word cut through Rastun's dark world of sleep. His eyes snapped open. Sherlock stood next to the battered old sofa in the Sheriff's Office break room.

"I just heard from Commander Umbarger," said the marshal. "There's going to be a briefing at oh-eight-hundred. They want us there, too."

"Thanks." Rastun rubbed his face, stubble scratching his hands. He grimaced at the stale taste in his mouth and pulled out his phone, which the SO returned to him last night, along with his Glock. The screen showed 6:02. He'd managed about four hours of sleep.

"Any word on Cassian?" he asked.

Sherlock shook his head. "He's still out there."

"Damn." After hearing that Cassian had wrecked his RV in a high-speed chase, Rastun figured it was only a matter of time before the cops caught him, or shot his psycho ass. But he'd blown up his vehicle to cover his escape, and it worked. Resources had to be diverted to fight the rapidly spreading fire and evacuate nearby homes. Blefary had taken a team of deputies into the woods to find Cassian and his accomplices. When they didn't answer repeated calls, another deputy checked on them. He'd found them all dead, their bodies torn apart. Definitely not the work of Cassian. They'd been attacked by lizard men.

Rastun's eyes lingered on a misshapen gray spot on the faded tile floor. He thought back to the night before, arguing with Blefary about the way he took down Lansford, thinking what a fuckhead the guy was.

That didn't mean he wanted to see the detective die.

He closed his eyes, thinking of two of the deputies who died with Blefary, Clay and Wills. Both were good guys. Friendly, helpful. To die the way they did . . .

He didn't know if they were married. Did some woman get a late night visit from the SO telling her her husband was dead? Did that woman have to tell her children why daddy wouldn't be coming home again?

Rastun pushed himself off the sofa. As bad as he felt for Blefary and the deputies, he still had a job to do.

He walked over to another sofa on the other side of the break room. Karen was curled up on the cushions, sleeping.

"Wake up, hon." He patted her shoulder.

She moaned and shifted, mumbling something.

"No time for the usual routine. We've got places to be."

"Mm-riiii." Karen rose, eyes half-open.

After using the restroom, Rastun poured coffee into a couple of Styrofoam cups, adding liberal amounts of sugar. The stuff was lukewarm and tasted like crap, but it gave him the extra kick he needed.

"Oh, this is wonderful." Karen came over, staring at her phone.

"What?"

She held out her phone, which showed the headline of an article. LEE COUNTY OFFICIAL BLASTS FUBI, CALLS GROUP "INEFFECTIVE" AND "UNCOOPERATIVE."

A sharp breath shot out Rastun's nose. "Let me guess. Sawyer is said county official?"

Indeed it was. He skimmed the article, in which Sawyer criticized the FUBI's failure to find and kill all the lizard men, adding, "Dr. Ehrenberg, Jack Rastun. They're more concerned about studying these monsters than protecting the people of Lee County, even after all the deaths and injuries they've caused."

The local newspaper also ran an online poll. "Are you satisfied with the way the FUBI has handled the hunt for the lizard men?"

Rastun sneered at the results. Sixty-seven percent of respondents voted dissatisfied. People he doubted ever had to search for creatures who were masters at staying hidden, or fight them off when they did appear. How many followed the hunt for the lizard men closely, and how many others just read a headline or heard a soundbite from that fuckhead Sawyer and thought themselves experts on the situation?

Karen rubbed his arm. "We've dealt with bad publicity before. We'll get through it."

He grunted, picturing himself using Sawyer as a punching bag.

After draining their coffees, Rastun and Karen followed Sherlock to his rental car and headed back to their hotel. The radio was tuned to a local news station, which reported on the forest fire started by Cassian. The blaze had spread to fifty acres, but it appeared firefighters were getting a handle on it.

Sherlock pulled into the parking lot of their hotel and walked them to their room.

"Just let me check the room to make sure it's safe."

Pistol out, he entered the room. Rastun hung outside, hand near his own gun in case Sherlock needed back-up.

"You really think Cassian or one of his asshole friends is in there?" Karen whispered. "They're probably too busy hiding from the cops."

"You're probably right. Still, when someone screams at me, 'I'm gonna fucking kill you,' I tend to take it seriously."

"A little paranoia helps keep you alive." Karen used one of his favorite phrases.

"It's worked so far." Rastun had no plans of letting go of that paranoia, not when Cassian believed him to be turning into some half-human/half-Reptilian being. All because he'd been scratched by that one lizard man.

I thought that was a werewolf thing. But who the hell knew how Cassian's insane mind worked. And who knew if that nutcase wanted to cap his ass to keep him from joining the ranks of the Reptilians.

And what if he wants to kill Karen, too? He glanced at her, icy pricks of fear crawling up his spine.

"Clear," Sherlock called out.

Rastun and Karen went inside, while the marshal stood guard outside. After showering and brushing his teeth, Rastun felt refreshed. He ran his electric razor over his face while Karen showered.

They changed into fresh clothes, then drove to the East College Street Gym, which served as the command center for the lizard men hunt. Vehicles from various city, county, and state agencies, along with police cars and National Guard Humvees, crowded the parking lot. Clusters of men and women in gray-brown-green pixelated Army Combat Uniforms stood under the shade trees that flanked the old red brick building with its slanted roofs. News vans and satellite trucks lined the edges of the parking lot, with several reporters talking in front of cameras.

They pulled into one of the few remaining parking spaces and walked to the arched front entrance, where Geek waited for them. He eyed Rastun and Karen and shook his head.

"What?" asked Karen.

"Lizard men, crazy ex-Army cooks, conspiracy theorists. Is there anybody around here that's *not* trying to kill you two?"

Rastun opened his mouth to retort, but Karen beat him to it.

"There's our pizza delivery kid from last night, though with our luck he'll turn out to be some crazy stalker fan who wants to stab us."

Rastun grinned. It seemed his sarcastic wit had rubbed off on Karen over the past year.

"You guys have any luck tracking the lizard men that killed Blefary and the deputies?" he asked Geek.

"Negative. Between the forest fire and Cassian still running around, the cops didn't want us anywhere near that area."

"Damn." Rastun couldn't blame the cops for that. Still, they may have missed a great opportunity to neutralize this pack.

"You guys eat yet?" Geek asked.

"No," Rastun answered, with Karen and Sherlock shaking their heads.

"Good, 'cause your ol' sergeant came through again." He reached down for his field pack resting on the walkway and pulled out three MREs. "I bummed these off some Guardsmen. I didn't even have to trade anything, just mentioned your names and they gladly handed 'em over."

Karen elbowed Rastun in the arm. "See. Fame does have its perks."

Geek handed them the MREs, smirking as he handed the beige plastic pouch to Rastun. "This one came from a cute little corporal. I think she wanted to give you a lot more than just an MRE."

Karen's eyes narrowed. "I'd like to see her try."

Rastun rubbed her shoulder. "I only have eyes for you, hon."

"Good save, sir." Geek gave him a thumbs up. "You guys eat. I'll see you inside."

Rastun, Karen, and Sherlock sat on the steps and dug into their food. A dark gray, puffy column of smoke stained the blue sky above them. Rastun said a silent prayer to the men and women battling the fire, hoping they could get it under control soon and go home safely. There'd been more than enough deaths in Lee County these last few days.

After they finished eating, the trio headed to the gym, where rows of folding chairs had been laid out and a small movie screen set up in the front. Rastun counted a few dozen people, the din of many separate conversations hovering around the room.

One conversation stood out among the rest, as it grew louder by the second.

Councilman Sawyer stood near the bleachers on the other side of the gymnasium, making emphatic gestures at Sheriff Haddix. Ehrenberg stood off to the side.

"That doesn't look good." Karen nodded toward them.

Lines etched across Rastun's forehead. He clenched a fist, starting toward Sawyer and the others.

"No more," the councilman snapped. "We're done helping these people, and you need to get on board."

"Actually, I don't." Haddix's face stiffened in resolve. "The council didn't hire me. I was elected by the people. I answer to them, not you."

"And we're in charge of the budget. Let's see how well your department does when you can barely afford to put gas in your cars."

"Gentlemen," Rastun said in a flat tone, glaring at Sawyer, trying hard not to go off on the jackass. He took a half-breath and turned to Haddix. "Sheriff. Good to see you back."

"Thank you, Mister Rastun." Haddix shook his hand, but kept his eyes on Sawyer. "The doctor said I should rest for a few days because of this concussion, but after last night . . ." His jaw tensed. Sorrow filled his eyes. "I lost four men. There's no way I'm going to sit on my ass with monsters and cold-blooded killers running around out there."

Haddix turned back to Sawyer. "And there's no way I'm going to turn away help from people who hunt things like these lizard men for a living. Especially considering how many lives they've saved. Or have you forgotten about those girls and the people at the town hall?"

The skin around Sawyer's nose wrinkled. His face reddened.

"Problem, Councilman?" Rastun said the second word like a curse.

Sawyer glowered at him. "I already told Doctor Ehrenberg. The county is done cooperating with you. I've instructed all our departments to stop assisting you. Most of them agreed." He returned his sharp gaze to the Sheriff and pointed at him. "I'll remember this."

He stormed off, many others in the gym watching him.

"I'm sorry about this, Sheriff," said Ehrenberg. "We certainly don't want to cause you any problems."

"Don't fret over it, Doctor. It's not the first time I've tangled with Sawyer. And don't worry. My department will keep cooperating with the FUBI. Besides, I owe you for saving my ass back at the town hall."

"I appreciate it, Sheriff." Rastun shook his hand.

"Ladies and gentlemen," a balding man with glasses stood at the microphone stand at the front of the gym. "If you'd all take your seats so we can begin."

People made their way to the rows of folding chairs. Rastun and the FUBI contingent sat in the second row.

The man at the microphone introduced himself as Scott Menke, the administrator of the state Emergency Management Division. "What we have here are three different emergencies rolled into one. A forest fire, a murderer on the loose, and a pack of wild animals that have killed several people. First, let me update you on the fire, since it had an impact on our other two situations."

Menke moved the mouse on his dais. The cursor on the movie screen clicked on a map icon, opening an image of Lee County, one section circled in red. The fire, Rastun assumed.

"According to the incident manager, what we're calling the Gum Springs Fire has burned fifty-five acres. All homes within a ten-mile radius have been evacuated. Luckily, no structures have been destroyed. We currently have ninety local, state, and federal personnel working the fire, and brought in two helicopters to conduct water bucket drops. We hope to have this fire fully contained within twenty-four to thirty-six hours."

Menke placed both palms flat on the dais. "Due to the risk of the flames spreading, searches for Alex Cassian and the lizard men could not take place within the Gum Springs Fire area of operations last night and early this morning. Because of the success of our initial attacks, we can allow search parties into certain areas. I'm now going to turn the briefing over to Captain Robinson of the Highway Patrol, who'll talk about the search for Alex Cassian."

A tall, unsmiling man in a gray tunic and pants stepped to the dais. "As Administrator Menke mentioned, the fire hampered our search efforts for Cassian and his two companions, so they were able to get a good head start on us. Still, their RV was destroyed in the fire, or rather, it was the cause of this forest fire. They no longer have transportation, and we believe they have limited resources."

Rastun silently disagreed. If Cassian had a gun and a knife, those would be all the resources a Marine, or ex-Marine, needed. Plus, like Army Rangers, the Force Recon guys could live off the land if they had to.

"All law enforcement agencies in the Carolinas are on the alert for them," said Robinson, "We've also requested aid from the FBI and the U.S. Marshal's Service. Alex Cassian's face has been shown on local and national news programs, web sites, and newspapers. The state government and the government of Lee County have pooled together ten thousand dollars as a reward to anyone whose information leads to the arrest of Alex Cassian."

Rastun folded his arms. He wondered if that kind of money would get one of Cassian's dumbshit buddies to turn him in. *Unless they're as committed to fighting the "Reptilian menace" as he is.*

Then again, nothing like a little money to make someone waver in their "unwavering loyalty."

"We unfortunately have no information about Cassian's two companions," said Robinson. "The man who tried to kidnap Jack Rastun and Karen Thatcher last night . . ."

Rastun noticed a few people in the audience turn toward him and Karen. He ignored them and concentrated on Captain Robinson.

" . . . has refused to speak since his arrest. All we know about Cassian's companions is that they are considered armed and dangerous, as is Alex Cassian himself. According to Mister Rastun, they are operating under the delusion that these lizard men are actually aliens trying to take over the world. Anyone who has survived an attack by them, in his mind, will turn into a Reptilian, as he calls them, and must be killed."

Several people in the audience shook their heads or scrunched their faces in disbelief.

"I'll now turn this briefing over to Colonel Davis of the National Guard."

Robinson stepped aside for the officer, who called up a map of Lee County on the screen.

"The red Xs indicate confirmed lizard men attacks. All indications are they are moving due east, toward Bishopville. Talking with Doctors Ehrenberg and Garland from the FUBI, they believe the Gum Springs Fire may have driven off the lizard men, but it's probably temporary. These animals are apparently expanding their territory, and that will likely include the outlying suburbs of Bishopville, putting hundreds, maybe thousands of people at risk of attack."

Davis brought up a photo of one of the dead lizard men from the town hall attack. "This is what we're up against. Doctors Ehrenberg and Garland have done preliminary exams on the bodies recovered from the attacks on the town hall and the McMurtry home. These creatures have an average height of seven feet and are roughly two or three times stronger than the average man. Their claws and teeth can easily go through flesh and bone. They're mainly nocturnal, so they have excellent night vision."

Davis turned to the photo, then back to the audience. "I don't think it's a stretch to say this is the deadliest land animal in North America."

He paused for a breath. "So what's our plan for stopping the lizard men? I'll be sending patrols into the woods throughout Lee County. Should these animals get past them, we'll have units from the 118th Infantry Regiment in a defensive line near the suburbs of Bishopville. When we spot these lizard men, we will have more than enough firepower to neutralize them."

Rastun slowly worked his jaw from side to side, mulling over Davis' plan. It appeared sound. But something gnawed at the back of his mind. Rangers weren't trained to sit in defensive positions and wait for the enemy to come to them. They went out and found the bad guys, and took them out.

If this were a human enemy, they might be able to draw them out, set up an ambush, and eliminate them.

Rastun straightened in his seat. His brow crinkled. A plan formed.

He raised his hand.

"Yes, Mister Rastun?" Davis pointed at him.

"Sir." Rastun stood. "I might have a plan for dealing with the lizard men."

"What is it?"

"One thing we know from all their attacks is that these creatures have no fear of humans."

"Yes. Your point?"

"I think that's something we can use to our advantage."

FORTY-FOUR

Colonel Davis stared at Rastun, eyebrows scrunched together in apparent contemplation. Rastun wondered if the man would be like Blefary and view him as someone looking to boost his celebrity status.

"All right." Davis nodded. "Tell us what you have in mind."

"Thank you, sir." Rastun strode past the dais to the map on the screen. He glanced at Sawyer, who sat with his arms folded, crossing one leg, then the other, scowling.

"Like I said, the lizard men have no fear of humans, even large groups of them. The attack on the town hall proved that. In a way, it's similar to how cheetahs hunt. A pair will go after a herd of thirty or forty wildebeest. The cheetahs may be outnumbered, but the wildebeest are prey animals. When they see those cheetahs, they all take off running, and the cheetahs pick off the stragglers."

"And I guess to the lizard men, we're like wildebeest," said Davis.

"Exactly." Rastun nodded. "There had to be between one hundred or two hundred people at the community center, and a handful of lizard men still attacked it. They may have thought it was an inviting target. I say we give them another one."

He pointed over to the map. "We know the lizard men have been pushing to the east. We need to find some place along their projected route and set up an encampment. Bring in tents or mobile homes, and a lot of people."

"What people?" asked someone from the audience.

"National Guardsmen, along with our FUBI team. Hopefully this will be too good a target for the lizard men to pass up. When they show up, we neutralize them."

Rastun turned to Colonel Davis. He eyed him, then the map, his jaw set, thinking.

"Do you really think that's a good idea, Colonel?" The question came from Sawyer.

Figures. Rastun clenched his teeth as the son-of-a-bitch went on.

"We have who knows how many of these monsters out there. I don't think we can afford to have your soldiers just sitting around doing nothing while our citizens are in danger."

"I'm not asking for hundreds of men," Rastun fought to keep his tone professional. "A platoon or two should be enough. And we won't be just sitting around. We'd be staging an ambush for the lizard men."

"Who's to say they'll fall for it," countered Sawyer. "What if they just go around you?"

"This can be considered a combat situation, and in combat, not everything goes as planned. Yes, the lizard men could bypass our position. Or they could take the bait. I think this is worth the risk."

"Well I'm endorsing this plan." Mayor McAllister looked at Sawyer, nodding. "I say we do everything we can to get rid of these damn monsters."

It didn't surprise Rastun the mayor backed him. The man had been nothing but helpful since the FUBI arrived here. Hell, he'd even fought off a lizard man at the town hall and helped evacuate some people. McAllister had earned his respect, unlike Sawyer, who'd bolted the moment the lizard men attacked.

"You really want to go with a plan from the FUBI?" Sawyer jabbed a hand at Rastun. "They've been here, what, over a week now. The lizard men are still out there and still killing people. You really think this plan is going to work?"

"Do you have a better one, councilman?" Rastun glared at him. "One that doesn't result in one of my people getting shot?"

The mouths of several people in the audience fell open. Sawyer straightened, eyes wide, head trembling in anger.

That probably hadn't been the most professional thing to say. Rastun didn't care. He was sick of this shithead trying to fuck up everything.

"I think it's worth a shot," said Davis.

"Thank you, sir." Rastun took an instant liking to the colonel. He seemed the sort of commanding officer Rastun had prided himself in being. Willing to listen to his subordinates, and never afraid that one of them might have an idea better than anything he could come up with.

"I'll task two platoons to implement this plan." Davis held up a finger. "But I'm going to maintain the defensive line near the city. If your plan doesn't work and these things slip past you, I want us to be ready for them."

Rastun nodded, not taking any offense. Any commander worth his salt made contingency plans.

"I'll send out some of my recon troops to scout potential ambush sites," said Davis. "When we find a suitable spot, we can set up some of our larger DRASH shelters, make it look like a small community."

"What are DRASH shelters?" asked Petal.

"Deployable rapid assembly shelters. Basically the modern version of Army tents with flooring, generators, even air conditioning." Davis turned back to Rastun. "Mister Rastun, I want you and Doctors Ehrenberg and Garland on my company commander's staff. You're the experts on these lizard men. Give them whatever advice you can to help them deal with these animals."

"Yes, sir," said Rastun.

"You got it," replied Ehrenberg.

"Um, sure." A frown formed on Petal Garland's face. Rastun didn't think the biologist was too keen on killing the lizard men. Heck, he would have preferred to attach an electronic tag on them and track their movements for research purposes.

The deadly attacks, however, made that option impossible.

When the briefing wrapped up, Colonel Davis asked Rastun and the other expedition members to join him to go over their plan for the ambush.

"So how about it?" Rastun slapped Sherlock on the shoulder. "Feel like sitting on your ass in the middle of the woods waiting for some big-ass lizards to show up?"

The marshal gave him a slight grin. "As exciting as that sounds, there's something I want to look into with Cassian."

"What?"

"It's the RV he had. I did some checking. Even a used one can run thirty or forty thousand dollars. He obviously has to gas it up. Then he needs food and other supplies. He also has at least three semi-automatic rifles, figure a thousand to fifteen-hundred dollars a piece. Cassian hasn't filed a tax return in two years, hasn't had a physical address in two years."

"That's a lot of expenses for someone who doesn't have a job," said Rastun. "So where's he getting his money from?"

"That's what I'm going to find out."

***

"Help! Help!"

Cassian tried to break free. Clawed hands squeezed his arms and legs to the point he feared his bones would snap.

"Help!" He pulled to the left, then the right, screaming with every movement.

The Reptilians wouldn't let go.

Four snouts hovered over him, saliva dripping from their sharp teeth.

"No!"

The teeth rushed toward him.

"NO!"

Cassian jerked awake, his heart pounding at a rapid fire pace. He sat up, sucking down air, willing his heart to slow.

He looked down at the bed he'd slept on. *Where am I?*

Memories from last night ate away the remnants of his nightmare. He, Smith, and Proly had been on the run from the cops. They came upon this house just as the couple that owned it pulled out of the garage and drove off.

Cassian decided to break in through the back door and scrounge whatever supplies they could. Aside from guns, Proly's laptop, and whatever they had in their pockets, the rest of their stuff had gone up in flames with the RV.

Proly had turned on a TV while Cassian and Smith rifled through the kitchen cabinets for food. Their run from the cops was all over the news. They also learned all the homes within several miles of the forest fire had been evacuated, including this one. Cassian decided they should crash here for the night. He doubted the cops would come by. They wouldn't want to get their asses burned up.

"Hey, *I* don't want to get my ass burned up," Smith had said.

Cassian set up a sentry rotation to make sure the fire didn't get close to the house. After his watch ended, he'd gone up to the main bedroom to sleep.

He slowed his breathing, his heartbeat coming back down to normal. His hands pressed into the mattress, relishing the softness. How long had it been since he'd slept in a real bed? How long had it been since he'd spent the night in an actual house?

Cassian reluctantly pushed himself off the comfortable bed and padded the short distance down the hallway to the bathroom. It had to be four times the size of the one in his RV, maybe even bigger. His teeth clenched as he recalled the vehicle exploding into a ball of fire. He still couldn't believe he'd actually blown up his own home.

I wouldn't have had to do it if fucking Jack Rastun hadn't sold me out.

Cassian shook with rage. He had actually dreamed of being like him. Imagined him the greatest warrior in the world. He thought Rastun was different, that he could actually defy the Reptilians.

But no. The son-of-a-bitch was one of them, had proven his loyalty by betraying him, betraying the whole human race.

"One day," Cassian growled. "One day."

He showered, then took some aspirin he found in the medicine cabinet. His neck and back still hurt from the RV crash. He could blame Rastun for that, too.

Cassian went through the dresser drawers and took a shirt and bluejeans. Both fit loosely on his lean frame. In all the pictures of the homeowners he'd seen in the bedroom, the husband and wife were both fatasses.

He grabbed the phone from the nightstand. Time to call for help.

"It's me . . . No, this isn't one of the burner phones you gave me . . . that's because the burner phones got burned up along with my damn RV . . . Don't worry. I'm calling from one of the evacuated homes. Look, we are up shit's creek, and we need help now . . . I had to shoot them. They were turning into hybrids. I told you that's how it works."

Cassian stood still, listening to the person on the other end. His right cheek twitched, frustration rising.

"Dammit, these things are about to overrun the town, maybe the whole state. This is what I've warned you about. The Reptilians are coming out in the open. If we don't stop them, this comfy little illusion of a world we live in is over. We're all going to live like slaves . . . We need wheels . . . Dammit, we don't have time."

He sighed loudly, pressing a hand against his forehead, as his contact rattled off one excuse after another.

"All right, all right. We'll try to steal something. But that's temporary. I need another RV for a mobile command post . . . Okay, I'll call you and we can arrange a meet. Thanks."

Cassian hung up and went downstairs. Proly sat at the kitchen table stuffing a donut in his face while resting his injured left ankle on another chair. Smith peered through the shade over one of the living room windows.

"All good?" asked Cassian.

"Yup." Smith nodded. "There's a lot of smoke in the distance, but no fire coming near us."

He slapped Smith on the shoulder and headed to the kitchen. They'd lucked out breaking into this house. Mr. and Mrs. Fatass had a shitload of food. Cassian helped himself to oatmeal, toast, bagels, scrambled eggs, a donut, coffee, and a beer. Sure, it was breakfast time, but he wasn't one to pass up a beer whenever he had the chance. *Who the hell knows when I'm gonna enjoy one again?*

He wiped his mouth with a napkin when Smith entered the kitchen and asked, "So what do we do now?"

Cassian slowly put the napkin down. His jaw tightened, trying to come up with a response.

"We can't stay here forever," Smith continued. "I was watching the news. They almost have that forest fire under control. The people that live here are gonna come back soon."

"And what about Todd?" asked Proly. "What are we gonna do about him?"

Cassian slowly rubbed the corner of his napkin. The police. The Reptilians. Jack Rastun. Todd Lansford getting arrested. Their RV gone. Who the hell knew when his "friend" would get him a new one. There was just too much damn shit to process.

"Alex," Smith pressed him.

"I'm thinking!" Cassian slammed a palm on the table. The empty beer bottle swayed and fell over.

What the fuck am I supposed to do? He rubbed his hands over his face. When he looked back up, Smith and Proly still stared at him. They were looking to him for leadership, for confidence. And he had no idea what to do. What the hell did he know about leading? He was a grunt. He'd never even made corporal. Now these two expected him to get them out of this shit alive.

That's when he recalled what many Marine officers and NCOs had said about making decisions. *"It's better to do something than do nothing."* Doing something gave you a chance, no matter how small, at surviving and accomplishing your objective. Doing nothing left you at the mercy of your enemy.

Cassian pushed himself back in his chair and squared his shoulders, ignoring the stinging pain in his back and neck. "We keep going. We stay one step ahead of the cops and the Reptilians. Then we regroup and figure out our next move."

"And Todd?"

Cassian bit down on his lip. The Marines taught him you never leave a man behind, but . . .

"We'll figure that out when we put some distance between us and the town. Hell, we don't even know where he is, how much security's around him. We . . . We also have to accept the possibility the Reptilians already have him."

"In which case he's as good as dead," said Smith.

Proly lowered his head.

Cassian tapped his fingers on the table. "We need a ride."

"You can forget about hotwiring the car the people here left in the garage," said Proly. "It can't be more than two years old. The steering column's designed to be hard to crack open and most of the necessary wiring's hidden. Plus," he waved a hand around the kitchen, "this couple looks pretty well off. They probably got LoJack."

"We'll find a car to steal," said Cassian. "Then we'll head . . . somewhere."

Smith shook his head. "Meanwhile, the Reptilians take Bishopville. Then it's probably on to Florence, Columbia. Shit, they could take over half the state before we do anything."

"What do you want me to do?" Cassian threw up his arms. "Every cop in the state's looking for us. There are probably more Reptilians heading here to get us. We lost our RV, we're down to three men, we've got a limited supply of ammo. It's not like we've got a nuke lying around to wipe out every Reptilian in this county."

He dropped his arms onto the table and looked toward the living room. He thought of the smoke coming from the forest fire, and it gave him inspiration.

"We may not have a nuke, but we might have the next best thing."

"What's that?" Smith's brow furrowed.

"When I blew my RV, look how fast the fire spread through the woods. If the fire department hadn't jumped on it quick, this whole area coulda burned up."

"So?" Smith shrugged.

"So," Cassian leaned forward, "if we wanna take out the Reptilians, and anyone they've infected around Bishopville, we start another forest fire. A really, *really* big forest fire."

FORTY-FIVE

Dozens of National Guardsmen milled about the cluster of tents and mobile shelters. Atop three of those shelters were soldiers with SAWs. Other men sat in dug out fighting positions, with armed Humvees and Strykers parked around the edges of the encampment.

Rastun took in the scene, memories flooding back of field maneuvers. He glanced down at his olive-brown-black Woodland BDU pants and shirt, then back at the Guardsmen. Damn, but it made him feel like he was back in the Army. He even felt the urge to roam through the ranks, checking on the men, offering advice, keeping up morale.

He didn't. Those weren't his men. They had their own officers and NCOs to do that. It wasn't his place to butt in.

Even though there are a few things where I probably should butt in more.

Rastun didn't agree with the company CO, Captain Hunt, on having two-man teams in hides beyond the camp watching for lizard men. Camouflaged or not, the creatures might be able to smell them. Plus, they had Alana's drone and the webcams observing the woods beyond the camp. Rastun also would have kept a quick reaction team close by in the event they couldn't repel an attack. He'd suggested both ideas to Hunt, who rejected them. He explained he needed other sets of eyes watching for lizard men, and that he did not want to take Guardsmen off the defensive line around Bishopville if the lizard men bypass them.

Despite the disagreement in tactics, Captain Hunt struck Rastun as a competent soldier. He didn't have an inflated sense of ego, seemed fair with the men under him, and listened to suggestions from other people, even if he didn't always agree with them.

Hunt had, thankfully, bought into Ehrenberg's idea of not having all the Guardsmen assume defensive postures around the camp.

"Prey like wildebeest stand around in large herds," he had said, "until a predator runs after them. If we want to attract the lizard men, we should behave like wildebeest."

So the soldiers congregated in groups, talking, playing cards, watching videos on their phones or tablets. A handful puffed on ecigarettes. Rastun wondered how many of those soldiers would rather have a real cigarette.

No way that's happening out here. He looked at the brown grass around him. After the forest fire started by Cassian two days ago, everyone was mindful of the extremely dry conditions. The Guard had several fire extinguishers on hand and the Forest Service even brought in one of its firefighting vehicles.

Rastun heard a shuffle and crackle of dry grass behind him. He turned to see Geek walking toward him. The big ex-Ranger slapped him on the shoulder, almost separating it. He let out a sigh and stared at the National Guardsmen.

"Feels like the old days, huh, Cap'n?"

"Old days? We've only been out of the Army for two years."

"Yeah, well, sometimes it feels like a lifetime ago." Geek's gaze remained on the Guardsmen, then shifted to Rastun. "You still miss it?"

"I'd be lying if I said I didn't. You?"

"Oh yeah. Let's face it, there aren't a lot of guys who can do the things we do. Being a Ranger's special. It's not something that's easy to walk away from."

"Especially when you weren't ready to walk away," said Rastun.

Geek nodded, staying silent for several seconds. "Still, there are benefits to not being in the Army. Number one is no crazyass jihadis shooting at me. I also don't have to put up with dumbass officers. Present company excluded, of course."

"Of course." Rastun grinned.

"It's also nice to work fifteen miles from home instead of eight thousand, and I really like coming home to the family every night." Geek elbowed Rastun. "Nice feeling, isn't it?"

Rastun cocked an eyebrow. "What are you talking about?"

"C'mon, Cap'n. You and Karen are practically husband and wife, minus the ring. And Emily, you're the closest thing to a father she's ever had."

Rastun said nothing. He looked at the tent the FUBI team used, thinking of Karen, thinking of Emily.

If the Western Sahara mission hadn't gone to shit, I'd probably still be in the Rangers, and I'd never have met Karen, never known Emily. His throat tightened at the thought. Not having them in his life was unimaginable.

The morning passed, slow and uneventful. For lunch, Rastun had an MRE of brisket entree with garlic mashed potatoes which wouldn't make the cut at a two star restaurant. He left a few pieces of his meal unfinished and chucked them into a plastic garbage bin, reminding himself *not* to close the lid. That was the exact opposite of what to do when in the field. Food attracted wild animals. But that's what they wanted. They had to make the camp as inviting a target as possible.

As the afternoon wore on, the only animals the open trash bins enticed were ravens. Rastun walked the perimeter with one of his field security specialists, or did a shift at the laptops monitoring the Flapjack drone and the webcams, or did push-ups and sit-ups, or napped. Just like in the Army, downtown dragged on for what seemed an eternity. As always during these lulls, he feared it would breed complacency, which could be fatal if and when shit went down.

Rastun sat on his cot, field stripping his Steyr AUG rifle when Ehrenberg and Petal entered.

"Jack, looks like you're in charge for a while," the cryptozoologist told him.

"Where are you going?"

"Sheriff Haddix wants us back in Bishopville. The fire department finally let them haul away Cassian's RV. Well, what's left of it. They found something in there they want us to check out."

"What?" asked Rastun.

"Beats me," Petal shrugged. "They wouldn't even give us a hint. They're acting like it's all top secret. Pretty bogus, if you ask me."

"Well, if things keep going the way they are, you're not going to miss anything while you're gone."

The two scientists left in a Humvee driven by a Guardsman.

Afternoon turned into evening. All remained quiet. Rastun joined the other FUBI members in their tent for dinner, minus Norgay, who had monitor duty. MREs were on the menu, again. He pulled his chicken pasta pouch out of the green, plastic flameless ration heater when Ehrenberg and Petal entered the DRASH.

"Welcome back," said Karen.

"So what was the sheriff so excited about?" asked Geek.

Ehrenberg's shoulders sagged. Petal grimaced, looking away from the others.

"I take it you found something unpleasant?" said Rastun.

"That's an understatement." Petal shook her head. "That guy is sick. Just . . . sick."

Ehrenberg glanced at the biologist, then back at the others. "They got burned pretty bad, still there was no mistaking them. It shows Cassian's been hunting the lizard men for a while, and he's been successful at it."

Rastun's eyebrows knitted together. "What did you find?"

"Skulls. Four of them. All lizard men."

***

Cassian and Proly bumped shoulders again, as the pick-up rattled along the darkened, dirt road. He grunted, maintaining a tight grip on the steering wheel. He wondered if this POS would fall apart before they completed their mission.

We shoulda got a better truck.

They bounced over another rut. Proly collided with Cassian's shoulder.

One with actual fucking shock absorbers!

Unfortunately, they had to make do with what they could get.

He stared beyond the beams from the truck's headlights, thinking back to the day before. After leaving the house, they hid in the woods.

"What the hell, man. We should just keep going," Smith had said to him.

"No way. This is a trick I learned in Force Recon. Sometimes the best thing to do when the enemy is looking for you is hunker down in their own backyard. The cops think we're going to get as far away from here as possible. When they don't find us, they'll expand their search farther away from the city. We should be safe."

They made an improvised shelter of branches and leaves and slept on the ground. It was far from the first time Cassian had used dirt and rocks for a bed. Not so for Proly and Smith, evidenced by the fact they'd been dragging ass all day. Sentry duty also cut into their sleep, but with Reptilians around, someone had to stay awake for a stretch to keep watch.

They stayed in their shelter until mid-afternoon, then set out to check the homes on the outskirts of town. That's where they found this pick-up. The damn thing had to be older than him, and much of its original blue paint had given way to rust. It also had no anti-theft devices, making it easy to hotwire.

"This looks like as good a place as any." Cassian stopped and got out, keeping the engine running. He reached into the bed while Proly and Smith stood watch.

Cassian picked up a gas can he found along the front porch of the pick-up truck owner's home. It was about half-full. Good enough for his purposes.

He walked into the field, briefly tilting the can every few steps. Gasoline spilled onto the dry grass. After about fifty paces he jogged back to the pick-up and put the can back in the bed. Cassian reached into his pocket for the kitchen lighter he took from the fatass couple's house. He reached out to the gas-soaked grass and flicked it on.

Flames blossomed in front of him.

"Whoa!" Cassian jumped back, feeling the heat from the fire as it swept over the grass.

"Damn," blurted Smith. "Look at it go."

"Let's get outta here before this whole place goes up," said Proly.

"I second that." Cassian slid back into the pickup. "Besides, we're just gettin' started."

FORTY-SIX

Rastun yawned as he approached the DRASH after finishing another hour of monitor duty. As with the previous watches, neither the drone nor the webcams picked up anything. His eyes flickered around the little tent city. Not for the first time, he wondered if this plan of his had become a waste of time and resources.

We haven't even been out here for two days. Patience.

His mind drifted to Cassian. As if the man wasn't dangerous enough, he'd managed to track and kill four of the most dangerous cryptids in the world. Rastun wondered why Cassian hadn't gone to the authorities with the lizard men skulls as proof of their existence.

Maybe they'd think they were fake. Or maybe he thought the cops were in league with the Reptilians. Or maybe he just likes to keep mementos of his kills.

He stopped wondering about Cassian's motives. He'd only taken a couple of psychology courses at Marshall University. That sure as hell didn't qualify him to be a criminal profiler. And how much analyzing did he have to do? Cassian was nuts and a killer. End of story.

He wondered if Sherlock had any luck tracking down the person funding Cassian. He had expected to hear from the marshal by now. If he had to put money on the likeliest suspect, it would be Staub. The man seemed to make a good living with his crackpot shows and books, and he was just as big a nutjob as Cassian.

And if it's not Staub, then who?

Rastun rubbed his heavy eyelids as he entered the DRASH. Cots lined either side, most occupied by sleeping FUBI members. His gaze fell on the cot Karen slept on, lying with her back to him.

A pleasant quiver went through his chest as he sat on the empty cot next to hers. He just stared at her, thinking about what Geek had said earlier.

Coming home to family. Rastun thought back to a year ago, out of the Rangers, working as a zoo security guard, no purpose in his life. Then Colonel Lipeli offered him the job with the FUBI, giving him purpose again. The day after he took the job, he met Karen. That changed his life.

He recalled all his girlfriends since high school. A few he'd been deeply in love with. Others were good women, but things didn't work out between them. A couple, including his ex-fiancé Marie, turned out to be shallow and manipulative.

None of them compared to Karen. None of them had saved his life on numerous occasions. No matter how dire the situation, Rastun knew Karen wouldn't crack. She'd have his back, just like he had hers. He could depend on her, confide in her, just being around her made everything better.

He clasped his hands together. How many women out there could accept the sort of job he did? Could he come home every night to a woman who begged him to do something that wasn't dangerous? He needed a job that challenged him, even if that challenge involved just staying alive. Not many people understood that sort of mindset.

Karen did. She knew what it was like to have a job with inherent risk. As much as they worried about each other, they also knew they didn't have the personalities to be office drones.

You think you'll ever find another woman like that?

He leaned over and gently kissed Karen's cheek. She moaned and stretched out her legs. Rastun pressed his forehead against her hair, closing his eyes, forgetting about Cassian and lizard men and –

"Everyone up!"

Rastun sprang to his feet and spun around. A tall, dark-haired man with a narrow face and wearing an Army Combat Uniform stood in the DRASH's entrance. It was Captain Hunt.

"What is it?" Rastun asked as the others stirred in their cots.

"We need to pull out, now."

"What are you talking about?" Ehrenberg swung his legs over his cot. "The lizard men haven't even shown up yet."

"We have something more important than lizard men to worry about," said Hunt.

Rastun's brow furrowed. "What is it?"

"A bunch of forest fires just broke out, and some of them are headed our way."

FORTY-SEVEN

Fires? As in plural? Rastun opened his mouth to ask how so many forest fires could break out at once.

Hunt didn't give him a chance. "Grab your stuff. I want you all ready to go in five."

The National Guard officer hurried away.

Rastun considered following him, wanting more information about the fires. *Forget it. Hunt's got more important things to do, and so do we.*

"You heard the man." He turned to the FUBI members. "Let's move it."

Rastun shoved his toiletries and iPad into his pack and slung it over his back. Next he grabbed his Aster 7 dart gun and Steyr AUG rifle. He checked around the DRASH. The others were also stuffing items into their packs.

Three Guardsmen waited outside for them. Two looked like they couldn't be older than twenty. The third had a thick build with three chevrons with two "rockers" on his upper sleeve. A sergeant first class.

"Okay, listen up," said the sergeant. "We have transport arranged for all of you. Dr. Ehrenberg, Mister Rastun, Miss Thatcher, and Mister Hewitt, you're in the Humvee with Private Heisler. Everyone else, Private Fetter will take you to the Stryker."

Geek swung his head left to right. "Hang on. We're missing Alana."

"She's in the ops tent bringing home your drone," said the sergeant. "As soon as it's secured, she'll join the others in the Stryker. Now let's move it."

"This way." Heisler waved for Rastun, Karen, Ehrenberg, and Geek to follow him. They jogged toward a nearby Humvee. The rest of the group hurried to a Stryker on the other side of the camp.

Rastun watched them go, catching sight of soldiers tearing down DRASHes and carrying various equipment. He clenched his teeth, tendrils of guilt crawling through him. It didn't feel right, leaving soldiers behind while he was taken to safety. Officers were supposed to be the last ones out of the danger zone.

You're not an officer anymore. That still didn't give him any comfort.

"Just give me one second." Heisler opened the rear door and climbed into the Humvee. He slid up into the vehicle's pintel mount and fiddled with the .50 caliber machine gun.

"What are you doing, Private?" asked Geek.

"Removing the firing pin. We can't have 'em in when traveling through civilian areas. Don't want to risk an accidental discharge."

Heisler dropped back into the Humvee and slid into the driver's seat. "Everyone in," he called through the open window.

Rastun took the passenger's seat, while the others got in the back.

"Where are we going?" asked Karen.

"Back to the command center in Bishopville." Heisler started the engine.

"We need to wait for the rest of the group," said Ehrenberg.

"They'll be following soon." The Humvee lurched forward.

"Private," Rastun said in a firm tone. "We are not leaving without them."

Heisler tensed. "Um, s-sorry, sir. I have my orders. Get the civilians out ASAP."

The private twisted the wheel, throwing the vehicle into an arc. It rumbled over the uneven ground.

Rage billowed within Rastun. Did some private just tell him no?

"Stop this vehicle, now!"

"I-I can't."

"Private!" He glared at the young man.

Heisler cringed. "P-Please, sir. With all due respect, you . . . you can't give me orders."

Rastun pressed his back against the seat, balling a fist. Damn this kid, he was right. He may retain some – *a lot* – of his officer's bearing and mentality, but without those captain's bars on his collar, he had no authority over anyone in uniform.

Still steaming, he reached into his pocket for his phone and called McClure.

"Yeah, Jack?"

"Pete, we're already mobile. This . . ." Rastun glanced at Private Heisler, then drew a slow breath. "Our driver wouldn't let us wait for you guys. Sorry."

"Don't worry about it. I can already see the drone coming in. We should be on our way in another minute or two."

That gave Rastun some relief. Still, he'd rather have the entire group evacuate together. "Copy. We'll see you back in Bishopville."

He looked over his shoulder, no longer seeing the camp in the darkness. "Well, so much for my brilliant plan."

"Not your fault, Jack." Ehrenberg tapped his shoulder. "Who could've predicted a forest fire?"

"Forest *fires*. That's what Captain Hunt said." Rastun looked out the window and spotted a couple of orange hues in the distance. It couldn't have been lightning that caused those fires. No thunderstorms had been predicted for tonight. He also didn't believe in multiple accidental fires breaking out all at once. That left one possibility.

Someone set those fires deliberately.

***

Cassian set the lighter to the gas-soaked grass. A line of flame raced across the field. He smiled. That was the sixth fire he'd started. He gazed southwest. Orange glows hovered over the darkened forest. The other fires were spreading quicker than he expected.

"Shouldn't we get out of here?" Proly shifted his weight from one foot to the other, looking around nervously. "I think we're pushing our luck."

"No." Cassian walked back to the pickup. "The more fires we set, the more the fire department and the cops have to stretch their resources, and the likelier it is Bishopville, and all the Reptilians there, burn up."

He put the gas can in the bed. The thing was nearly empty. Cassian thought about finding a gas station and refilling it, but nixed that idea. It wouldn't surprise him if every one in Lee County had a wanted poster of him. *Besides, the forest is so dry we can get a good fire going without gasoline.*

Cassian drove back down the dirt road, checking his side mirror. The fire grew rapidly behind him. A grin spread over his face. He thought of the millions of dollars the military spent on bombs and cruise missiles that could level entire city blocks. *Me, I'm gonna take out an entire city with a can of gas and a lighter.*

The smile stayed on his face as he reached the paved roadway. In the past, all he'd ever been able to do was take out one Reptilian here and one there. This time . . . this time he'd deal them a massive blow. How many would the fires kill? How much would this set back their plans for world domination?

But he couldn't stop here. Cassian learned in the Marines once you had momentum, you pressed on. You didn't give the enemy a break. He just had to figure out how to hit the Reptilians after Bishopville burned to the ground.

Cassian drove south. The six fires had gone in an arc from west to north. He didn't want to keep going in that pattern. The cops could jump ahead of him and catch him.

With six forest fires going on, they're probably too busy to look for me now. They had to be handling evacuations and traffic control and . . .

Shit. He pulled over to the side of the road and slammed on the brakes.

"What the hell, man?" Smith turned to him.

"Cops are gonna be evacuating people because of the fires. What if some of them are hybrids? We can't let 'em get away."

Cassian hopped out of the pickup and pulled out his kitchen lighter. He touched the flames to blades of grass and tree branches on the side of the road, then drove away.

I need to do that a few more times. Cut off vital transportation routes, keep any infected people within his planned circle of fire.

A few cars passed him the opposite way. Cassian grinned again. They'd be in for a surprise a few miles up the road when they came across the fire he set.

He searched for another dirt road to turn on, listening to a news broadcast on the radio. They talked about evacuations and calling in fire departments from nearby cities and counties to battle the forest fires. That convinced him even more that he was right to stick around and start more fires. He thought back to what one of his instructors in the Marines had told him.

"No one, not even big countries like us or China, have infinite resources. There's a limit to the number of fires anyone can put out at once, so to speak, before their efforts become ineffective."

Cassian straightened in his seat. That man had no idea how right he was.

Another pair of headlights approached. He paid them little mind, looking to his left for another dirt road.

"Oh shit," Proly stammered. "Oh shit."

"What?" asked Cassian.

"Look, man." Proly pointed.

Cassian followed the other man's finger. The other vehicle had pulled off to the side near an intersection. He leaned forward, squinting. Was that a lightbar on the car's roof?

Bright red and blue lights flashed ahead of him.
A blade of panic tore through Cassian's stomach. *Cops!*

FORTY-EIGHT

Rastun spied two pairs of red dots on the road far ahead of them. Taillights. Most likely people fleeing the forest fires.

He stared past Private Heisler and through the driver's side window. Between the darkened trees he saw a staggered, broken line of bright orange. Was the fire getting closer?

Rastun glanced at the Humvee's speedometer. The needle hovered around fifty-five. He'd been down this road a couple of times before. They ought to hit an intersection in another two miles. Then it was east to Bishopville, and safety.

Unless the fire spreads into the city.

His stomach tightened. The Stryker carrying the rest of the FUBI expedition was already on the road, but a few miles behind them. He prayed they'd get to safety before the fire reached the road.

He stared ahead just as they passed a one-story house on the left. They should be coming up on the intersection soon.

Something moved out the corner of his eye.

"Look out!" yelled Karen.

"Shit!" Heisler stomped on the brake. Tires squealed.

Rastun jerked forward, the seatbelt digging into his torso. A large, dark figure rushed in front of the Humvee. Did it have a snout?

A dull *thud* rattled the vehicle.

"Oh shit!" Heisler's voice cracked, his eyes wide. "Oh shit, I hit him. I hit him."

He turned to Rastun, shaking. "You saw it. He-He just ran out in front of me. Oh shit. Oh shit."

Heisler threw open the door and got out.

"Private. Get back in here." Rastun ordered.

Heisler hurried around the hood. He stopped, gawking at what lay in front of the vehicle.

"Private!" Rastun shouted. "If you want to live, get back in here now!"

Heisler shuddered, stumbling back to the open door. "Oh God. Oh God."

"Get it together." Rastun reached out to pull the young private back into the Humvee.

Something outside growled.

"To the left!" Geek hollered, going for his pistol.

Rastun went for his Glock.

Heisler turned toward the woods, and screamed.

A dark shape smashed into the Guardsman. His head cracked against the top of the doorframe. Heisler's limp form dropped into the driver's seat. The lizard man fell upon him, jaws clamped down on his neck.

Rastun fired twice. Both rounds tore into the creature's shoulder. It jerked, letting out a high-pitched hiss.

Geek jammed the barrel of his pistol into the side of the lizard man's head. A muffled *pop* echoed through the interior. Blood and brains spattered against the windshield. The creature slumped on top of Heisler.

Rastun looked down at the private. Blood poured from his neck. His lifeless eyes stared at the Humvee's roof.

More growls rose from the darkness. Rastun looked over the bodies in the driver's seat.

More lizard men charged out of the woods.

FORTY-NINE

Sweat drenched Cassian's palms. His heart beat at a rapid fire pace as he stared unblinking at the cop car. The officer got out, waving a flashlight, signaling him to pull over.

"Shit, shit, shit." Cassian slowed. Did the cop think him just an ordinary civilian? Even if he did, he had to have a description of him. He might even have a description of this truck. How many old, rusted POS pickups had been stolen in Lee County in the past twenty-four hours?

What if he's with the Reptilians?

"What are we gonna do?" Proly's voice quivered. "What are we gonna do?"

Cassian crushed the steering wheel. "Only one thing to do."

He floored it.

***

Deafening cracks filled the Humvee's interior as Rastun and Geek fired their pistols. Two lizard men staggered. Others kept coming.

Rastun glanced at the bodies of Heisler and the creature that killed him sprawled across the driver's seat, their legs hanging out the open door. No time to shove them out and start the Humvee. He also had no time to retrieve the .50 caliber's firing pin from Heisler's body.

"Make for the house! Go!"

Ehrenberg opened his door and jumped out, followed by Karen. Rastun fired his Glock as they dashed for the house.

The pistol clicked empty. He snatched his rifle and Aster 7 dart gun and scrambled out of the Humvee. He threw the rifle's strap over his shoulder when he heard thumps atop the Humvee.

A lizard man perched on the roof on all fours, eyes glowing red, rows of sharp teeth bared.

Rastun brought up the Aster 7. It fired with a soft *pop*. A dart stuck out of the creature's shoulder, pumping Golden Poison Frog toxin. One milligram could kill a dozen people.

This dart contained thirty milligrams.

The lizard man tumbled off the roof.

Another lizard man rounded the hood. Rastun shot it in the chest. It took one step before pitching face first onto the asphalt.

Rifle fire burst behind him. Geek with his Steyr AUG. Rastun ran past him. The darkened house sat thirty yards away. Karen and Ehrenberg were almost to the front lawn.

Several lizard men dashed around the Humvee. Rastun fired his remaining two darts, one toxin, the other standard tranquilizer. The toxin dart missed. The tranq hit one of the creatures. It growled and kept running. With all the adrenaline coursing through it, it could be minutes before the drug took effect.

He brought up his Steyr AUG and fired two bursts, following Geek to the house. A lizard man twisted and stumbled. Ahead of him, Geek ran a few more yards, then turned and fired. One of the beasts fell to its knees.

Ehrenberg and Karen reached the front door and tried to kick it open. It wouldn't budge.

"Stand back!" Geek yelled.

The two jumped aside. Geek put three rounds into the lock and slammed a booted foot against the door. It flew open.

Rastun swung around as the others hurried inside. He counted eight lizard men nearing the front lawn. He backed through the door and fired. One of the monsters went down. The others let out guttural roars.

Rastun yanked out the empty magazine from behind the rifle's trigger guard and inserted a fresh one. Glass shattered to his right. Geek knelt on a sofa, stuck his rifle out the broken window, and fired.

Rastun aimed at the closest creature and pulled the trigger. It staggered back. Four more shots and it toppled over. Geek gunned down another one.

The surviving lizard men split up. Three loped into the woods to the left, the others going right. Were they running away, or attacking from another direction?

"Geek, cover the rear. Doc." He threw him the Aster 7 and a plastic container with twelve darts. "Take the north side." He pointed toward the dark hallway to his right. "And call McClure. Tell him to get his ass here ASAP."

"You got it."

"Karen. Find something to use as a weapon and watch the south end."

"Okay." She hurried to the hall closet.

Rastun scanned the front lawn and the surrounding woods. Concern mounted as the orange glow from the forest grew more intense. The odor of smoke tinged the warm air.

A sharp *bang* rocked the walls. Another followed. Another. Next came deep, prolonged growls.

"Jackpot." Karen pulled an aluminum bat from the closet. Either the homeowner – who probably evacuated – was involved in recreation softball or had a daughter who played for her school. Whatever the case, the family had unknowingly left them a weapon.

Bat in one hand and pepper spray in the other, Karen sprinted through the living room and into the kitchen.

"Lizard men to the rear!" Geek threw back the glass patio door. The Steyr AUG crackled, tiny winks of orange seeping through the rifle's flash suppressor. A large silhouette went into spasms and collapsed. Geek fired a few more rounds, then stopped, rifle still up.

"Guys." Ehrenberg dashed back into the living room. "We've got big problems."

"Heh! No shit, Doc," said Geek.

"Sorry. I mean, we've got even bigger problems."

"What now?" The veins in Rastun's throat stuck out.

Ehrenberg turned to him. "I just talked to McClure. One of the forest fires jumped the road ahead of them. They had to turn around and find another route."

"Fuckin' A wonderful." *There goes our reinforcements and extraction.*

Rastun held his breath. Worry swelled. Would McClure, Petal, and the others get out all right before these forest fires overwhelmed them?

Would any of them get out of this alive?

"He did say he's going to call the command center and try to get a helicopter to come get us."

The lizard men banged on the side of the house again.

It better be one very *fast helicopter.*

Rastun checked outside. No lizard men to the front.

Something flickered overhead. Something orange. He looked up at the two trees near the driveway.

The tops of them were on fire.

Ehrenberg stepped beside him, also staring at the burning trees. "They must've started from embers carried by the wind."

Rastun's face twisted. He cursed himself. They couldn't leave the house without getting picked off by the lizard men. If they stayed here, more embers could set fire to the house.

I trapped us in here. Geek, Randy . . .

His throat clenched. *Karen.*

Rastun shut his eyes. Beating himself up wouldn't do him or anyone else any good.

The sound of breaking glass carried down the hallway. A snarl followed.

The lizard men were inside.

Heavy footfalls came from one of the rooms to the left. A large figure tramped through the doorway and swung toward them, snarling.

Rastun and Geek fired. The lizard man twitched and fell backwards.

"They're coming this way!" Karen yelled from the kitchen. She had what looked like a plastic bottle in her hand, spilling its contents on the tiled floor.

The shadowy form of a lizard man emerged from the small hallway next to the kitchen. It rounded the stove, red eyes aimed at Karen.

"Karen!" Rastun ran toward her, rifle up. Karen was in the line of fire.

The lizard man charged her.

"Karen, get -"

The beast slipped and fell on its back. Karen shot it in the face with pepper spray. It hissed in fury. Karen brought down the aluminum bat on the creature's stomach.

"Move!" ordered Rastun.

Karen jumped back. Rastun lowered the barrel of his Steyr AUG and fired. The lizard man jerked, then went still. He saw thick liquid around the creature's body. Probably cooking oil.

He glanced back at Karen and nodded. "Good thinking." It didn't matter how big and ferocious these things were. They couldn't do shit on their back.

Rastun carefully stepped over the puddle of cooking oil and checked around the kitchen corner. Clear. He moved down the small hallway into the laundry room. The window had been broken. He looked outside. No lizard men in sight. Fire engulfed the two trees by the driveway. Burning leaves and branches fell on the lawn, setting the grass on fire.

Flames crept toward the house.

FIFTY

Sweat soaked Cassian's stubbly face. His eyes shifted between the road and the rearview mirror. The cop car was getting closer.

"He's gonna get us." Proly's voice cracked. "He's gonna get us."

"Shut up!" Cassian yelled, mashing the pedal to the floor. The old pickup's engine groaned as it sped down the rural road. The temperature gauge climbed a few ticks shy of the red.

"Fuckin' piece of shit!" He thumped his palm against the steering wheel. No way could he outrun the cop, not in this POS.

They still had their guns. He could pull over and shoot it out with the cop. It would be three-on-one. They could kill the pig and –

"Look out!" Smith shouted.

Cassian's eyes widened. The pickup's headlights washed over a Humvee in the middle of the road.

He stomped on the brake. The tires screeched like a chorus of banshees. That didn't drown out Proly's scream.

A loud *crunch* tore through the cab. The pickup shook. Cassian caught a blur of movement out the corner of his eye. A deep *thud* followed.

His sweaty hands gripped the steering wheel when he heard another set of tires squeal. He glanced at the rearview mirror. It dangled from the ceiling. Cassian was aware of red and blue flashing lights when another quake rocked the pick-up.

It felt like an eternity before he released the steering wheel and breathed again. His heart beat at a machine gun pace. He took a shaky breath and looked at the windshield. Dozens of cracks spread across its length, originating from a circular form in the center. Blood soaked the middle of that circle.

Gritting his teeth, Cassian turned. Sparks of pain shot through his back.

Oh my God.

Proly was slumped between the seat and the mangled dashboard. Blood coated his face.

"Web?" Cassian touched Proly's shoulder. "Web, come on."

Weber Proly did not move.

"My legs!" Smith cried out. "My fucking legs!"

Unlike Proly, Smith had worn a seatbelt. But the dashboard was pushed against his legs. He threw back his head and banged a hand on the crumpled passenger side door. He screamed again.

"It'll be all right, man." Cassian grimaced, more bolts of pain ripping through his back. He stared through the windshield again. The right front half of the pick-up had melded with the Humvee's hood.

What the fuck is a Humvee doing in the middle of the road? He was just lucky he hadn't hit it full on, otherwise his legs might have been crushed like Smith's.

His friend kept screaming.

"Hang on, buddy. Just hang on."

Out the back window, Cassian saw the police car, its crumpled front end pressed against the pick-up's rear. He didn't see any sign of the cop. Maybe the fucker was dead.

He pushed open the door and stumbled out. He groaned and rubbed his sore back. *What do I do?* He couldn't leave Smith, but how could he free him? Even if he did, could he walk? Cassian knew he wouldn't get far lugging him. The cop who chased them had to have radioed for back up. How long before they got here?

Two big lumps lay on the road next to the Humvee. Brow furrowed, Cassian stepped toward them. He stopped, eyes wide when he recognized them.

Reptilians.

He yanked out the Smith & Wesson SD40 pistol from his waistband and moved closer to the creatures. Neither moved. Chest tightening, he touched the nearest one with his toe.

No reaction. Cassian did the same to the other one, with the same result. He looked over the Humvee, which had a .50 caliber machine gun on the roof. Inside were the bodies of a soldier and another Reptilian in the front seat. Another monster lay not far from the Army vehicle, this one in a pool of blood. He looked again at the pair lying beside the Humvee. Neither showed any visible wounds.

What killed them? Who killed them?

He bent over, a stabbing pain running up and down his back. A dart with red feathers stuck out of one Reptilian's shoulder. He took a quick breath and held it. *Wait a minute. Doesn't the –*

Rapid cracks came from down the street. Cassian tensed. He instantly recognized the sound. Gunfire. Could it be from the same people who killed these Reptilians?

One of the burning trees near a house exploded into a mass of flames. Fire spread across the lawn. His eyes caught something else near the side of the house. Two large figures. Dark in color, with stubby snouts.

Oh my God. Oh my God.

The Reptilians turned and spotted him. Even from this distance, he could see their blood red eyes.

The monsters ran toward him.

The sweat drenching Cassian's body turned ice cold. He brought up his pistol, then turned back to the Humvee. His gaze settled on the .50 caliber.

"Fuck, yeah." He stuffed the pistol back in his waistband and scrambled onto the pickup's crumpled hood, gritting his teeth against the sharp pain in his back. He traversed the Humvee's equally crumpled hood, climbed onto the roof, and slid into the pintel mount. He swung the big machine gun at the Reptilians, now barely thirty feet away. He thumbed the trigger.

Nothing.

"What the hell?" Cassian hit the trigger again. The big gun still didn't fire.

"Shit!"

One of the monsters snarled and scrambled up the Humvee's rear.

Cassian pulled out his pistol. The Reptilian was only a few feet from him, maw opened.

He fired three times into its mouth. A gusher of blood and brains exploded out the back of its skull. The creature collapsed on the roof.

Where's its buddy?

A scream came from the pickup. Smith. A higher pitch than before, from simple pain to agony and terror.

"Doug!" Cassian pushed himself out of the pintel mount. He slid off the roof and ran to the pickup's cab.

The Reptilian was inside, tearing out a chunk of Smith's neck. His screams turned into raspy gurgles.

"No!" Cassian emptied his pistol into the monster. It jerked and fell.

"Doug!" He leaned halfway inside the cab.

Doug Smith lay against the door, his throat and shoulder ripped open, blood pouring down his torso.

"Dammit!" Cassian pounded the driver's seat. "Dammit!"

Gone. They were all gone. His unit, his friends. Proly, Smith, and Lansford. Yes, the cops had Lansford, but how long before the Reptilians finished him off? They probably already had.

"Fuckers! You mother fucking bastards!" The Reptilians had taken his parents, his friends. He trembled. Never in his life had he felt so alone.

He caught sight of the wrecked police car. Was the cop still alive? The cop who made them crash? The cop who killed his friends?

Cassian ejected the empty magazine and shoved in a new one. He stomped over to the police car and looked through the shattered driver's window. The officer inside lay back in his seat, the dashboard pressed against him.

Cassian fired six shots through the window. The officer slumped to the side.

He bared his teeth, rage and fear drowning his soul. He wanted to kill more. More Reptilians, more cops, more . . . anything.

He swung back to the house. The flames from the trees illuminated the surrounding woods. That's when he saw them. Two more Reptilians fleeing through the woods.

"Oh no." Cassian shook his head. "Oh no, no, no. You're gonna pay. Every last one of you fuckers is gonna pay."

He ran back to the pickup, grabbed his P415 rifle and took off after the Reptilians.

***

Standing halfway out the patio door, Rastun scanned the woods to his right. Two lizard men ran away. The bodies of half-a-dozen more lay scattered throughout the backyard.

"I'm clear," Geek said from behind him.

"Clear." Rastun lowered his rifle. Something flickered above him. One of the trees in the backyard caught fire, maybe from another windblown ember. Smoke wafted over the roof, the stench stinging his nostrils.

He stepped outside and moved away from the patio, facing the house, his head raised.

"What's up?" asked Geek.

Rastun didn't answer. He backed up a little further.

Flames spread across the roof.

"Shit."

"Don't tell me," said Geek. "Another problem?"

"The roof's on fire." Rastun hurried back inside.

Ehrenberg stood in the middle of the living room, cell phone to his ear. "It's McClure," he told him. "He says there's a National Guard helicopter on the way."

"Good. Call the command center and have them patch you through to the chopper. We're gonna have to move to another LZ."

"I'm not surprised." Ehrenberg turned to the shattered window. "That fire's getting pretty close."

"Closer than you think." Rastun pointed up. "The roof just caught fire."

Ehrenberg lifted his gaze to the ceiling. "Yeah. I don't wanna stay here any longer. What about the lizard men?"

"The ones that aren't dead ran off. Now let's -"

"Jack!" Karen stood near the window, waving for him.

"What is it?"

"Someone crashed into our Humvee." She pointed out the window.

Down the street, Rastun saw the mangled remains of a pick-up truck and police car. He wondered how none of them could have heard an accident that bad.

Hard to hear when you're shooting lizard men.

Someone ran across the lawn, avoiding the flames. Someone with a semi-automatic rifle. The glow from the fire illuminated his face.

I don't believe it. Rastun pushed aside his shock. "Cassian!"

Alex Cassian stopped. His head snapped toward the window. The man's eyes went wide.

"Don't move!" Rastun brought up his Steyr AUG.

Cassian stood frozen . . . then dropped to the ground.

Rastun fired and missed.

Cassian rolled over the grass. He lay prone and raised his rifle.

FIFTY-ONE

"Down!"

Rastun threw himself on the carpet a split-second before Cassian fired. Bullets cracked through the remaining glass in the window and thudded against the wall. Rastun checked around the darkened room. Karen, Geek, and Ehrenberg all lay flat on the floor, none of them hit.

The firing ceased. Rastun eased himself into a crouch and peeked out the window.

Cassian ran toward the house.

"Front door!" Rastun swung around. The flames threw Cassian's shadow on the doorway.

Rastun fired. Splinters of wood jumped off the doorframe. The shadow backed away.

A crash of wood and glass rang out through the room as Rastun jumped to his feet. Geek had pushed over a cabinet and pulled Ehrenberg behind it. Rastun rolled over the coffee table just as Cassian fired from the doorway. Rounds snapped overhead. Geek shot back as Karen crawled over to Rastun.

"Rastun!" Cassian yelled. "I'm gonna fuckin' kill you!" He got off three rounds. "You and that hybrid photographer bitch of yours!"

"I do have a name, asshole," Karen yelled back.

Rastun fired over the coffee table until the rifle clicked empty.

"Shit." That had been his last mag.

Cassian fired again. So did Geek. Rastun tossed aside his rifle and pulled out his Glock.

"Mister Cassian," Ehrenberg called out. "Jack and Karen aren't hybrids. Look around. If they were, why would they kill so many Reptilians?"

"You're lying! It's a trick."

A rifle barrel poked through the doorway. Three cracks followed. Rastun fired three rounds of his own.

"Forget it, Doc," said Geek. "He's punched his one-way ticket to Loonyville."

Rastun fired two more times. "Cassian, that fire's crawling up your ass. You don't give up, you're gonna burn up." *And so will we.*

"At least I'll take some Reptilians with me!" Cassian sprayed the living room. Geek fired around the cabinet until he emptied his rifle.

A flash of orange appeared in Rastun's peripheral vision. He looked down the hallway. It was lit up by flames sweeping over the ceiling.

They had to get out of this house now.

Cassian unleashed another mini-barrage. A couple of rounds thumped the coffee table. Rastun fired around it, driving back Cassian.

"Geek!" He gave him a series of hand signals. Geek gave him a thumbs up.

Rastun fired at the doorway, then looked at Karen. "Geek and I are gonna lay down cover fire. When we do, you and Randy crawl for the patio door and get outside."

Karen's lips drew into a thin line of worry. She jerked when Cassian and Geek exchanged fire.

"We'll be right behind you." Rastun put a hand on her shoulder.

Karen nodded. "You better."

Rastun gave her a quick grin, then put a full magazine into his Glock. "On three. One, two . . . three!"

He opened fire. So did Geek. Bullets shredded the wooden doorframe. Karen and Ehrenberg crawled across the floor.

Rastun emptied his magazine and inserted a new one. He glanced behind him. Both Karen and Ehrenberg were out the door.

The fire in the hallway crept down the walls. Flaming pieces of ceiling fell to the floor. The smoke grew thicker. He coughed, his throat and lungs stinging.

"Go!" Rastun jumped up and ran for the patio door, firing on the move, Geek in front of him.

Once outside, Rastun moved against the wall and shoved his last magazine into the Glock. He got to one knee and swung around the doorframe. No sign of Cassian by the front door.

"Hey," Ehrenberg said. "You hear that?"

Rastun kept his eyes, and gun, on the front door. Even with the buzzing in his ears from the gunfire, he heard a steady thumping in the air.

A helicopter.

Finally, something's going our way.

"It's Randy . . . we're in the backyard now." It sounded like Ehrenberg was on his phone with the command center in Bishopville.

"Yeah, we can hear the helicopter now . . . Karen, use your flashlight to let 'em know where we are."

Rastun didn't turn around. His gaze remained on the front door. Cassian hadn't fired at them, or shouted any more threats. He hadn't done anything at all.

Maybe I hit the crazy shithead.

Something moved to his left. Rastun turned.

Cassian rounded the hallway into the kitchen.

"Shit," Rastun spat. He must have come through the broken window in the laundry room.

Cassian charged into the kitchen . . . then went flying through the air and vanished from sight. His rifle clattered on the tiled floor.

"Geek, keep the others covered." Rastun ran back into the house. "I'm going after Cassian."

Flames worked their way into the living room. Smoke hovered in the air. Cassian was sprawled on the kitchen floor, his legs lying across the dead lizard man. He must have tripped over it.

The ex-Marine tried to push himself up.

"Don't move!" Rastun aimed his Glock at Cassian. He put a foot on the fallen rifle and kicked it behind him into the living room.

"Face down on the floor. Hands on your head and interlock your fingers."

Cassian didn't budge. His face twisted in anger, narrowed eyes aimed at Rastun.

"You've got three seconds before I put a bullet in your damn brain."

Cassian continued glaring at him.

Rastun drew a slow breath. Smoke scratched his throat. His finger tightened around the trigger.

Something crashed behind him. He spun around.

The northern half of the house caved in, burying the hallway and bedrooms in a pile of flaming debris. The fire rushed across the living room, cutting him off from the patio door.

Rastun heard booted feet running across the kitchen floor. He turned.

Cassian tackled him.

FIFTY-TWO

Rastun and Cassian crashed to the floor. Fiery hammers battered Rastun's injured ribs. He let out a cry of pain.

Cassian wrapped his hands around Rastun's throat. He gritted his teeth and sent three quick jabs into Cassian's side. The ex-Marine grimaced and leaned to the left. Rastun pushed him off. Teeth bared, he got to his feet, pain squeezing his ribs.

Cassian reached for his waistband and pulled out a pistol. Rastun shifted to the left and thrust out his right leg. He nailed Cassian in the gut with a sidekick. The other man stumbled into the counter. Rastun kicked him again. The pistol fell from Cassian's hand. Rastun lunged for it.

Cassian snatched a coffee pot from the counter and threw it. Rastun ducked. The pot soared inches over his head and shattered against the wall.

Cassian kicked him in the gut. Rastun howled, pain searing his insides. Cassian drove an elbow into his back, driving out the air from his lungs.

Forget the pain. If he succumbed to it, he was dead.

Cassian tried to kick him again. Rastun blocked it with his left arm. He drove his right fist into Cassian's sternum. The ex-Marine stumbled back.

Rastun inhaled . . . and coughed. The smoke grew denser, burning his eyes. Flames spread closer to the kitchen.

Cassian slid around the counter, trying to get to his fallen rifle. Rastun grabbed him from behind, trying to slide his arm around Cassian's throat to get him in a chokehold. Cassian grabbed him by the wrist, trying to push his arm away. He thrust his right elbow behind him. The point grazed Rastun's side.

Pain exploded across his ribcage. Rastun bellowed, his legs sagged. Cassian grabbed his arm and bent over. Rastun flew over him and slammed into the floor. Spears of agony tore into his mid-section. He cried out and hacked on the smoke.

Something crashed behind him, a hard rain of metal and wood. Rastun rolled on his side. Cassian had pulled out a kitchen drawer. Dozens of utensils lay on the floor. Cassian grabbed a steak knife and brought it down.

Rastun grabbed the ex-Marine's forearm. His own arm trembled as Cassian pushed down. Rastun's right hand shot up. His fist cracked against Cassian's chin. Rastun felt more than heard another crack as his knuckle dislocated. A vice crushed his right hand. Rastun ignored it and hit Cassian again.

Cassian swayed to the side. Rastun pushed him into the corner of the kitchen counter. Rastun reached out for the utensils, coughing on the smoke, and snatched the nearest one.

A potato peeler.

Cassian grabbed the edge of the counter and pulled himself to his feet. Rastun stood and twisted around. He slashed with the potato peeler. It ripped into Cassian's right ear. He shrieked and pressed his free hand against his wounded ear.

Pain battered Rastun's right hand. He lost his grip on the peeler. He swung back to the mess of utensils on the floor, coughing again. He picked up a carving fork with his left hand. Rastun started to turn when he noticed movement behind him.

Cassian thrust out his knife.

Rastun dodged left. Cassian stumbled past him, righted himself and swung around.

Rastun drove the two-pronged fork into Cassian's throat. The man froze, eyes wide. His mouth opened, emitting a gurgle.

Rastun withdrew the fork, and stabbed Cassian in the throat again. Blood poured down the man's torso. He clutched his throat with both hands, trying in vain to stem the river of crimson. He staggered back into the stove, then took several shaky steps toward the rifle on the floor. Rastun moved toward Cassian, ready to stab him again.

Cassian careened past the rifle, looking like a marionette with only half its strings working. He stumbled through the archway and pitched face first into the fire that blanketed the living room. Flames swept over him. Rastun grimaced as Cassian went into spasms. He let out a wet, choking cry. The eerie noise ended moments later. Cassian stopped moving.

Rastun doubled over, hit by a coughing fit. Each cough pounded his ribs. Smoke stung his eyes and burned his throat and lungs. The stench of burning flesh floated into his nostrils.

"Cap'n!" someone called out.

He looked to the left, coughing again. Geek hurried into the kitchen from the hallway.

"You're too late to get here in the nick of time." Rastun jerked his head toward Cassian's burning body, then hacked.

"I think it's time to go." Geek grabbed him by the arm. Rastun let the big man guide him into the hallway and through the broken window of the laundry room. They hustled around to the backyard, where a Blackhawk helicopter hovered overhead. A medic stood in the middle of the yard, one hand on a rescue hoist, the other waving for them to hurry up.

"Where's Karen? Doc?" Rastun spoke and coughed at the same time.

"They're already on the chopper."

When they reached the medic, Geek looked at Rastun. "You're first, sir."

"Like hell." He hacked, and gritted his teeth against the pain blazing through his ribs. "I'm in charge. I go la . . . ast." He broke into a coughing fit.

"Like hell. You're in worse shape than me." Geek turned to the medic. "Get his dumb ass on that bird."

"Yes, sir."

Rastun tried to argue, but ended up coughing.

The medic secured him to the winch and gave the crew chief on the Blackhawk a thumbs up. They ascended toward the helicopter. Rastun looked around. Another section of the flaming roof collapsed. Most of the trees in the backyard had caught fire. Across the street, the flames had swept through the woods and onto the street. The Humvee, pickup, and police car all burned.

It felt like he was in the middle of hell.

They made it onboard the chopper. The crew chief removed Rastun from his harness and leaned him against the door on the other side. Karen practically jumped on him, wrapping her arms around his shoulders. She planted a long kiss on his cheek.

"I'm okay." Rastun coughed and rubbed Karen's arm.

The medic returned a minute later with Geek. The engines roared and the Blackhawk surged eastward, leaving behind the inferno.

The medic gave Rastun a quick examination. "Here." He handed him a portable oxygen cylinder. Rastun pressed the clear, plastic mask against his face and took a few breaths. Clean, fresh air flowed into his lungs.

"You're suffering from smoke inhalation," the medic yelled in his ear to be heard over the pounding rotors. "You also have broken ribs and a dislocated knuckle. We're taking you to Lee County Memorial Hospital. You're going to be fine."

Lee County Hospital, again. Maybe he should just move into the place permanently.

After another deep gulp of air, he lowered the mask and looked to Karen. He traced his fingers along her cheek. She took hold of his hand, tears in her eyes.

He leaned in close to her ear. "I've come to a decision."

"What?" Karen squeezed his hand.

"As soon as I'm healed up, we're going on vacation. A *long* vacation."

FIFTY-THREE

From the back seat, Sherlock noted the splash beneath the Sheriff's SUV as it drove through a puddle. In fact, many puddles stood out on the streets and sidewalks of Bishopville. Rain finally fell on the city yesterday, snapping the heatwave and helping firefighters hold back the forest fire.

He gazed at the sky. Wisps of smoke mingled with gray clouds. Another round of rain was forecast for today. Hopefully it would knock out the remaining hotspots of the fire. More than forty homes had been lost to the blaze.

It could have been a lot worse. Without that rain, there might not be a Bishopville, South Carolina.

They turned down Main Street, Sherlock studying the storefronts. Posters, statues, and other images of the Lizard Man, once a part of the city's identity, were nowhere in sight. After all the deaths the creatures had caused, most residents probably couldn't view them as a fun local legend any more.

I wonder how many are left? Between the fight at the house and the fire, Dr. Ehrenberg figured most, if not all, of the lizard man pack terrorizing the county were dead.

Sheriff Haddix turned into the parking lot of Bishopville City Hall. Chief Gibson, sitting in the passenger seat, drew in a long breath, his face stiff with hesitation.

"Are you ready to do this?" asked Sherlock.

Gibson turned to him, nodding. "Yeah. Yeah, let's get this over with."

The three men walked into City Hall. They found Mayor Bud McAllister in his office.

"Gentlemen. Good morning." He nodded to them. "What brings you by?"

"Some unfinished business concerning Alex Cassian."

"Oh?" McAllister straightened in his seat, clasping his hands. "What's the point looking into him now? He's dead. Case closed."

"Not necessarily." Sherlock shook his head. "Cassian hadn't worked for the last two years, yet he was able to buy an RV, the gas for it, and weapons and ammunition. He'd need money for that. Quite a bit of money. We couldn't find any bank accounts in his name, any indication he'd saved up a significant amount of money. That means someone was funding him."

"Oh?" McAllister's gaze shifted to the papers on his desk.

"That someone was you, Bud," Haddix said in a harsh whisper.

"What?" McAllister blurted, his voice higher than normal. "N-No. What are you talking about? I didn't know Alex Cassian."

"Then why did you get a phone call from him?" said Sherlock.

McAllister froze, mouth agape. "I-I . . . I never did."

"A couple who lives outside of town reported their home was broken into," Haddix explained. "This happened after they'd been evacuated during the forest fire, the first one Cassian set when he blew his RV."

A sheen of sweat appeared on the Mayor's forehead.

"The crime techs went through the house," said Sherlock. "They found a few partial prints. It looked like Cassian and his accomplices did a decent job of cleaning the house before they left. But they weren't thorough enough. The techs found hair samples in the shower and sink drains. We checked them against Department of Defense's DNA database. Several were a match for Alex Cassian."

McAllister wriggled in his chair, unable to look at him, Sheriff Haddix, or Chief Gibson.

"We checked the homeowners' phone records," said Sherlock. "One call was made from the house while they were evacuated. That call went to your cell phone."

He moved in front of the Mayor's desk. "I started checking into your financials. Nothing looked suspicious with your development business or your personal bank accounts . . . except one you have set up at a bank in Florence. It's linked to some stocks you have, stocks that are doing quite well. You established this account two years ago, right around the time Cassian went off the grid, and have made cash withdrawals of several thousand dollars at a time every three months on average. The last one, two days after the story on Phil Welsh's death broke."

McAllister lowered his head.

"My God, Bud." Gibson stepped forward, shaking his head. "Why? Why would you give money to a psychopath like that?"

"He . . . He said he could kill them all." McAllister's voice cracked.

"What, the lizard men?" Gibson tilted his head, a baffled look on his face. "You believed him?"

McAllister nodded.

"How did you meet Alex Cassian?" asked Sherlock.

More sweat formed on McAllister's face. "He came to see the police, two years ago, before you came onboard." He glanced at Chief Gibson. "He killed one of those monsters, cut off its head. He took it to the police department in a cooler to show them. The old chief happened to be in the lobby and Cassian showed it to him. He thought it was fake and told him to get the hell out."

McAllister drew a shaky breath. "I had a meeting with the chief there, and saw Cassian walking to a pickup with the cooler. I asked the chief about it, and he told me the story. Said it looked convincing, that he oughta work in Hollywood."

He slouched in his chair. "I had to know for myself if it was real or fake. I hired a PI to track down Cassian. All I knew about him then was he drove a beat-up gray pickup with a Semper Fi bumper sticker. The PI found him in two days. I met him, he showed me the head . . . and it was real. I agreed to support him if he could kill more of those monsters, and set up that fund."

"How did you get him the money?" asked Sherlock.

"We did dead drops, like in those old Cold War novels. I'd leave envelopes of cash in abandoned buildings or under rocks in a field." He looked up at them, face strained. "I didn't know he'd kill those people. I swear I didn't. I'm sorry. I just wanted him to kill the lizard men."

"Why?" asked Haddix. "Why did you want them dead so bad?" McAllister folded his hands tight and swallowed. "They killed my girlfriend."

The Sheriff and the Chief looked to one another in surprise.

"When was this?" asked Sherlock.

"When I was in high school. It was . . . Charlene Owens."

"Charlene Owens?" Gibson blurted. "Are you kidding me?" Sherlock turned to him. "You knew her?"

"I know about her. Charlene Owens was one of the most brutal murders in Lee County history. Happened back in the early seventies. They never found her killer."

"How do you know a lizard man killed her?" Sherlock asked the mayor.

McAllister shivered. "Because . . . because I saw it."

Gibson's and Haddix's eyes bulged. Sherlock folded his arms, keeping his face stiff and neutral. Inside, the story amazed him. He'd had a few theories as to why McAllister would help someone like Cassian. Blackmail had been his first guess. He also thought the mayor might be a conspiracy theorist who hid it better than Cassian or Staub. Something personal was another angle, though he never imagined it would be linked to a 40-year-old cold case.

"We were going to meet up at the millpond. When I drove up . . ." McAllister's lip quivered. "I saw her, on the ground. One of those things over her. She . . . it ripped her apart. It saw me and ran into the woods. I just sat there in my car, couldn't move. Didn't know what to do. Couldn't . . . couldn't believe she was dead. I . . . I just left. Left her lying there. I loved her, and . . . I didn't know what to do."

"That happened nearly two decades before the first official sighting of any lizard man," said Sherlock. "So you couldn't tell the police because they wouldn't believe you that a monster killed your girlfriend."

"That wasn't the only reason." McAllister looked at Haddix and Gibson. "You know why I couldn't say anything, to anyone. Not back then."

Sherlock turned to the police officials. Chief Gibson held the mayor in his gaze for a few moments before turning to Sherlock. "Charlene Owens was black."

Another surprise to the story. Still, Sherlock kept his composure. "So, South Carolina, early 1970s. A young white man and a young black girl dating would not be accepted by most folks."

McAllister shook his head. "It would have destroyed my family's reputation, killed our business. I couldn't afford to say anything. That . . . that's haunted me every day for over forty years. Seeing Charlene like that, not doing a thing about it. Being . . . being a coward. When I ran into Cassian, I thought that would be my way of making amends. I never thought he'd do so many horrible things."

His head hung low. His body jerked with a sob.

Gibson looked at Haddix, biting his lip, and nodded. The sheriff took out a pair of handcuffs.

"Bud McAllister, you're under arrest for accessory to murder, obstruction of justice, aiding and abetting . . ."

McAllister sobbed as Haddix helped him up and cuffed him. Sherlock almost felt sympathy for him. Almost. Yes, it had to be horrible for McAllister to see someone he loved mutilated like Charlene Owens had been. That pain, the guilt, drove him to Alex Cassian in a misguided attempt at revenge and redemption.

But Cassian had murdered two innocent people and two cops, nearly killed Captain Rastun, and set a massive forest fire. Because of McAllister's silence, the town he'd taken an oath to serve was almost destroyed.

Sherlock watched the sheriff escort McAllister out of the office, satisfied. Had circumstances been different, he might be back in Washington now, and McAllister would remain here, serving out the remainder of his term, preparing for a comfortable retirement, no one the wiser.

Thanks to him and many other law enforcement personnel, the soon-to-be former mayor would face justice.

FIFTY-FOUR

"Wow," Rastun muttered to himself. He removed his sunglasses, put them on his black and orange Philadelphia Flyers ballcap, and took in the panoramic view.

The craggy, humped form of Courthouse Rock stood in front of him. Shifting a few inches to the left, he saw the curved shape of Bell Rock. Another few inches to the left and the spires of Cathedral Rock came into view.

Absolutely beautiful. He took a swig from his water bottle and gazed at the dark reds, browns, and grays that made up the mountains around Sedona. He smiled, knowing he'd done right to pick Arizona for their vacation. Not only did the state have an abundance of natural beauty, but, aside from a few alleged sasquatch sightings along the Mogollon Rim, it wasn't a hotbed of cryptid activity. After Bishopville, he didn't want to deal with large, mysterious monsters that could kill him. At least, not for a while.

Sedona also provided him the perfect place to do something very, very important.

He spotted Karen and Emily hiking up the forest trail toward him.

"Check this out." He held out his hand.

"Oh my God." Karen gazed at the rock formations with wide eyes. "How beautiful."

"Whoa. Cool." Emily stopped to admire the scene.

Karen snapped photos of the surrounding landscape. A quiver went through Rastun's stomach, as it had every time he'd laid eyes on her today. He took another drink from his water bottle, still staring at her.

"What?" Karen turned to him.

"Um . . . nothing."

Karen grinned, shook her head, and went back to taking pictures.

Tremors stormed through Rastun's gut. *Better do this now before you lose your nerve.*

He walked over to Emily and handed her his phone, set to camera mode. "Em, do me a favor."

"What?"

240

"Take a picture of me and your mom, but do it when the time's right."

Emily's face scrunched. "How will I know that?"

"You'll see." He patted her shoulder and walked back to Karen, drawing a shaky breath. A twinge of soreness went through his ribs. They still weren't a hundred percent healed, but the pain was nowhere near as bad as it had been during the lizard man expedition.

"Can't beat the view, huh?" he said.

"No you can't." She flashed him a gorgeous smile.

Rastun swallowed and put an arm around Karen. She pressed herself against his side. His stomach knotted and his heart sped up. He opened his mouth. The speech he'd rehearsed for the past couple of days abandoned him.

"Um . . ." He bit his lip and looked out at the rocks. *What the hell, man. Spit it out.*

"Something wrong?" asked Karen.

"No. No, absolutely not. Just . . . thinking about the past year. How much . . . how much meeting you changed my life."

Karen beamed at him, then kissed his cheek. "I can say the same thing. I never thought I'd meet a guy as great, as wonderful as you, and someone who'd be so good to Emily."

"I'd do anything for that kid, and for you." He turned Karen so she faced him. She lowered her camera, letting it dangle from the strap around her neck. Rastun took hold of both her hands and drew a deep breath.

"I love you, Karen. I've never met anyone as . . . amazing as you. After everything we've been through, the sea raptor, the lizard men, I owe you my life about a dozen times over. I know without a doubt that whatever happens in the future, you'll be right there by my side."

"Of course I will," said Karen. "You mean the world to me, Jack. You talk about me saving your life, but if it wasn't for you, I wouldn't be standing here with you today."

Rastun squeezed both her hands. "I . . . um . . . I just think . . . aw hell."

He lowered his head, working up his courage. He finally forced himself to one knee. Karen gasped, her hands leaping to her mouth. Rastun glanced at Emily. The girl broke out in a wide grin and began taking pictures.

Rastun reached into his pocket and pulled out a small black box. He flipped it open to reveal the diamond-encrusted ring. Tears trickled from Karen's eyes.

"Karen Thatcher, will you marry me?"

Time froze. He stared at Karen, hoping, praying she said that one word.

She wiped at her tears, her head bobbing up and down. "Yes. Yes, yes I will."

Bolts of sheer joy shot through Rastun. He slipped the ring on Karen's finger, then leapt to his feet. He kissed her and wrapped his arms around her. Emily ran up to them and hugged both of them.

"This is the coolest thing ever," she said.

Rastun patted Emily on the head, refraining from correcting her. "Coolest thing ever" didn't come close to describing what just happened.

This was the greatest day of his life.

PRAISE FOR JOHN J. RUST'S BOOKS

SEA RAPTOR

"I really enjoyed this book. The character development and multi-layered plot held my interest. I didn't want to put it down."
Steve Yeager, author of *Raptor Apocalypse*

"There's a lot to like in this novel. Three-dimensional characters, lots of fast action-adventure in a complex who-can-you-trust plot, some fun gadgets, and a good knowledge of the military and the area it's set in help give this novel a sound foundation."
Matt Bille, author of *The Dolmen*

WAR OF THE WORLDS: RETALIATION (with Mark Gardner)

"It's an exciting rollercoaster of a ride, with sudden twists and heart-stopping drops-and one I wouldn't mind riding again."
James Rollins, *New York Times* best-selling author of the Sigma Force series.

About the Author: Born in New Jersey, John J. Rust studied broadcasting and journalism at Mercer County Community College and the College of Mt. St. Vincent. He spent three years with New Jersey 101.5 FM before moving to Arizona, where he became the sports director and play-by-play announcer for KYCA radio. Rust has published several sci-fi short stories, as well as seven other novels, including *Sea Raptor, War of the Worlds: Retaliation* (with Mark Gardner), *Dark Wings,* and the *Fallen Eagle* trilogy. Follow Rust at www.facebook.com/johnjrustauthor and on Twitter @JohnJRust.

SEVEREDPRESS

facebook.com/severedpress
twitter.com/severedpress

CHECK OUT OTHER GREAT
HORROR NOVELS

DEATH CRAWLERS
by Gerry Griffiths

Worldwide, there are thought to be 8,000 species of centipede, of which, only 3,000 have been scientifically recorded. The venom of Scolopendra gigantea—the largest of the arthropod genus found in the Amazon rainforest—is so potent that it is fatal to small animals and toxic to humans. But when a cargo plane departs the Amazon region and crashes inside a national park in the United States, much larger and deadlier creatures escape the wreckage to roam wild, reproducing at an astounding rate. Entomologist, Frank Travis solicits small town sheriff Wanda Rafferty's help and together they investigate the crash site. But as a rash of gruesome deaths befalls the townsfolk of Prospect, Frank and Wanda will soon discover how vicious and unrelenting these new breed of predators can be. Meanwhile, Jake and Nora Carver, and another backpacking couple, are venturing up into the mountainous terrain of the park. If only they knew their fun-filled weekend is about to become a living nightmare.

THE PULLER
by Michael Hodges

Matt Kearns has two choices: fight or hide. The creature in the orchard took the rest. Three days ago, he arrived at his favorite place in the world, a remote shack in Michigan's Upper Peninsula. The plan was to mourn his father's death and figure out his life. Now he's fighting for it. An invisible creature has him trapped. Every time Matt tries to flee, he's dragged backwards by an unseen force. Alone and with no hope of rescue, Matt must escape the Puller's reach. But how do you free yourself from something you cannot see?

CHECK OUT OTHER GREAT HORROR NOVELS

MONSTROSITY
by Tim Curran

The Food: It seeped from the ground, a living, gushing, teratogenic nightmare. It contaminated anything that ate it, causing nature to run wild with horrible mutations, creating massive monstrosities that roam the land destroying towns and cities, feeding on livestock and human beings and one another. Now Frank Bowman, an ordinary farmer with no military skills, must get his children to safety. And that will mean a trip through the contaminated zone of monsters, madmen, and The Food itself. Only a fool would attempt it. Or a man with a mission.

THE SQUIRMING
by Jack Hamlyn

You are their hosts.

You are their food.

The parasites came out of nowhere, squirming horrors that enslaved the human race. They turned the population into mindless pack animals, psychotic cannibalistic hordes whose only purpose was to feed them.

Now with the human race teetering at the edge of extinction, extermination teams are fighting back, killing off the parasites and their voracious hosts. Taking them out one by one in violent, bloody encounters.

The future of mankind is at stake.

And time is running out.